Books

Giant Wars Series
Loving His Fire
Grounded By Love
Melted By Love
Wicked Flames of Desire

Galactic Courtship Series
Xacier's Prize
Claiming His Champion
Captivating the Doctor
Escaping the Hunt
Abducting the Ambassador
Wicked Prisoner
Seducing the Enemy
Cuff Me Now
Challenging the Arena
Dark Desires in Space
His Fallen Star
His Human Temptation
Racing Toward Desire
Zro'eq's Fallen Star
His Human Doctor
The Spy and The Alien

Ice Age Alphas
The Sabertooth's Promise
The Sabertooth's Mate

Direwolf's Desire

Direwolf's
Desire

Lily S. Thomas

Enjoy your Cruise!

This book is a work of fiction. Names, characters, places and incidents either are products of the author's imagination or are used fictitiously. Any resemblance to actual events or locales or persons, living or dead, is entirely coincidental.

Cover created by SelfPubBookCovers.com/ KimDingwall

Copyright © 2020 by Lily Thomas

All rights reserved, including the right to reproduce the book or portions thereof in any form whatsoever. For information email lilysamanthathomas@yahoo.com.

www.lilythomasromance.com

ISBN: 9781661419745
ISBN: (ebook) B083XKDT5B

I've always wanted to be an archeologist. There's something about being the first person to pull out an artifact, to see the history right in your hands. There are no words for it. Why didn't I become an archeologist? I didn't think pursuing a career that would force me to travel would be fair to my birds, so instead of digging up artifacts, I write about people who do.

I did draw on some of my life experiences for Andrea, so I hope you enjoy. Sometimes including scenes from your own life can be way too amusing!

Enjoy!

Chapter 1

There wasn't a single cloud in the bright blue sky to bring any respite from the sunlight that beat down on the team of archeologists who dug painstakingly in the dirt. A couple of shade tents had been set up, so the archeologists could rest and have some water while cooling off, but while they were in their pits, they were vulnerable to the rays of the merciless sun.

Andrea wiped a gloved hand across her sweaty brow before the sweat dripped into her eyes and blurred her vision. "Is it me, or is it just getting hotter out here?"

"Maybe you should take a break," Emma said from beside her, her broad-brimmed sun hat shading most of her body.

"Maybe you should tell me what store you bought that at." Andrea pointed the sharp metal tip of her trowel at Emma's amazingly large hat.

"Oh, this?" Emma reached up and gripped the edge of the hat. "I have no idea. My mother likes to buy me things out of catalogs," she shrugged, "not that I mind. Saves me some much-needed money, if I don't have to worry about buying clothes."

"Well, let your mom know I'd enjoy one of those hats, and if she's looking for another daughter to buy clothes for, I'm her girl!" Andrea was only half-joking, because her wardrobe really did need some new items. She was the kind of woman who bought clothing from second-hand stores and then wore them until they had too many holes to be worn another day. Only then would she go out and buy new ones. Well, new to her. It was rare for her to visit a department store.

"I'll be sure to pass it along." Emma's blue eyes twinkled from under the shade of her hat before she turned her attention back to brushing the dirt off of what might be a bone hidden in the ground.

Turning back to her own dig site, Andrea continued to slowly peel back the layers of dirt, careful in case there were any bones or artifacts hidden under the ground. This site meant a lot to her because it was the first time she had been hired onto an ice age dig.

The head archeologist, Clyde Manning, had given her a ring a few weeks ago and asked if she wanted to be on this dig. To say she squealed in delight would be an understatement. This was her dream dig, and everything they dug up was amazing.

Most people would look at the brittle bones and dirty artifacts and think, eh. But Andrea just saw the thrill of discovering history. These bones and artifacts were thousands of years old and showed how life once was for the human race. The ice age life was as different as one could get from the twenty-first century living.

To think, the people buried in this site had faced the teeth of sabertooth tigers and had to hunt mighty mammoths as a source of food. She could only imagine seeing those creatures in person. She'd probably wet her pants, at least when it came to the sabertooth, but even the idea of standing beside one of those beasts brought a sense of awe to her chest. Sadly, and maybe gratefully, she would never see one of those beasts in real life.

"I've been thinking about switching hotel rooms. There's this weird noise…"

Andrea tuned out Emma's words as her trowel brushed something under the dirt. Pulling out a small brush from her kit of tools, she began to whisk away the dirt with gentle strokes.

As she uncovered whatever it was, she could tell it was made of wood. It even looked intact, which was amazing. After so many years of being used and then hidden in the dirt, she was astonished to see the carvings on the surface were so clear as she brushed off the dirt. As she leaned closer, she could see the flecks of red paint that once adorned the surface of the wood. It was faint, but the paint was there.

"What's that you found?" Emma's voice was right in Andrea's ear, and she startled a bit.

"I'm not sure," Andrea said as she continued to brush away the dirt until she finally revealed what it was.

"A bracelet." Emma breathed. "Besides the faded paint, it's in spectacular condition." She pointed a long slender finger at the bracelet. "I can't see any cracks in the wood."

Andrea gently removed the bracelet from the earth with both of her hands and marveled at it.

"Makes you wonder who wore it and what story or stories it might have witnessed," Emma commented, and this was why they were friends as well as colleagues. They were both fascinated by the past.

"I should bring this up to the table," Andrea said, referring to the metal table where any finds were brought to be studied at a later time.

"Nice find, Andrea." Emma said as she walked back over to her side of the pit.

Standing, Andrea had a difficult time taking her eyes off the bracelet. She knew she must be insane because she could have sworn she heard it calling her name. As she left her pit, she finally glanced away from the bracelet, so she could climb the rickety ladder. Their pit was about ten feet in the ground. The moment her feet hit solid ground though, she glanced back down at the bracelet.

Then for some strange reason, she didn't fight the compulsion to slip the wooden bracelet over her hand and onto her wrist. Maybe the sun had fried her brain, but as the cool wood warmed around her wrist, she smiled, despite the fact she was breaking several rules of her job.

The ground under her feet shifted, and Andrea threw out her arms as she tried to catch her balance, but the ground was gone, and she fell and fell. Her arms whirled wildly at her sides, but she never hit the ground. It was as if she was falling, and there was no ground below her.

Then the ground hit her. Hard. The breath knocked out of her lungs, and as she struggled to suck in some much needed air, she glanced around her frantically. There were bushes and grass instead of dirt, archeologists, and tents. Where was everyone?

When Andrea finally sucked in a shaky breath, she sat up and looked around in bewilderment. The land around her was drastically different. The sun still shone down on her, but there was a chill to the air, and she was alone.

"Hello?" Andrea called out cautiously as she rubbed a hand against her chest, still recovering from her fall.

No answer came.

Maybe the sun had gotten to her, and she'd passed out from heat exhaustion. It was possible she was now dreaming as her unconscious mind sought a refuge for her. She only hoped her fellow archeologists would look up from their work long enough to notice she'd passed out.

The skin on her arms prickled in the cooler air of her dream, bringing her gaze down. She gasped when her eyes fell on her body.

She was naked!

Her clothes were gone!

Calming her racing heart with some deep breathing, Andrea reminded herself that she was in a dream, and her lack of clothing was nothing to panic about. She'd analyze her strange dream once she woke up… in a hospital. She was sure once her colleagues saw she was passed out in the dirt, they'd rush her to the emergency room, and everything would be good again.

Rising to her feet, Andrea figured she couldn't go wrong by exploring her dream. Her dream had really vivid colors and sounds. The tweets of birds could be heard off in the distance as they went about their lives.

She thought dreams were supposed to be fuzzy around the edges. Then again, maybe it would be fuzzy once she woke up, and it only seemed vivid right now because she was currently in the dream.

Crossing her arms across her chest, she

vigorously rubbed her hands over her arms to get rid of the slight chill in the air. She'd gone from a desert like setting to a milder environment.

Leaves rustled above her head as Andrea pushed herself onto her feet and began to walk through the trees as she took in the scenery around her. It was quiet in her dream. Sure, there were birds and rustling noises from small critters, but there was an overall silence to the air. Her dream didn't seem to include the noises of the twenty-first century because she couldn't hear the hum of airplanes and cars which were always around.

It was peaceful, and the lack of white noise didn't bother her. It actually pleased her ears, like it was giving her brain a break from having to process all the sounds out for her entire life.

Walking even further into the forest, she enjoyed the feel of the grass under her bare feet. Pausing briefly, she wiggled her toes in the soft grass. As she busied herself with studying the plants around her, she heard a growl rip through the air.

Spinning on a foot, Andrea glanced around with wide eyes as she tried to find the source of the growl. When she heard a loud crack as a branch snapped, she darted into the forest without a second thought. She flew past tree trunks, branches reaching out as if to halt her progress, but she was having none of that. Dream or no dream, she didn't want to know what had growled at her.

Flailing her arms, Andrea beat back the branches as they scraped at her skin.

There was a primitive side to her brain that screamed at her to run. Run for her life!

And she did just that.

Then the sounds of something crunching after her reached her ears. She puffed and huffed as her arms pumped by her side, and her feet pounded over the ground.

This wasn't a dream.

This was a nightmare.

Her lungs burned as they tried to keep up with her legs. Great. Not only was she slightly out of shape in real life, but also in her dream. If she could dream her clothes away, couldn't she dream herself with a six pack and ripped legs?

Andrea did her best to keep ahead of whatever crashed after her, but it was only a matter of time. Her legs were slowing, and whatever was behind her was gaining ground. She could hear it breathing down her neck.

Then a large mass hit her as something tackled her to the ground. A large weight slammed into her back, and as she landed, she twisted in its grasp and let out a squeak of terror at what she saw.

A sabertooth tiger's mouth gaped down at her. Her eyes widened as she took in the size of the canines that were right in her face. She could have stuck out her tongue and licked a canine, it was so close. As its mouth came down for a killer bite, she screamed as she thrashed her arms and legs.

With the jerking movements of her arms, the bracelet rolled off her wrist as she shut her eyes tight and wished to be home.

Andrea let out a scream.

"What's wrong with you?!" A voice snapped in irritation.

"Don't yell at her." Emma's voice said sternly from nearby. "She's clearly ill."

Andrea's eyes snapped open to find a swarm of archeologists surrounding her. "What happened?" She asked as she tried to take in the fact that she was lying on the ground and only a moment ago, she'd screamed like a moron in front of her colleagues. Talk about embarrassing.

"You must have passed out." Clyde's bearded face came into view. "We didn't notice you on the ground until we heard you screaming."

"It was like you just suddenly appeared out of nowhere." Emma agreed as she nodded her head vigorously, the rim of her broad hat bobbing up and down.

"Here," Clyde took one of Andrea's arms, "let me help you to some shade. You may have fainted because you overheated."

"Thanks." Andrea murmured as she saw the wooden bracelet resting on the ground nearby. With a quick blur of movement, she scooped up the bracelet and pocketed it before anyone could see the artifact.

"Grab her other arm." Clyde directed another man, who quickly stepped in to take her other arm.

"I don't think–"

"Shush, you." Clyde cut her off. "I don't need you dying on the job. Too much paperwork, and then I'd have to find another archeologist with as much eagerness as you."

Andrea rolled her eyes. "I'm not going to die."

"Heatstroke is serious. Do you know how many people die each year of heatstroke?"

"No, do you?" Andrea challenged.

"A lot," Clyde said without losing a beat.

"Fine." She grumped, seeing the hard line of Clyde's mouth. "I'll rest in the shade for a bit and re-hydrate."

"Good. Glad you're thinking clearly now."

As they walked under a tent, she could feel the air cool down by about ten degrees. The two men guided her over to a metal folding chair and didn't let go of her arms until she was firmly seated. Then Clyde rushed to grab her a water bottle and shoved it into her hands.

"Thanks." Andrea accepted the sweating bottle and cracked the plastic seal on the water bottle and raised it to her lips, and took a few gulps. The cold liquid felt so good on her sore throat. Her screaming had been no joke. She'd thought for a few seconds that she might actually die in her dream.

Clyde pointed a finger at her. "You drink that whole bottle and spend at least thirty minutes under this tent before you even think about rejoining the rest of us out in the dig site."

"Aye aye, sir." She raised a hand to her forehead and saluted him.

It was his turn to roll his eyes at her before walking away from her.

Andrea slowly sipped at the water as she watched the time click by on her watch. When she finished the bottle, she tossed it into a nearby bin before reaching a hand into her pants pocket and fiddled with the wooden bracelet.

That dream of hers had been so vivid. The colors of the trees and the noises still rung in her head. Then there was the foul breath of the sabertooth as it opened its mouth. It had smelled of rotten flesh. A shiver rolled through her as she jumped a little in her seat.

The images of that sabertooth seemed more like a memory than a dream. Those fuzzy lines still didn't appear in her mind. Those long canines were seared into her brain. They'd been stained brown after years of use.

Shaking her head, Andrea laughed at herself. Her mind had been fried by the sunlight, and she was being silly. If her dream had been real, then that meant she'd time traveled, and as far as she was aware, that couldn't happen… unless magic was involved… and if she believed in magic, then she was definitely losing her mind.

Time travel and magic.

Andrea snorted.

The sun and heat had taken more of her sanity than she would have liked to admit.

"How you feeling?" Emma walked up beside her chair.

"Much better." Andrea smiled over at her friend as she leaned against the metal back. "So much better now that I'm in the shade with some water."

"Good." Emma crouched beside her. "I was worried you might need a hospital visit when you were spotted on the ground." Emma placed a hand on Andrea's knee. "And what was with that screaming? You gave us all heart attacks."

Andrea blushed. "Sorry. I had a nightmare while I was passed out." Andrea reached a hand behind her head and yanked the scrunchy out of her hair, letting the auburn locks fall loose around her shoulders.

"And?" Emma persisted.

"And what?" Andrea leaned back against the chair as she stretched her legs out in front of her and studied the tan cargo pants she loved. Almost all of her pants were cargo pants, although there were the occasional blue jeans in her closet.

"Your nightmare had you screaming like a banshee, so it must be something worth discussing. You definitely have my interest piqued." Emma gave up on squatting next to Andrea's chair and plopped her butt down on the ground, before crisscrossing her legs and turned her blue eyes up at Andrea like a three-year-old ready for a story.

"In my nightmare, I woke up naked." Andrea started since she had no idea what Emma wanted from this conversation.

Emma nodded her head. "And…?"

"Which was weird, but I guess that's a dream for you." Andrea shrugged her shoulders. "They don't have to make sense, and then I walked around until a loud crunch behind me had me sprinting through the forest."

Emma nodded her head.

"Then a sabertooth jumped me, and right as he was about to rip out my throat, I woke up here." Andrea waved a hand at the dig site.

Emma's nose scrunched as she continued to nod her head. "I can see why you'd scream like a maniac. Nightmares can seem so real until you wake up, and being chased by a sabertooth?" Her friend shuddered. "I'd be screaming myself awake as well."

"Am I paying both of you to sit on the job?" Clyde walked past them to grab a water bottle for himself.

"I needed a little break from the sun and to check up on Andrea." Emma bounded to her feet in a fluid motion that would rival any gymnast. The woman was fit, tan, blue-eyed, and blonde.

Andrea wasn't one to be jealous, but she did envy Emma a bit for her perfect figure. Her own auburn curls were pretty, but if she ever went out to a club or bar with Emma, she knew who would get more attention from men.

"How are you doing?" Clyde snapped the seal on the bottle as he walked over to them.

"Much better." Andrea stood. "And ready to get back to work."

"Love the eagerness." Clyde took a swig of water, a bit trickling out as he guzzled it. "Now, get back out there, you two." Then he swiped his wrist over his mouth to wipe away the water.

"We're moving, we're moving." Andrea grumped as she left the shade of the tent behind and walked over to her dig site. Her work boots kicked up a bit of dust, just proving how brutal the sun was. There wasn't an ounce of water in this soil.

Gripping the sides of the ladder, Andrea slid all the way down until her feet hit solid ground. As she knelt by her digging supplies, she heard Emma's boots clattered down the rungs of the metal ladder.

"Want to hit up that Chinese restaurant near our hotel tonight?" Emma asked from her side of the dig site. "I don't usually eat out. I like to stick to a strict diet, but it's been calling my name ever since we started this dig, and I need something spicy and slathered in sauce."

"Not tonight." Andrea glanced up from her supplies and sent Emma a smile. "How about we go there tomorrow?"

"Sounds like a plan!"

It might be nothing, but Andrea wanted some time alone in her hotel room to study this wooden bracelet she'd found. That dream or nightmare, whatever it had been, spun in her mind, and she needed to know more about it.

Chapter 2

The moment her workday was done, Andrea leaped into her rented SUV, and with a quick wave to Emma, she pulled out onto the dirt road and drove the thirty minutes back into town.

Eager to relax in her room, she'd barely thrown her car into park in the parking lot before leaping out, and racing up to her hotel room. Slipping the key card into the top of the hotel mechanism, she opened her door the moment a green light blinked on the device, and then closed it behind her.

Once Andrea had the security lock flipped into place, she kicked off her shoes and reached a hand into a pocket on her cargo pants. Her fingers caressed the wooden bracelet as she moved to the kitchenette in the hotel room. It had a microwave, a small fridge, a hot plate, and plenty of counter space. Super basic and just enough to keep her comfortable.

She grabbed one of the bottles of red wine off the counter and a glass. Walking back into the combined living room and bedroom, she flopped onto the queen-sized bed. She uncorked the half-full bottle and poured the crimson liquid into a glass.

Then Andrea grabbed the remote and threw something on in the background as she took a couple of sips of wine and pulled the wooden bracelet out of her cargo pants pocket.

"I could so get fired for this," Andrea said as she studied the faded red paint in the designs of the bracelet. Removing an artifact from a dig site was a big no no. If Clyde found out, he would have no choice but to fire her, and then good luck finding another job in this field.

Even as she thought about how much trouble she'd be in if someone found out, she leaned in closer to study the bracelet. As much as she told herself she hadn't traveled back in time, she still couldn't convince herself it had only been a dream.

Those colors of the trees and grass, the sight of the grass wiggling between her toes, and the smell of the sabertooths breath had been so distinct. Every time she thought back on them, they felt more like a memory rather than a hazy dream.

Reaching over to her bedside table, Andrea grabbed her wine glass and sipped from it while staring at the wooden bracelet. If it hadn't been a dream, then she was sure this bracelet had something to do with it.

As the night waned, and Andrea polished off the rest of the red wine, and as her head hit her lumpy hotel pillow, she slipped the bracelet onto her wrist and closed her eyelids.

Andrea cracked her eyes open to find herself once more in another world. She could feel the damp grass under her bare back, and the cool air rushed over her naked body. Whether or not this was a dream or time travel, she'd prefer to be dressed. Clothing was a twenty-first century weapon, and she felt stronger with it covering her body.

She took a moment to watch the lazy puffy white clouds drift over the blue sky before she slowly sat up. Placing her hands behind her back, she pushed until she was on her butt. Tall green grass surrounded her. It waved lightly as a soft breeze blew through the area. When she pushed herself up on her feet, she could see over the grass that came up to her waist. Lifting a hand, she skimmed her palm over the tops of the grass as she walked through it.

As far as Andrea could see, there weren't any sabertooths nearby.

Then again, in this tall grass, she would never know if there was a sabertooth lurking nearby... watching and stalking her. Nervously, she eyed the waving grass around her as her heart thundered in her chest. The last time she'd been tackled by a sabertooth had been plenty for her.

Andrea continued to walk through the grass as she marveled at the clarity of her dream. Green leafed trees spotted the landscape, and blueish grey pine trees stood in stark contrast to the rest of the scenery.

Within minutes, she heard the trickling of water. Her curiosity piqued, she followed the sound until she wandered across a small stream. The water was crystal clear, allowing her to see straight down to the reddish brown and tan rocks that had been worn smooth by years of constant running water.

Taking a deep breath, Andrea stuck a bare foot into the gurgling water, and let out a small squeak of a gasp as the cold water sucked the warmth right out of her foot. She plunged her other foot into the water and hopped to the other side of the stream, causing droplets of water to splash through the air wildly.

As the water droplets on her skin dried, a chill spread across her lower legs and feet. Walking into the grass on the other side of the stream, she bent over in the grass, grabbed handfuls, and used the thick stemmed grass as a towel.

Once done, she surveyed the area, saw a forest of towering trees ahead, and began to make her way towards them.

Andrea paused as the ground began to shake under her feet.

"What the hell?" She cursed as she ducked low in the grass. She wasn't sure what to do, and the ground was still trembling under her feet. Her first thought was an earthquake, but it didn't feel quite right, and she'd lived in California for a few years.

A loud trumpeting noise echoed through the air.

Andrea's head whipped up, nearly giving her whiplash, as her eyes searched the area for the source of the shaking ground and loud trumpeting noises.

A small herd of mammoths walked along the outline of the forest. Her jaw dropped as she observed the large beasts. Their shaggy coats swayed around their massive bodies as they walked across the landscape. Their long trunks waved in front of their faces as they searched the ground for any fresh shoots. Her eyes then went to the massive curved ivory tusks.

They were stunning.

Andrea had seen plenty of mammoth bones, and like most people who visited museums, had seen a couple of skulls or re-created mammoth bones, but she'd never seen one like this. It was awe-inspiring and caused her to tremble in excitement.

What she needed was a camera!

Of course, a camera would do her no good. If she did bring back a photo to her time, people would assume it was either art or photoshopped. No one would believe her if she said she went back in time and photographed these wonderful beasts. They would call her crazy and send her to a psychiatric hospital.

As the herd of giant beasts entered the other side of the forest, she saw the cutest thing ever. A baby woolly mammoth trailing after its mother. The goofy little creature had a bounce to its step as it frolicked through the tall grass.

Another blur of movement caught Andrea's eye, and when she glanced to her other side, her breath caught in her chest.

A sabertooth.

The intimidating creature trailed after the herd of mammoths. Her eyes sought out the baby mammoth, but it was too close to the adults for the sabertooth to be a threat… at least for now. She hoped the sabertooth wouldn't get the opportunity to kill that adorable little baby.

Ducking down in the tall grass, Andrea slowly slid back towards the stream. As much as she would like to keep watching the beasts, she didn't need the sabertooth spotting her and attacking. One sabertooth attack was enough for her.

As she slid back into the water, she barely

noticed the cold, her focus on making as little sound as possible. Crouched like she was, she ended up soaking more than just her legs, but she didn't care. It didn't matter if this was a dream. She still didn't want to imagine being attacked by a sabertooth. When she'd crossed to the other side of the stream, she continued to crawl through the grass.

Her main concern was the sabertooth prowling around on the other side of the stream. She'd worry about drying off later.

After a couple of minutes of scuttling around in the tall grass, she popped her head up and glanced around. There were no sabertooths or mammoths around that she could see, so she assumed she was safely away from them.

Good.

Standing to her full height, Andrea walked around aimlessly. The flora and fauna fascinated her archeologist's mind. Some of these animals and plants didn't exist in her time, and it was hard for her to pass up the chance to study them.

When she spotted a herd of horses in the distance, she paused to take in the sight. The animals were a bit smaller than the ones she was used to, more like an Icelandic pony than a thoroughbred.

Not wanting to disturb the horses, Andrea moved on until she found some plants. The leaves were something she'd only found preserved in stone, so she picked some leaves, clutching them in her hand in the hopes that she could bring them back to her time if this truly was time travel.

Andrea glanced around, wondering how she could carry the leaves. If only she had her cargo pants, then she would be able to stuff the pockets full of these leaves.

Twitching her nose in annoyance, she huffed and puffed and eventually let the leaves fall from her grasp. They fluttered in the air, waving back and forth until finally landing on the ground.

It was wishful thinking. So far, she hadn't been able to take anything between this world and hers.

It seemed she would have to settle for the leaf imprints they found in the dig sites. Andrea glared at the bracelet on her wrist. It appeared that the only thing that could come with her was the bracelet.

Too bad.

Walking away from her pile of discarded leaves, Andrea proceeded to explore the immediate area. Small birds flew away in a flutter of frantic wings as they shot out of the tall grass at her rude interruption.

Then as Andrea neared a pocket of trees, she heard something that had her ears perking up. It almost sounded like talking. It was guttural, and she couldn't understand it, but it did sound like people speaking to each other.

Crouching low to the ground, Andrea crept across the ground, barely making a sound. As she peered over a medium sized green leafed bush, she saw where the talking was coming from.

Neanderthals.

As an archeologist, she'd studied the difference between Neanderthals and homo sapiens. The Neanderthals were stockier in their build, looking like beefed up shorter men. Their foreheads were more prominent, and these were definitely Neanderthals. She studied the group with growing interest. They all appeared to be men, and all of them had long black or brown hair that was tied back with a rawhide band.

The group of Neanderthals stood in a tight group, seeming to discuss something.

Andrea's eyes wandered across the weapons they held or had tied to their bodies. One had what appeared to be a stone ax tied to his waist, and each of them also carried a spear in one hand. The wood shaft had a sharply carved stone tip that had been tied to the top with animal sinew. Maybe this was a Neanderthal hunting party, and if she was quiet enough, perhaps she could follow and watch them hunt.

There were many people in her time who were under the false impression that Neanderthals were primitive compared to their homo sapien counterparts, but there was a lot of evidence to the contrary.

As much as she wanted to think this was a dream, she was beginning to think it was real. Glancing down at her bracelet, she shook her head in wonderment. She wasn't sure if she was sane, but this was her archeologist wet dream right here.

Looking back at the group of Neanderthals, she found them walking away from her. Whatever they'd been discussing, there'd been a decision made. Stepping lightly to her side so she could follow them, her foot landed on a stick, and before she could jerk her weight back...

Snap!

The sound seemed to echo in the air around her, and Andrea cringed as her eyes shot up to see if the Neanderthals had heard the noise.

They had!

All of their heads shot up, and their eyes began searching the area. She still held hope they would continue with their day, and she wouldn't be spotted. Keeping one hundred percent frozen behind her bush, she prayed they wouldn't come over to where she hid.

No such luck.

The lead man began to steer his men over to where she was hiding.

Andrea kept firmly in place behind her bush, but when the men were about to stride right into her, she leaped to her feet, spun around, and sprinted in the other direction.

A guttural cry went up behind her as they caught sight of her, and her heart flew into her throat as her bare feet pounded across the hard ground.

Risking a glance behind her, she saw the Neanderthals hot on her tail. There was a glimmer of eagerness in their dark eyes. Facing back to the direction she was running, she pumped her arms at her side. They were probably eager because she was butt ass naked, and they were primitive men. They most likely were thinking about conking her over the head with a wooden club and dragging her back to their cave for wicked deeds.

Like hell that would be happening.

Dream or no dream, she wasn't about to let an orgy happen with her. She was a one man kind of gal.

Andrea raced through the tall grass area, and when she reached the stream, she leaped into the air and cleared it easily, before landing on the other side and continuing towards the forest.

Small rocks and branches pinched and prodded at the soft skin of her feet, but she ignored the nuisances.

What she needed to do was lose these men in the woods. Then again, they were primitive hunters, and she was beginning to wonder if she'd ever be able to lose them. Glancing over her shoulder, she found the men still hot on her trail.

Dammit all to hell!

Her lungs burned like someone had shoved kindling into them and lit them on fire.

Facing forwards, Andrea leaped over a tree root that did its best to trip her, but her adrenaline helped her zero in her focus on survival.

A whirring sound from behind her, had her mind racing with thoughts as it tried to figure out what that might be. She didn't have time to look back and see though. With how fast she was moving through the woods, she had to keep her gaze facing forward. Then something wrapped around her ankles, and she found the ground rushing up towards her face.

"Shit!" Andrea screamed as she raised her hands in front of her face to protect it as she sailed towards the ground.

Someone's hands wrapped around her ankles, and with a ferocious scream, she rolled onto her back, rose up, balled her fist, and decked the closest Neanderthal in the face. He let out a grunt of pain but didn't release his hold on her. Right as she was about to deck him again, another Neanderthal caught up, grabbed her hands, and with a yank held them behind her back. She felt him wrap something around her wrists, and when he was done, she found her arms completely useless to her.

Leaning forward, she screamed in the Neanderthal's face, "Let me go! Now!"

The Neanderthal's lips simply curved up in a smile, revealing his yellowing teeth. He growled something at her, but all she could do was shake her head in confusion. She couldn't understand him, which didn't surprise her. She was thousands of years in the past. There was no way she would be able to communicate with him.

Andrea glared at him. Unless she wanted to head butt him or bite him, she was out of options.

The rest of the men caught up, and she counted five of them. If this was a dream, it could end now… but it didn't. It kept going.

The Neanderthal in front of her removed the throwing weapon that was wrapped around her legs. It was made of rawhide strips with decently sized rocks wrapped around the ends.

A lot of modern people thought Neanderthals were simplistic and stupid, but they would be dead wrong. Archeologists had proven that they were intelligent over and over again. There were several caves discovered in the European region where there were Neanderthal cave drawings and sophisticated weapons.

When the Neanderthal in front of her was done freeing her ankles, she was tempted to bolt to her feet, but she dashed the idea. Assuming she did get away from them, her hands would still be tied behind her back, which would only result in her being defenseless until she could figure out how to shed the ties.

The Neanderthal growled something at her, and his putrid breath washed over her nose. It crinkled her nose in disgust as she pulled back slightly.

When he stared at her expectantly, she shook her head, her loose hair waving over her shoulders.

He huffed with obvious irritation but decided there was nothing he could do about their lack of communication. He stood up. Then he motioned for the Neanderthal behind her to hoist her up onto her feet.

Hands dipped under her armpits, and the Neanderthal behind her lifted her, and the tips of his fingers brushed over the sides of her breasts. She barely suppressed a growl of outrage. Now wasn't the time to lash out for a brush that might have been an accident. She needed to bide her time.

Once Andrea was on her feet, she skittered away from the Neanderthal's touch because she was pretty sure he had skimmed her breasts on purpose. Not that she could read his mind, but when she whirled and faced him, he stared openly at her exposed nudity. Her eyes narrowed.

Andrea glared at all the men who surrounded her. "Since we can't communicate, I'm going to name each of you."

The Neanderthals around her shrugged as they growled words at each other and watched her.

She was going to name the head Neanderthal Nick. The one with a scarred face, like he'd been mauled by a cave bear, she was going to name Allen. The next one would be named Bob because he kind of looked like a guy who would be named Bob. Robert was the one with his hair braided into one large braid that ran down his back. And the last one would be named Mike, because of his bushy beard, which rivaled the other mens'.

Nick grabbed a hold of her arm in a rough grip and yanked her towards him. He growled something at her, and Andrea didn't need a translator for this one… she was his. There was a gleam of excitement shining bright in his brown eyes as he scanned her face.

Andrea scrunched her face up and tried to yank back out of his grasp, but it was like trying to rip her arm free of a band of steel. These Neanderthals were made of pure muscles.

Suddenly, he spun her around, and she felt

him doing something with her bindings. Was he letting her go?! Excitement built in her as her heart thundered and adrenaline pumped through her system, readying itself for a fight or flight situation.

When he spun Andrea back around, she glanced down at his hand, and her heart dropped. He was holding a rope made of tanned animal skin. He wasn't letting her go. He'd been putting a leash on her already tied hands.

Chapter 3

This whole situation would be so much better if she were dressed. Even a bra and underwear would be nice. Andrea hunched over herself as she walked after Nick, who still held her leash in his hand, trying to hide her nudity.

The rest of the Neanderthals walked around her. Every once in a while, she could feel their heated gazes drift over her. She would have sworn there must have been scorch marks all over her skin by now with all those heated gazes glancing over her exposed body. Nick may have claimed her as his, but clearly the others were wishing for their own opportunity with her.

Andrea wasn't sure where they were headed, but the men seemed to know where they wanted to go. They walked through the forest for the better part of the day before Nick, the lead Neanderthal, stopped in a small meadow. The sun was beginning to set, and brilliant reds, oranges, and pinks flew across the sky, mixing in with the blackening starry sky.

The rest of the men spread out a bit, and she noticed them gathering wood. This appeared to be the place where they would make camp for the night. Nerves and the cold had her shaking a bit. As night settled on them, she had no doubt the massive predators of the ice age would come out to hunt.

Nick yanked her towards him with the animal skin leash. The jerking movement had her plowing into his barrel chest, but he barely seemed to register her weight. A smile spread across his lips as he raised a hand to play with her loose auburn curls.

He growled something guttural at her, and she prayed to whatever gods they had back then that he wasn't going to try and use her tonight.

This nightmare was getting worse with every minute that passed.

Where was a sabertooth when someone needed it?

Another of the Neanderthals called out to Nick, and he used his hands on her shoulders to press her down until her bottom was firmly planted on the ground.

He told her something while giving her a stern look.

Andrea shrugged her shoulders to let Nick know she had no idea what he was saying, but at least he was trying to communicate with her. It gave her hope for the upcoming night.

Nick held out a hand and pushed it to the ground.

"Stay seated?"

He did the movement again before deciding that was enough and left her side to join Bob. The both of them walked into the forest and disappeared from sight.

Peering around herself, Andrea found the other three Neanderthals still around her. She could get up to her feet, even with her hands tied behind her back, but with three Neanderthals within sight, it wasn't like she would get anywhere before they caught her.

Rolling her shoulders, she tried in vain to get them into another position, because her muscles in her back were beginning to cramp and cause her some discomfort.

Allen, with the scarred face, walked up to her, a bunch of wood in his arms. Then he dropped the wood, before kneeling before the sticks and logs. She watched as he rearranged the kindling and wood. Then he pulled a pack from off his waist, opened it, pulled out some animal skin, and then pulled back the folds until he exposed a red-hot coal. Allen placed the coal among the logs and blew until it lit the kindling. The flames licked hungrily at the logs, putting off a lot of heat as the sun disappeared under the horizon, allowing the cold to creep up and prickle her skin.

When Allen leaned back and focused his brown eyed gaze on her, Andrea shifted uncomfortably and dropped her gaze. She hoped taking a demure demeanor would help her with fending off these primitive men.

A scooting noise reached her ears, and when she glanced back up, she found the spot on the other side of the fire empty. A growl in her ear, had Andrea's head zipping around to see Allen right next to her. He was invading her personal space.

Trying to scoot away, she paled when his hand flew through the air and grabbed her upper arm.

"Leave me alone!" Andrea barked. Screw being demure. That clearly hadn't worked, and it was hard for her to suppress her inner fighter.

Allen growled something at her as he threw her back against the ground and attempted to climb up on her.

"Hell no!" Andrea rolled out from under him, and when his head turned to face her, she kicked out a foot and nailed him in the chin with her heel.

The clink of his teeth reached her ears, right before a roar of raw anger pierced the air.

Flipping around, she glanced at the other two men who were simply staring at her and Allen, but neither of them seemed interested in helping her. They must be the two at the bottom of the totem pole then, and she was dealing with a guy who held some rank in the group.

She was doomed.

Leaping to her feet, in an athletic grace she didn't know she had within her plumper body, Andrea ran. Who needed the use of their hands when adrenaline pumped through them? Not her.

Sadly, Andrea didn't get far, before Allen had her pushed up against a tree trunk, still in view of their camp, still with the other two just watching with blank stares. The rough bark prodded at the soft skin of her back and butt cheeks as he pressed into her.

Allen leaned his face close to hers as he growled. His bulbous nose nearly brushed hers as his foul breath washed over her, nearly choking her with the repulsive odor. Despite the dark around them, she could clearly make out the hundreds of scars that coated the tanned skin of his face.

When his hands began exploring her curves, Andrea tried to side step away from him, but he had her pressed tightly between his body and the tree. Unless she wanted to lose some skin, she wasn't going anywhere.

So… she chose her last defense.

Andrea sucked in a gulp of air and then let out the highest pitch screech a human throat could make.

He grimaced, but there was a determined glint in those brown eyes as his hands continued exploring.

Andrea continued screaming. She would have tried to knee him in the balls, but the length of his body pressed her up into the tree, leaving her lungs as her only weapon since her hands were still tightly tied behind her back.

Then a roar of fury from behind them had them both freezing, and Andrea's screaming caught in her throat. Someone was coming to her rescue.

Peering over Allen's shoulder, she found Nick and Bob striding back into camp, and Nick didn't look too happy if his drawn brows and puffed up chest meant anything. It wasn't like she wanted to sleep with any of them, but right now, she was hoping Nick, the nicest Neanderthal of the group, would come to her rescue.

Allen turned, but he kept a firm grip on her arm as he brought her into his side. He growled something at Nick that didn't sound very nice to her. Clearly, Allen thought Nick should at least share if not give Andrea over to him completely.

Nick's eyes flickered back and forth between them. He was searching... seeing if she wanted Allen?

Andrea shook her head swiftly. She didn't want anything to do with Allen.

Allen crushed her to him when he caught her silently communicating with Nick. Nick let out a growl as he marched towards Allen.

Deciding it was time for a fight, Allen thrust her away. If she had use of her arms, she could have righted herself, but with her hands tied behind her back she ended up landing on the ground like a sack of potatoes.

The men collided in the next second.

Andrea's jaw dropped. Men fighting over a woman was a fantasy most women dreamed of, but it was a fantasy, meaning they didn't really want it in real life. If they had been two attractive men fighting over her, she might have been rejoicing a bit more, but she had two Neanderthal men fighting over her. Not really her fantasy.

Their stocky bodies were thicker than a human, and she had to wonder if they might have a little more muscle than the average human as well. The two men pummeled each other with their fists. Nick landed a blow that had Allen's head snapping back with a pained grunt, but when he recovered, he came back at Nick.

Andrea wasn't sure who she wanted to win this fight because she was fairly certain the winner would think her theirs. And she didn't want to be anyones.

Ripping her eyes off the fighting men, she saw the other three Neanderthals just standing around.

"Aren't you guys going to stop them?" She gaped at the other men from where she laid on her side like a fish on land.

One of them, Mike, turned his head towards her, but deciding she was less interesting than the fight, he turned his attention back towards the fight.

When Andrea looked back at Allen and Nick, she found them tumbling around on the ground. Nick held Allen down, pressing a hand to the man's neck until Allen grumped something at him. Pulling back, Nick stood and offered the man on the ground a hand. Allen looked as though he would reject the hand, but then he slapped his into Nick's, and Nick hauled him up to his feet.

It seemed they had come to a decision.

Nick left his clan mate and strode over to her. He reached down, grabbed her upper arms, and yanked her up to her feet. Then he guided her over to the fire, which was still gleefully burning in the middle of their camp.

"Thanks." She whispered under her breath, and Nick spared her a quick glance and an utterance of his own. They didn't need to understand each other's words to know she was thanking him, and he was saying, you're welcome.

Bob pulled a couple of dead rabbits off his belt as he knelt by the camp fire.

"Dinner?" She turned to Nick as she let him help her down.

He shook his head at her.

"I'm just going to assume yes. I've never eaten rabbit before." Andrea shifted her attention back to Bob as he began to skin and gut the rabbit. She blanched and looked away. Yeah, no. She was a fan of buying her food in a grocery store. It didn't have eyes, usually, and it never looked cute and fuzzy.

If she forgot she was surrounded by several scary Neanderthals, she might have enjoyed the camping feel of this moment. The fire light lit up the immediate area, while the rest of the land was covered in dark.

Tilting her head back, Andrea gazed up at the stars above her in wonderment. It was like a giant had blown a handful of sugar into the sky.

Within minutes, Bob had those rabbits skinned and roasting over the fire on a spit, which he turned every once in a while. As the smell of cooking meat drifted over to her, she couldn't stop the growl that rumbled from her stomach.

All the men turned to stare at her, and she cast them a sheepish grin. "Sorry. Been a while since I last ate."

Of course, they didn't understand her, and their attention quickly returned to the fire, the rabbits, and whatever they were discussing in their primitive language.

Now that things were moving at a slower pace, Andrea was able to take in their tanned animal skin clothing. She wasn't entirely sure what animal they had used, but with the light brown fur tufts that they'd left on the tanned skins, she was going to guess deer. The clothing was simple, in that, they hadn't appeared to decorate it with any beads.

Nick leaned over to her and presented a fur in his outstretched hands.

"For me?"

He unfurled the fur and swung it up and over her shoulders.

"Thanks."

It wasn't a lot, but it was already warming her back up. As was the fire. The heat from the flames warmed her legs and her front half. She wished she could hold her hands out to the fire, but Nick was never going to untie her.

As her eyes drifted from the camp fire and over her companions, she noticed the Neanderthals around her wore necklaces with teeth strung on them. Her eyes narrowed as she looked at a few around Allen's neck… some of those appeared to be human teeth. It was from a slight distance, or the firelight playing tricks on her mind, but those definitely looked like human teeth.

Bob pulled the crispy rabbits off the firepit, immediately grabbing her attention. He pulled out a stone knife and cut the meat up into rough pieces. Trickles of heat could be seen drifting off the slices, and her stomach let out another growl.

"Yum." Nick's brown eyes glanced over at her, and she pointed to the meat with her nose that was now being passed out. "I'd love some."

Nick reached out a hand and took some of the roasted rabbit meat. Then he shifted on his bottom until he faced her. He held up some meat, and she nodded her head eagerly as she twisted her tied hands to the side of her body and wiggled her fingers for the morsel.

But Nick just shook his head at her.

"What?" Andrea felt some disappointment soar into her chest as she thought that he meant to only tease her and not feed her.

Then Nick held the meat in the air with a couple of his fingers, and realization dawned. He wanted to hand feed her. Ugh. She wasn't so sure she wanted to do that. Then her stomach let out a horrendous growl.

Nick brought the meat to his mouth and ate it. Then he quickly grabbed another and offered it to her.

"Fine." Andrea gave up, leaned in, and right as she was about to snag the meat with her teeth, a howl echoed through the trees. Nick pulled his hand back, and her teeth clinked together on thin air.

"What the hell?" Andrea couldn't contain her anger. He'd just teased her! "I gave in. What more do you want from me?" She steamed.

Nick quieted her with a few waves of his hand.

Then another howl echoed through the forest, and then another from a different direction sounded.

"So, there are wolves in the forest." Andrea shrugged unconcernedly. With their brightly burning fire and how many of them there were, she wasn't too afraid of an attack. Wolves tended to stay away from humans, and she thought it'd be the same back in the ice age. No animal liked fire. It was instinct.

Andrea's heart leaped into her throat as she gazed around at the Neanderthals around her. Their eyes had gone wide, and their sudden fear had her worrying. Maybe she was wrong with her assumption that predators didn't like fire. Maybe predators didn't fear humans and Neanderthals in the ice age.

Suddenly, all of the Neanderthals leaped to their feet. Nick rushed to pull her onto her feet. The moment she was up, he spun her around, ripped off the fur, and cut the bindings on her wrists with a stone knife.

"Ummm, thanks?" Andrea wasn't so sure her hands getting untied was a good thing. It meant Nick thought she might need to use them.

Howls began to fill the night air, and it sounded like they were getting closer. Much closer. And the howls sounded like a pack that was communicating during a hunt, but a hunt of what?

Nick ushered her away. He waved his hands at her, and when she took some cautious steps away from him, he nodded at her.

Turning, she bolted.

When Andrea reached the edge of the forest, she glanced back at the group of Neanderthals, who were now armed and slightly crouched as they waited by the camp fire. Were wolves in this time really that much more daring?

Then the wolves broke into the small meadow, and a shiver raced up and down her spine. Those weren't just wolves. Those were dire wolves. A top ice age predator. She'd worked several digs where dire wolf skeletons had been uncovered. They were beefier wolves and slightly bigger than your normal wolf, and there were several of them bearing down on the Neanderthals right now.

The Neanderthals let out a war cry and charged the dire wolves, and Andrea decided she'd seen enough.

Dashing through the forest, she hoped to hell the Neanderthals, and the dire wolves would kill each other, and she could get away free. Once she found a new hiding spot, she ducked down, low to the ground.

Within minutes, Andrea heard something crashing towards her hiding spot. Staying hidden behind her bush, she waited to see who it was. Nick burst through the trees.

Leaping out, Andrea called out, "Over here!" She waved her hands frantically at Nick. What a turn of fate. She was now turning to her Neanderthal captor for help.

Rushing over to her, Nick grabbed her arm and resumed barreling through the forest. She wasn't entirely sure what had happened to the other men, and she didn't know if Nick being here was a good or a bad thing, but she was going with him anyway.

Howls of wolves once more rang out in the dark forest, and she didn't need any encouragement from Nick to sprint through the forest. No branch, no rock, and no root would stop her forward momentum. She felt like a deer as she leaped over anything in her way. Adrenaline hyped up her senses allowing her to feel a bit like a super human.

Her breaths came out as pants as she sucked in gulps of air cold night air. Sticks and stones prodded the soft under sides of her feet, but she pressed on. There was a lot of motivation snarling at her back.

A growl sounded behind them, and suddenly Nick was gone from beside Andrea. Risking a glance behind her, she saw two wolves facing off with him in the moonlight. Good luck, Nick, and she meant it, but she wasn't sticking around to see the outcome.

Chapter 4

Nose to the ground in his dire wolf form, Rokki growled in frustration.

One scent filled his nose.

Neanderthals.

These Neanderthals kept invading their territory, hunting their prey, and despite many warnings, they were still doing it. It was time to send a stronger message, a message the Neanderthals would understand. A message that would stick with them.

Ruub, a pack member, stepped up beside him, his grey fur waving in the slight breeze that drifted through the forest, carrying the scent of the Neanderthals, and... something else. Something Rokki didn't quite know, but he supposed he would find out soon enough.

Moonlight lit the meadow they were in, and even if it hadn't, his vision would have been more than adequate.

Glancing around, Rokki found the other three wolves with them. Naab sprinted over to them in his grey wolf form, with Grok and Dholk trailing behind.

With a simple flick of his black furred ears and tail, and Rokki sent his pack members racing ahead, with Rokki trailing after them. He would let his clanmates take care of the Neanderthals, while he tried to figure out what that strange scent was that tickled his wolf's nose.

Letting out ominous howls, they let the

Neanderthals know they were closing in for the kill. They dashed through a nearby forest, following the scent of their prey.

In no time, they broke into a meadow and saw five Neanderthal men facing them. Their spears were at the ready. Despite that, he knew this would be a simple fight.

Rokki crouched low to the ground and snarled at the Neanderthals in front of them. Only two of them shook visibly. The rest had a glint of determination shining bright in their eyes. Their camp fire lit up their faces, which were set in determined grimaces as they readied themselves to fight off the dire wolves.

Charging forward, Rokki picked a target in front of him. The man's face was covered in scars from previous fights, but Rokki wouldn't be adding any more for him to show off. He was going to kill him.

The man waved the sharp tip of a spear at him, and Rokki threw his large wolf frame to the side to dodge the sharp tip. Leaping back into action, he drew the man away from his group, slowly backing up, while doing his best not to make it too obvious.

Scar face followed him.

The Neanderthal was too stupid to realize Rokki want him alone. To have his back unguarded.

His men were attacking the other Neanderthals, but Ruub found a moment to turn and nip at scar face's calf. Scar face jerked around, but Ruub had already gone back to attacking his own Neanderthal, which left scar face open to attack by Rokki.

Rokki lunged. His black dire wolf form sailed

through the air, and his mouth full of sharp teeth clamped down on scar face's arm. Scar face let out a horrific scream as he dropped his spear. His other hand balled into a fist, and he hammered the top of Rokki's head.

Thrashing his head side to side, Rokki caused as much damage to the man's arm, before he released it and backed off. Shaking his massive head, he shook off the ringing in his ears from the hammering scar face had given him. Before scar face could grab another weapon, Rokki leaped onto him.

He went straight for the jugular. His sharp canines dug into the flesh of scar face's neck, and when he jerked back, he ripped the man's throat out. Blood covered the immediate area, including Rokki.

Opening his jaw, he let the flesh drop from his mouth.

His dire wolf drew its lips back in a grimace. Neanderthal did not taste good. He wanted to find the closest stream and wash out his mouth, but he had other things to do. Cleaning the blood off his body and out of his mouth could wait until later.

Raising his head, Rokki found three Neanderthals and all of his men, which meant one of the Neanderthals had escaped. Lifting his dark nose to the air, he caught the other scent, despite scar face's blood all over his snout.

Circling around the fighting, Rokki broke out into a lope as he followed the fresh scent that disappeared into the forest. The Neanderthal was delusional if he thought Rokki would just let him disappear into the night.

Breaking into a run, his dire wolf form was

perfectly built for this environment. Although large, his sleek frame was built for a wild dash through the forest. His ears pointed forward as he heard his prey crashing through the forest ahead, and there was that scent again. It was different than the Neaderthal's scent. This time it was slightly stronger, and it called to him. Called to his dire wolf. Told him to run faster, so he did just that.

Rokki caught sight of the Neanderthal in front of him in the dark forest, and he was running next to what appeared to be a human woman. She didn't smell like a Neanderthal.

Not giving the woman much of a glance, he clamped his mouth down on the Neanderthal's leg.

Once Rokki dispatched this Neanderthal, he would pursue the woman who was still running through the forest. His dire wolf demanded that they seek her out and explore her scent further.

The Neanderthal fell to the ground with a grunt of pain.

Something hard smack across Rokki's head, dislodging him from the Neanderthal's calf. He shook his large head, trying to stop the ringing in his ears and the trees from swirling across his vision.

The Neanderthal jumped on top of Rokki, wrapped an arm around his neck, and tightened its hold.

Rokki's dire wolf snapped its jaw, but he couldn't get to the Neanderthal's arm. There was only one thing he could do. It might leave him vulnerable, but he wasn't in a great position at the moment either.

Shifting, Rokki slipped through the Neanderthal's arms, his human form smaller than his dire wolf. Once outside of the Neanderthal's arms, Rokki shifted again, this time back into dire wolf.

Frustration coursed through him that the Neanderthal would get the better of him. The barrel-chested man had strength but very little brains. The Neanderthal whirled and faced him, a club gripped in one hand.

So that was the weapon that had knocked him in the side of the head.

Rokki hadn't spotted the weapon on the man. His lips pulled back on his snout as he snarled at the man in anger. The Neanderthal may have landed a blow, but it wouldn't happen again.

Circling the Neanderthal, he searched for an opening. His opening came when a deer sprinted past them, startling the Neanderthal enough for him to turn away from Rokki.

Without a single hesitation, Rokki dug in his back paws and flung himself towards the Neanderthal. His teeth latched onto the man's arms, crushing the bone and skin until the Neanderthal released the club.

Releasing his hold, Rokki backed off only long enough to launch himself back at his enemy and knocked the Neanderthal off his feet. With his front paws on the man's barrel chest, he sank his teeth into the Neanderthal's throat.

When he pulled away, the man gasped and gurgled as he choked on his own blood and a crushed throat.

Rokki ignored the man's death gurgles while he raised his snout to the air and searched for the woman's scent. She couldn't have gotten far. With a chuff of excitement, he started his hunt.

Andrea was so done with this. She was done with the ice age. She was done with Neanderthals, and she was done with wolves.

She'd given up on thinking this was a dream or a nightmare. People would wake up from this kind of thing. She'd never heard of someone who had experienced such a horrible dream and not woken up. Everyone woke up during nightmares.

Which meant she was back in the ice age. With dire wolves, sabertooths, Neanderthals, and whatever else this world wanted to throw at her. A modern woman was not equipped for this kind of thing.

What she wouldn't give for a twenty-first century weapon right now.

It wasn't long until Andrea bent over at the waist and sucked in some much-needed air. Her lungs felt like they were on fire!

Something behind her snapped with a loud crack, and Andrea ignored her protesting muscles and pushed herself back into a run.

Before she got far, something large landed on her, and she hit the ground. With her hands out by her face, she froze on the cold grass and waited for her death. She could feel the hot breath of whatever stood over her back.

It didn't come though.

No teeth sank into her flesh. No claws dug into her skin.

Andrea felt the beast staring down at her.

Why wasn't it killing her?

Not that she wanted to be killed. It wasn't like she was complaining. She just didn't understand why the beast was teasing her. Animals weren't usually this cruel with their prey.

Andrea bit her lip, refusing to let any whimpers escape her mouth. She could feel the fur on his legs on each side of her rib cage, and she could feel his furry back legs around her thighs. It was a huge dire wolf, even for a dire wolf.

When still nothing happened, Andrea flipped herself over onto her back.

The snout of a dire wolf was directly in front of her face, and she gulped back her fear, which had to be pounding out of her. She really hoped the wolf couldn't smell her fear.

Those large golden eyes skimmed over her face. The fire wolf's black fluffy fur was outlined by the stars high above their heads and the moonlight glinting through the night.

The beast leaned forward, and she let out an eek as its black cold nose pressed to her neck. She heard him inhale, before pulling his head back and sending her a wolfy grin. Those teeth though sent fear pulsing straight from her head all the way to her toes.

Then the unthinkable happened.

The dire wolf shifted into a man. A naked man who was now lying over her naked body, and he was drop dead gorgeous with his think head of black hair and striking blue eyes. Those eyes! They almost glowed in the dark, and her heart skittered around in her chest.

His body dropped, allowing his weight to press her body into the grass... his erection pressing into her thigh! Andrea began to squirm under him as she felt panic pump through her. It was time to get out of this situation. She was so done with predators and men pressing themselves on her in this crazy ass world.

Raising her arms, she attempted to punch the man in his chiseled jaw, but with a growl of irritation, the man leaned back on his haunches, grabbed a hold of her arms, and then forced them above her head. The movement had the wooden bracelet slipping from her wrist, and as it slipped off, she closed her eyes and wished for her bed.

Andrea's eyes popped wide, and she found the white popcorn ceiling of her hotel room above her. Her legs were tangled in the hotel bed sheets, and a tv show played faintly in the background of the well-lit room.

A smile spread across her face. She was back. Darting up in bed, she ripped the wooden bracelet off her wrist and threw it across the bed, where it landed in the fluffy covers with a soft whoomph.

How crazy.

Again, there was no fuzziness to her dream. It felt just as sharp as a recent memory like she really had been in a forest just a couple of minutes ago. The golden eyes of the dire wolf were burned into her memories as were the blue eyes of the hunk that had been pressing his erection into her thigh.

Her blood heated as she thought back to the man who had been pressed so intimately against her. Even with their brief contact, she'd felt his abs and how muscular he was.

Swinging her legs off the side of her bed, Andrea stood up on the carpeted floor and winced at the slight irritation on the bottom of her feet. Sitting on the edge of her bed, she lifted a foot and twisted it with her hands until she could see the bottom of her foot. There were small cuts after all her running around... which meant that had been more than a dream. She'd traveled to the past.

Andrea glanced over at the wooden bracelet on the bed.

"What the hell did I find?" She was half tempted to tell Emma, give her friend the bracelet, and see if Emma experienced the same things, but then she'd have to come clean on taking an artifact from a dig site.

Andrea shook her head as she got up and walked into her bathroom. She was going to lotion up her feet and get some sleep without the bracelet on her wrist, and she wasn't sure she was ever going to put it back on.

Rokki stared down at the empty ground below him with a slack jaw. He blinked. She was still gone... disappeared into thin air. Blinking, he stared down at the empty spot below him before shifting back into his dire wolf form.

Sniffing the air around him while he turned his large head, he could tell that this was where her scent ended. It wasn't like she'd somehow slipped out from under him and ran. She'd just... poofed away. He could still see her outline in the grass.

Using the claws on his paws, Rokki frantically dug at the grass, kicking up large clumps of the dirt. The clumps of dirt flew wildly, landing in the bushes nearby, shaking the branches and leaves. When his digging didn't result in revealing where the human had gone, he stopped, panting.

One sniff and she was gone. He'd been so close to claiming his mate.

She was his mate.

There wasn't a single doubt in his mind that she had been his.

And now he had no idea where she'd gone.

His dire wolf threw its head back and let out a howl at the full moon above them as frustration coursed through it. Every wolf wanted to encounter his mate, and he had before she'd suddenly vanished!

He and his men had saved her from the Neanderthals, and he'd expected her to be grateful. Instead, fear had gushed off of her because of him. That had his dire wolf growling in anger. Even if she hadn't been his mate, he still wouldn't have hurt her.

Throwing back his wolf's head, Rokki let out another slow torturous howl of pain and loss. Then he snapped his mouth shut with a clink of his teeth. Glancing around, he made sure that no one in his pack was close enough to have seen the woman and his reactions to her.

No one needed to know he'd found his mate, and then she'd used magic to disappear. There was a prophecy about a witch, and he didn't want this to reach his brother's ears. Not yet at least. Not until he knew more about his mate.

Rokki didn't want to admit defeat in losing her, but there was nothing he could do. She was gone.

With a growl of annoyance curling the lips on his dire wolf's snout, he turned and loped back to his men. His wolf wanted to go back to where their mate disappeared, but he quickly shut the beast down. There was nothing more they could do for tonight, and he wasn't ready for his pack to know he found his mate.

Breaking into the meadow, Rokki slowed down. The pads of his feet gently bent the grass under his weight. He loved this form. If he could stay in his dire wolf form, he would. His dire wolf was more adapted to this environment.

His eyes drifted over to his men in the meadow. One of the Neanderthals was still fending off his men. The Neanderthal spun with a spear gripped tightly in his hands. The sharp stone tip swooshed through the air, threatening to slice one of the dire wolves that circled him.

As much as Rokki wanted to jump in and help his men, he knew he needed to let them figure this one out on their own. If four dire wolves couldn't take out a single Neanderthal… well, that would be an embarrassment for his people.

A grey wolf with golden eyes that glowed in the dark night lunged towards the Neanderthal. The man spun, trying to aim his weapon, but the grey wolf was too quick. With a snap of his jaws, he captured the spear in his mouth, dug in his four feet, and refused to loosen his hold no matter how much the Neanderthal shook him.

Another wolf, this one covered in thick black fur, jumped forward and latched onto the man's leg. Together, the two wolves dragged the Neanderthal to the ground, and the other two wolves jumped into the fray.

Within a couple of seconds, the last Neanderthal was dead.

Shifting back into his human form, Rokki called out, "Let's gather what we can from the bodies and head back to our village." There was no need to waste the supplies on the Neanderthals. The predators of this forest would take care of the bodies, but those same animals would have no need of the supplies.

The grey wolf with golden eyes shifted into his human form. "Were you the one howling?" Ruub walked over to Rokki. The man's golden eyes reflected the light of the moon high above them.

"The human woman escaped me." Rokki still had to beat back his dire wolf. The beast wanted to go back and howl at the moon in misery, but he knew better. If his mate was a witch, then he needed to make sure she would be safe in his pack before he found her again. She'd disappeared right in front of him. It had to be magic... which made her a witch. It had to mean his mate was a witch, which meant the prophecy of the brothers was coming true.

Ruub's eyebrows rose high on his forehead in disbelief at Rokki's words.

"She didn't out run me." Rokki clarified. "She disappeared." He figured it wouldn't matter if he told his men about her... as long as he didn't say mate out loud. With all the scents around them, he knew it would be hard for them to recognize her smell if he found her and brought her back later... so for now, this could be a random witch with no consequences for their clan.

"Disappeared?"

"It must have been magic, but I did catch and kill the other Neanderthal." Rokki switched the subject. Even if he wasn't worried about his men recognizing her scent, he didn't need them remembering this event and putting things together when he did bring his mate back to the pack, because he would find her. There was no doubt in his mind. "Now, we know they are in our territory hunting and willing to take a female from our territory."

"She was human from what I could smell," Ruub said. "What do we care if they take a human? She wasn't a member of the pack."

Rokki shook his head. "She may have been human," And his mate, but he wasn't about to say that out loud any time soon, "but this shows the Neanderthals feel confident on our land. The human female could have been one of our females out hunting alone or a pack female on a moonlit run. The Neanderthals had no way to know the human wasn't a part of our pack and mated to one of our males."

Ruub nodded his head. "I see what you mean. The human could have been mated to one of our men."

"Darc isn't going to like hearing about the Neanderthals invading our territory," Rokki mentioned his older brother with a grimace. Darc and Rokki disagreed on most things, but they did agree on sending a strong and loud message to the Neanderthals.

"Your uncle won't be happy to hear of it either."

No one in the clan would be thrilled with this news. Rokki wasn't sure why the Neanderthals were invading their territory, but they were here, whether the dire wolves liked it or not. Now they just had to focus on protecting their clan.

"Was anyone injured?" Rokki asked a little louder so his voice would reach the other men who were shifting from their dire wolf forms and into their human ones.

"Just a few scrapes and scratches," Grok responded from where he searched the corpse of a Neanderthal for anything useful.

Naab walked over. His hands were full of weapons. "I've searched my Neanderthal. Their weapons are well built." The man commented as he studied one of the stone blades he'd taken from the body. "Better built than I thought they could make."

"We can tell you collected everything," Ruub commented with a glance at Naab's hands. "How do we plan on getting these weapons back to the village?"

"We will stash them and come back for them later," Rokki said.

"I wish we could get the Neanderthals to stop crossing into our territory," Ruub said. As a beta wolf, he was always ready to back up his alpha but also wouldn't mind finding a common ground between people. He was a peacemaker, and if he could think of a way to bring peace between their people, Rokki would listen. He always listened to his people.

"Brelk already tried to send a group to discuss terms with the Neanderthals," Rokki said. His uncle, Brelk, and the temporary alpha of the pack, had done his best with the Neanderthal threat, but the Neanderthals had simply sent them the heads of the wolves his uncle sent to negotiate. Ever since then, they'd killed any and all Neanderthals that'd come into their territory. It was war.

"I still don't understand how the human escaped you." Ruub suddenly jumped back to the human woman.

Rokki waved a hand in the air ready to get the topic back under control. He didn't want his pack members thinking about the woman again. "Perhaps she used a nearby stream to hide her scent. Either way, it doesn't matter. A human woman running around our territory isn't as much of a problem as the Neanderthals."

"If we keep a couple of men in human form, we can take the supplies off the Neanderthals and not have to come back tomorrow." Ruub threw out helping Rokki to switch the conversation.

Rokki wanted nothing more than to shut down the idea, because he wanted nothing more than to come back and search for his human, but he also didn't want to attract too much attention. "We will do that."

"Who will remain in human form?" Ruub asked, ready to deliver his alpha's orders to the rest of the men.

Rokki's uncle may be temporary alpha of the pack, but Rokki had already chosen his men for the day he became alpha... as long as his brother, Darc, didn't become alpha over him, since they were both alpha wolves.

"Have Dholk and Grok carry the supplies back to the village. The rest of us will remain in dire wolf form." Rokki said.

When the men were ready, Dholk and Grok stayed in their human forms, while the rest of them shifted into their dire wolf forms.

Rokki loved being in his wolf form. His senses were much better, and for some strange reason, it felt like the form he should always be in. As they set off through the woods, he made sure to brush up against several trees and bushes so he could easily find his way back to this area. If his witch came back, he would be sure to capture her before she could flee from him again.

Chapter 5

After another long day of digging in the dirt under the hot sun, Andrea was happy to drive back into town to meet Emma at a local Chinese spot. All that digging and brushing dirt off bones and artifacts had worked up her appetite.

As she walked into the restaurant, the man at the front greeted her with a wide smile as he slightly inclined his head, "Good evening, Andrea. Another to-go order?"

Andrea shook her head as she realized that not only did the man recognize her, but she also knew his name. It showed that she'd been eating out way too much while on this dig. Her hotel had a kitchenette. She should make a stop by the grocery tomorrow and grab some fresh fruits and vegetables. Her heart would thank her when she was in her seventies or eighties.

"Good evening, Jin. I'm actually here to meet a friend." Andrea said, feeling happy she could tell him that she wasn't a lonely person who didn't know how to cook.

"A friend?" Jin asked dubiously like she had to be a recluse or something.

"I have friends." Andrea folded her arms in front of her chest as she became a bit offended at his doubt.

"I thought you were here on business."

"I am, but she's my colleague." Andrea tried to explain.

"Ah," he held up a finger as if he'd just figured out what she meant, "a business dinner then."

"Um, sure." Andrea just wanted to sit and have some orange sesame chicken with a side of crunchy noodles and brown rice. Jin could call her dinner whatever he wanted. "I think she might already be here. Her name is Emma Wilkins."

Jin's head glanced down at the paper on his hostess stand. He pulled some glasses onto his nose, which were attached to a black strap around his neck so he couldn't misplace them. "Ah, here it is. Come with me." He waved for her to follow him.

Jin led her to the back of the restaurant, where a pretty blonde waited on one side of the booth. "Your waiter will be with you soon."

Andrea sent him a smile and a nod. "Sounds good." Then she slid across the faux leather red bench seat with a couple of disturbing squeaking noises. "Am I late?"

"No, I was early." Emma placed the menu down on the table and sent her a smile. "I haven't eaten here yet, so I wanted to make sure I had time to figure out what would fit into my calorie counting diet."

Andrea grimaced inwardly. She would hate to know how many calories she devoured a day since she'd been ordering from this Chinese restaurant almost every day since she came to this dig site.

"As long as you haven't been waiting for me, too long."

"Not at all."

"Hello." A cheery voice greeted them from beside their table, and they both glanced up at the young waiter. Then his eyes fell on Andrea's face. "Oh, hi, Andrea! Glad to see you've decided to eat in the restaurant rather than just get take out."

Andrea's face heated as she blurted out her order, and Emma followed suit.

The moment the waiter was gone, Emma asked, "You come here often?"

Andrea shrugged as her cheeks heated even more. "It's on my way back to my hotel, so I usually stop by for dinner. It's quick and easy."

"How often?" Emma raised her ice water to her lips and took a sip as her blue eyes studied Andrea over the rim of the glass.

Andrea ducked her head as she pretended to skim over the menu in front of her. "Every night."

"We could have eaten at another restaurant if you'd wanted. When I suggested this place, I didn't know you'd already eaten here."

"Nah," Andrea waved a hand in the air, "it's fine. I did agree to meet you here after all, and the food is really good."

"I try not to eat out too often, so I'm glad it has your recommendation." Emma leaned back in her seat with a sigh. Her blonde hair had been painstakingly curled into a perfect hair do, and she'd put on a full face of makeup, but not a gaudy amount, just enough to highlight her already perfect features. She looked like she should be a model, rather than an archeologist sweating and digging out under the sun, but looks could be deceiving.

Andrea raised a hand to her knotted auburn locks, trying in vain to dislodge some of those rats' nests, as her mother had fondly called them throughout her childhood. At least she had the green eyes going for her. Men seemed to like the auburn air and green-eyed look.

The waiter returned to their table, took their orders, disappeared for a few more minutes, and then showed back up with steaming platefuls of food.

"Ooooo, it does smell good," Emma said as she leaned over to sniff at the scents floating off her dish.

"It'll taste even better," Andrea promised as she looked down at her own dish, which glistened up at her from the plate. Unable to wait, she unwrapped her silverware and dug in.

The dinner was eaten in semi-silence as each woman focused on the food in front of them. After a day of digging under the sun, they'd each worked up an appetite to rival a football player.

When the fortune cookies were dropped off on the table, Andrea held out a hand, stopping Emma from breaking the plastic wrapper around the cookie. "Have you ever heard of the game of putting 'in bed' at the end of a fortune cookie fortune?"

Emma shook her head, her blonde curls swinging wildly around her face.

"So," Andrea took her own cookie, "this was something my mother told me back when I was about twelve years old. Of course, she now claims she never told this to me, but I have a very clear memory of it." Her mother loved to say she never told Andrea about it, but Andrea had a clear memory of going to that Chinese restaurant on her twelfth birthday. "Anyway, you open the fortune and read it, but you add 'in bed' to the end."

"Sounds like fun!" Emma said as a smile

crept across red-tinted lips. Her friend didn't wait. With a pop of the plastic wrapper, she grabbed her cookie with two fingers, and with a snap, she pulled out the tiny white piece of paper. On one side, there was a word in Chinese, and on the other, there was the fortune. "Do not dwell on differences with a loved one – try to compromise… in bed."

They both burst into laughter.

"Oh my goodness, this is fantastic!" Emma wiped a tear from the corner of her eye as they calmed back down. "I'm not sure I could compromise in bed! I know what I like and how I like it."

"That was the perfect example of how fun this can be." Andrea smiled, pleased that her game was off to such a great start and that she was making a better friend out of Emma. Traveling the world to find dig sites meant that she didn't get many close friends, so she was eager for any chance that came her way.

"Open yours! Open yours!" Emma discarded her fortune as she munched on the crunchy cookie.

"Okay. Hold your horses." Andrea popped her wrapper open, cracked the cookie, and drew out the fortune. "Someone is looking up to you. Don't let that person down… in bed!"

They both cracked into a fit of laughter that drew curious gazes from other diners in the restaurant.

"Oh my goodness. Your mother sounds like a hoot!" Emma cried streaks forming in that perfect makeup mask.

"Sometimes, she came up with the best stuff." Andrea agreed as she sucked in a greedy breath of air.

"Should I get you some more cookies?" The waiter materialized out of thin air by their booth. His amused face smiled down at them.

"I think we could use some more cookies." Emma nodded her head enthusiastically.

The waiter strode away and came back with a couple of handfuls before leaving once more.

"Screw having a diet!" Emma announced. "I need to hear some more of these 'in bed' fortunes!"

Andrea cracked open another cookie. "Your efforts have not gone unnoticed... in bed."

They cackled like a couple of witches who'd cast a spell on an unsuspecting person and couldn't wait to see the mess they'd created.

Not to be outdone, Emma cracked open another and announced louder than necessary, "Why not treat yourself to a good time instead of waiting for someone else to do it... in bed?!"

Scowls were cast their way as they bust a gut with their laughter. Andrea sank to the side, laying down on the faux leather cushion. Emma's chest collapsed on top of the table as she buried her head in her arms.

"Guess... you should... whip out the... vibrator tonight." Andrea gasped out between breathes of air as laughter continued to rock her body.

"Oh... my... god!" Emma clamped her teeth down on her hand to keep from bursting into an uncontrollable fit of laughter. "I didn't even think about that, but you're right! That's how I could treat myself in bed."

"Oh dear," Andrea righted herself on the seat. "Maybe we should save the rest of these for another night so we don't get kicked out before dessert."

"True." Emma smiled. "I wouldn't mind something more interesting to eat than a plain fortune cookie."

With that decided, they placed a couple of orders in for some red bean buns.

Once the buns arrived at the table, Andrea broached the subject she'd been waiting to talk with Emma about. "Since I told you about my last dream, I thought you might listen if I told you about another dream I had."

"You've got me interested," Emma said as she grabbed one of the decent sized red bean buns. "Was it anything like the last one?"

"It has some similarities." Andrea nodded her head. "I woke up yet again in the nude in what appeared to be the ice age."

Emma nodded her head enthusiastically as she ripped off junks of the red bean bun and popped them into her mouth.

Andrea then proceeded to tell Emma about the Neanderthals, which had her friend raising her delicately plucked eyebrows. Then when she got to the werewolf part, a smile spread across Emma's face.

"Sounds to me like you've been reading too many paranormal romance novels, and your brain is just processing them while you sleep."

Andrea took a bite of a red bean bun. She wanted to deny what Emma was saying, and tell her how real it had all felt, but she wasn't sure Emma would believe her. It was even hard for Andrea to come to terms with what she was thinking, and she had experienced them first hand.

"Or maybe your unconscious is telling you to get a boyfriend because there are some needs you need taken care of that you can't quite itch by yourself." Emma leaned back, having finished her red bean bun in record time.

Andrea stuck her hand in her pants pocket and fiddled with the bracelet. After her last dream, she'd told herself she would return it to the dig site and never give it another thought. Yet here she was with the bracelet in her pocket.

"It didn't seem like a dream though," Relief entered her chest as she admitted it to another person.

"Some dreams can seem like reality. Sometimes I think I'm remembering a memory, but it turns out it was just a dream that messed up that memory." Emma added helpfully.

Andrea bit her tongue lest she tell Emma that she took an artifact from the dig site. She wanted nothing more than to tell Emma that the bracelet was sending her back into time. If only she could hand the bracelet to Emma and tell her to try it on for a night. Andrea was sure her friend would experience the same thing, and it would all become clear to Emma.

Darn.

She couldn't do it.

If Emma reported her to Clyde, it would be bye-bye fun job and good luck finding another. Once it spread through the industry about what she'd done, no one would want to hire her. She'd stolen an artifact! This was a big no no in the archeology world. And she loved her job. If she was banned from holding another artifact, a piece of history, she would lose her mind and her purpose for breathing.

Touching history was life.

Removing her hand from her pocket, she left the bracelet where it was, and Andrea squashed the very idea of telling Emma.

For the rest of their dinner, they talked about dinner and how they managed to have a life outside of work with all their travel and months on dig sites. Neither of them had boyfriends, and they communicated to their families through letters or emails with the occasional phone call.

After dinner, they rose from their booth, embraced, and went on their separate ways for the rest of the night.

Andrea found her heart thundering away in her chest as she drove back to the hotel. Eagerness had her palms sweating, and her hands jittering around on the steering wheel. The bracelet was singing her name, and she found it so hard to resist. The moment she arrived at the hotel, she rushed up the stairs, taking them two at a time.

Closing the hotel room door behind her, Andrea turned the lock, stripped off her shoes, and jumped onto her bed with a slight jostle. Reaching into her pocket, she pulled out the bracelet and moved it between her hands.

She had to be crazy. Every time she went back to this other world, she was attacked by something. Not by fluffy stuffed animals but by sabertooths and dire wolves with really sharp teeth. Yet she couldn't help the yearning that caused her heart to ache as she wished to travel back. The sun had clearly fried her brain since she couldn't get enough of it. Sure, it was scary going back in time, but there was also a thrill factor that was hard to resist.

Slipping the wooden bracelet onto her wrist, Andrea laid her head down on the soft downy pillow and shut her eyes.

Andrea woke up in a field. The soft grass cushioning her body, which was once more naked. The only thing that came with her from her world was the bracelet, which she now had a theory about. Since the bracelet had been created in the ice age, it was allowed to come back and forth with her. The wooden ring felt cold around her wrist, her body heat having not warmed it.

Birds sang around her. Their joyous noises rang through the trees around her. Closing her eyes, she let the natural noises wash over her senses. Modern humans didn't realize how many mechanical noises there were around them. No one in the twenty-first century actually knew what silence was… not like it could be.

As Andrea pushed herself onto her bare feet, she listened carefully to the noises around her. She could hear small animals rustling around in the leaves that covered the ground, but she didn't hear anything large and dangerous. There was no growling. Nothing to make her fear for her life.

After studying the ice age for years, she knew the time was wild and dangerous. But every time she'd been here, she'd been jumped, and she figured she was owed a better visit by now. Three times was the charm or something like that.

Not knowing where to go, Andrea picked a direction at random and just walked. The first few steps were a bit hesitant, but soon she walked through the area with a bit of a bounce in her step. She was in the ice age!

After a couple of hours of walking, the excitement wore off, and her feet began to ache, and she knew she'd just walked several miles since she arrived here. There was so much to see and process. This land kept pulling her in, even with all the dangers.

Right as she was about to plop a seat on some soft looking grass and massage the soles of her feet, a desperate trumpeting sound rang through the air.

Andrea's head shot up as her heart stopped in her chest. "An elephant?"

Then she remembered when she was. The ice age. If something out here sounded like an elephant, then it had to be... a mammoth! Picking up her pace, she sprinted towards the desperate sound that pumped through the air.

Andrea knew she should run in the opposite direction. The animal could be trumpeting because of predators or something dangerous, and here she sprinted right towards it.

Breaking out of the forest, she stopped dead in her tracks.

There was a gradual slope from where she stood, and below her was a tar pit. She'd excavated plenty of these as an archeologist. Tar pits were fantastic for preserving history, but they were horrible for animals who didn't know better. There were even tar pits that laid undercover, like water.

Her green eyes widen as she saw a massive mammoth struggling in the black sticky goo of the tar pit, and her heart went out to the poor creature. The poor thing would most likely die of dehydration or drown in the tar pit. If a predator arrived on the scene, it would probably...

Speak of the devil.

A sleek tan furred sabertooth strolled into the area below her.

Andrea sank onto her knees as she attempted to blend into her surroundings. She knew she should turn tail and leave the area, but this was too interesting for her to leave alone. Her life was all about studying the ice age, and here she was about to get a first-person view. It was too hard to resist.

The mammoth caught sight of the sabertooth and let out a horrible noise that had Andrea clamping her hands over her ears. It struggled greatly, but only sank deeper into the tar pit, which sloshed around as the massive legs strained.

The poor thing!

Andrea's heart broke in her chest. She wished she could help the creature, but there was nothing she could do except watch. This was the ice age. There weren't any bulldozers around, because it would take a bulldozer to pull that massive animal out of the tar.

The sabertooth circled the large tar pit. His pink nose pressed low to the ground as he sniffed and tried to figure out if he could make a meal out of the mammoth.

Andrea expected to see him jump onto the back of the mammoth, but the sabertooth seemed too nervous about the situation. And she didn't blame the animal. She would never go near a tar pit. She already felt too close, and she was a fair distance away.

A sudden wind blew her loose hair into her face as it shook the branches above her with a rattle.

Brushing her hair down, she caught sight of the sabertooth who's large head was high in the air. Sniffing. Then the black eyes shifted in her direction.

Andrea's heart froze as she waited for the sabertooth to make a decision. She didn't want to dart and crash through the forest if the sabertooth decided to ignore her scent.

With a ginormous leap, the sabertooth sprinted in her direction. It's short, but muscular legs ate up the distance.

"Shit!" Andrea leaped to her feet and darted back into the forest. She was tempted to climb a tree, but she wasn't too sure if a sabertooth could climb or not. Most cats were able to climb to some extent, so she continued to zig-zag through the forest.

How many times did she need to be chased by predators to stop coming back here?

Unfortunately, it was too late for her to do anything about it. The sabertooth crashed through the forest after her, and the animal was eating up the distance between them. She didn't even bother sparing a glance behind her. She was either going to make it or not, but if she didn't, then she prayed this was just a dream.

A tree root reached out of the ground, and Andrea hopped over it, but her toes skimmed the root just enough to trip her. Throwing out her hands, she spun in the air and let her back take the brunt of the fall, so she didn't break her wrist.

Oomph!

Raising her eyes, Andrea found the sabertooth barreling towards her. Its massive canines stretched from its top jaw down past its lower jaw and ending in a sharp tip. The ginormous hairy paws ate up the ground.

All Andrea could do was gape at the sabertooth with a slack jaw as her brain tried to catch up with what was happening.

A blur of black fur leaped over her head, landing straight in front of her.

Andrea's jaw hit the ground as she stared at a straightened black furred tail, and the hind legs of a giant dire wolf. She'd dug up one of these animals in her job, but it hadn't been quite this large. Dire wolves were larger than the twenty-first century grey wolves, but still, this one was quite the specimen.

Even from her position behind the dire wolf, she could see all the muscles rippling under its thick pelt of fur. She wanted to reach out a hand and stroke its fur, but this was no house doggy. This was a mean fighting machine who could easily rip her hand off.

The hair on the haunches of the black wolf raised as it let out an ominous growl.

The sabertooth and the dire wolf collided with snapping jaws, glinting teeth, and ferocious growls that ripped through the air. Every time the sabertooth tried to skirt past the dire wolf, the wolf would reangle itself, so it stood between the sabertooth and herself.

For whatever reason, the dire wolf had come to her rescue, and she wasn't about to let it go to waste.

Andrea's brain finally caught up with what was happening, and she dashed to her feet and darted deeper into the forest. The sounds of the fight carried through the forest and spurred her on. Her feet might hurt, and branches might scratch at her naked skin, but nothing was going to stop her from putting distance between herself and the dangerous predators behind her.

Chapter 6

Rokki had come sniffing around the area where his human had disappeared a day ago. He wasn't sure if she would come back or if she would even come back to the same area, but he couldn't restrain his dire wolf. The beast wanted to find her and keep her safe.

She was his mate.

This world they lived in was not an easy one at all. There were predators behind every tree and bush, and it wasn't just the predators one would need to worry about. Mammoths and woolly rhinoceros were known for their ill tempers and killed plenty of people.

With his wet black nose pressed to the ground, he followed any scents that might lead him to her.

It wasn't long before the trumpeting of a mammoth carried through the forest. With no sign of his human mate, he couldn't help the curiosity of his beast. Rokki loped through the woods, the paws of his wolf form barely making a noise as he prowled closer to the racket.

As Rokki approached, the sounds of the mammoth became desperate. Another predator must have come to see what the commotion was about. And within a few more steps, he heard something crashing through the forest.

Then a sabertooth let out a horrific growl that had even Rokki's heart fluttering around inside his chest. Sabertooths and dire wolves were competitors when it came to being on the top of the food chain.

His fluffy wolf ears pricked forward as he heard a female voice utter something. It was either another language, or he was too far away to understand her, but the voice had his dire wolf lifting its head in interest.

Sprinting, all four of his muscled legs propelled him over the forest floor. Trees, rocks, and bushes blended together in a blur of green and brown as he streaked through the forest.

When Rokki caught the scent of the sabertooth, he knew he was getting close. A woman's cry of despair echoed through the trees, and Rokki pushed his beast as much as he could.

Flying out from behind a particularly large trunk, he flew over the female's head to land in front of her, presenting her with his rear. Her scent drifted over him and filled his nostrils. The pungent odor of sweat and fear filled his nostrils. Now that he was here, she didn't need to worry about the sabertooth.

Rokki and his dire wolf would sacrifice their life if the sabertooth forced it. No one touched their mate.

The beast charging at him showed no signs of slowing down or turning tail.

For a split second, a spear of fear pierced his heart, but then determination set in. Failure wasn't an option for him because he had a mate to protect.

With a leap forward, Rokki crashed into the sabertooth with a snarl of fury. The woman behind him was human and his mate, meaning she was vulnerable and precious. If he lost her to the teeth of a predator, his life would be at an end as well. He'd never heard of a dire wolf getting a second mate. He would lose his opportunity for offspring.

The sabertooth swiped a set of dangerously sharp claws through the air. Rokki felt the air swoosh the fur on his snout, but thankfully the beast hadn't landed a blow. He snapped his jaw of menacing teeth at the sabertooth and almost got some flesh, but the beast spun away from him, getting closer to the human female.

Rokki jumped to place himself between her and the sabertooth once more. He snapped his jaw with a click before leaping back at the sabertooth. This time he barreled into the beast and tackled it to the ground.

Large canines snapped dangerously close to Rokki's neck, and he shivered at the thought of one of those puncturing his flesh. With a swipe of his back paw, he dug in his rear claws and scraped a couple of long gashes on the sabertooth's leg.

The sabertooth let out a howl of pain, and Rokki backed off, allowing the beast to go on its way. And it took the opportunity. The sabertooth slinked away, trailing blood as it disappeared into the thick forest around them. If he didn't have to kill the sabertooth, then he was happy to let it go. It was nothing but an animal driven by needs like hunger.

Rokki turned with a wolfy grin plastered across his snout until his eyes fell on empty space behind him. There was nothing but grass, trees, and bushes around him.

Where in the gods had his mate gone?

With a snarl of frustration, Rokki sprinted through the underbrush as he let his nose lead him true.

So far, each time he'd encountered his mate, she'd been in trouble. And now he feared that she would put herself in danger once more. He still didn't understand why she chose to run around naked. Most humans preferred to cloth themselves.

As Rokki followed the scent of his mate to a less dense part of the forest, he spotted her running not too far ahead. Slowing down to a lope, he followed behind her. Her wide hips swayed at him, tempting him to chase after her and plant his bite on her neck, but he restrained himself. He could still smell the fear drifting on the air.

His eyes drifted up her body until he saw one of her hands pressed into her side. It appeared his mate wasn't one who was used to running. Good, because as much as he loved a chase, like any wolf, he wanted to plant his mark on her neck.

Rokki's mate placed a hand on a tree trunk and glanced over her shoulder, her green eyes meeting his. Her eyes widened, and then she burst into another sprint.

With a growl that carried through the air, Rokki launched into a full out run. His front legs stretched out fully as the wind whipped through his shaggy black hair.

His mate turned and saw him closing the distance.

Then she did the unpredictable. She jumped, hooked her hands on a branch, and began to climb a tree. He couldn't believe his mate. Sure, she was human, and humans could do some questionable things, but he couldn't believe he was currently watching her climb a tree.

Coming to stand next to the tree, he plopped his haunches on the ground, wrapped his long thick tail around his body, and lifted his eyes to see his mate halfway up the tree. If she thought that would save her from the big bad wolf below her, then he was happy to ruin her dreams.

But he was going to take a second to appreciate the view above him.

From down here, Rokki had the most spectacular view of his mate. She knelt on a branch high above him, and his wolf eyes were able to spot the sweet area between her thighs. It was in the shadows, so he couldn't make out much, but it still had his wolf growling in pleasure. Soon, very soon, he would know that sweet center of hers.

Then his eyes shifted to her plump breasts, which dangled high above like some berry waiting to be plucked. Another growl had his lip curling up in a wolfish smile. Her rosy nipples were hard and pointed like the tip of a spear. Too bad she was all the way up there in the tree. He was a wolf, not a damn cat, and he wasn't keen on going up after her... but if going up after her meant in a delicious reward afterward... well, who was he to fuss about climbing a tree.

Letting the shift overtake him, Rokki felt his body snap back into human form, his bones and skin cracking back into place as his fur receded into his body. What felt like an eternity to him, was in actuality, just a few seconds.

As Rokki finished the transformation, he heard a startled gasp above him.

Glancing up, he met the wide green eyes of

his human mate. Her grass-green eyes slowly narrowed on him while she yelled intelligible words and pointed an accusing finger at him.

Rokki simply shrugged his shoulders as he shook his head. He had absolutely no idea what she was saying, but she didn't appear pleased with his transformation. Perhaps she came from a human clan that didn't trust weres. There weren't many humans who trusted them, and he didn't blame them. People who could turn into killer predators were a bit scary.

Rokki pointed a long finger at her and then pointed at the ground, while his eyes never left her.

His mate shook her auburn curls. Her eyes flashed in defiance.

Mmm, a bit of fire. He liked a woman who had a fire burning inside her body. She would need some spunk if she wanted to last in his pack.

Rokki didn't want to climb the tree, but if he had too, then there was no other choice for him.

This had to be a dream. Now that Andrea had just witnessed the massive black dire wolf shift into a human man with a ripped body and a devilishly handsome face. This wasn't time travel, and her heart sank a bit at that realization. She'd really been hoping it was time travel, but no, it was a dream, because no such thing as a werewolf could exist… even in the ice age.

Once the shock wore off, Andrea narrowed her eyes at the man below her. Even if he was nothing more than a dream, he was hot to trot. Boy, oh, boy. Yum yum! She resisted the temptation to lick her lips.

Those abs were rock hard. Even from this distance, she was positive she could wash clothes on that abdomen, not that she would since that would be awkward. Then her eyes drifted up past his chest to his chiseled facial structure and noticed the scar over one eye. The ice age was a dangerous place, whether it was a dream or not, and his scar was just proof of that.

Then she noticed all the reddish tattoos all over his skin. She had no idea what they meant, but they mesmerized her. There were dots and swirls, and if she remembered correctly, the ice age way of tattooing wasn't as easy or simple as the twenty-first way.

A thought entered Andrea's mind, and slowly her gaze shifted lower... and lower until she spotted his cock hanging between his legs. He was flaccid now, but she had a good idea that he would be quite hung once rock hard.

Even though he was a werewolf, he definitely had a body that would soak her panties, if she had any on right now.

The naked man below her pointed a finger at her and then pointed at the ground in clear communication.

"Umm, no," Andrea replied as she shook her head. "There is no way I'm coming down there. Dream or no dream." She clutched tighter to the branch under her. "There's such a thing as stranger danger, and a werewolf is definitely dangerous."

His upper lip curled in a growl, and his golden eyes flashed at her, but she still didn't budge from her crouched position.

They stared each other down as each studied the other.

A slow smile of success crept across her lips, and a fire leaped into his golden eyes as he caught the smirk. Then he strode towards the tree, hooked a hand on the first branch, and hauled himself up. Then he climbed to the next branch.

"Stop!" Andrea flung out a hand with an open palm.

The naked man halted as he was about to hook a hand on a third branch and glanced up at her.

"I'll come down." She didn't want to get into a fight with mister hunky when they were high up in a tree. One of them could fall and break a neck. If she was going to fight him, then she would do it on the ground.

His golden eyes stared at her blankly. Great, they had a language barrier. Then again, what had she expected?

Andrea pointed to herself, and then the ground. "I will climb down." She motioned to the ground again.

His eyes narrowed on her, but he leaped to the ground straight from the branch second branch, landing with a grace only a man like him could possess.

Great. And now he was going to watch her as she climbed her unfit body down the tree. She wasn't fat by any means, but she also didn't keep up with exercising, and the fact she got up this tree was a miracle due to adrenaline. Now she was worried she might not make it down as gracefully.

Slinking from her branch, Andrea reached a cautious toe blindly for the next branch. When she felt the welcoming scrape of bark under her foot, she planted her foot firmly, and let the toe from her other foot explore. When she felt the branch, she planted her second foot and let go of the branch above her head.

Andrea smiled with her success. Now she just had like five more of these to go. As she eased herself onto the next branch, she planted her feet and let go of the branch above her. Then the bark slipped, and her arms pinwheeled next to her.

With a gasp, she felt the branch slip out from under her feet. She tried in vain to grab hold of a branch or anything.

But no such luck.

Her loose hair whipped around her face as she fell backward. She was going to die! Maybe she'd wake up in her hotel bed… but if this wasn't a dream, then she was going to go splat on the ground… or at least break a leg, and a broken leg in the ice age wasn't the best thing. She didn't even want to think about their shamans treating her. A broken leg could be a death sentence.

All these thoughts flitted through her mind as though she fell in slow motion, but all these thoughts floated through her mind in the blink of an eye.

Then Andrea landed against something hard and… soft at the same time.

Her eyes had slammed shut sometime during the fall, and when she determined she was truly still alive, she popped one eye open to see the naked man's face right next to her face.

"Eeek!" Andrea screeched as she realized he had caught her against his firm chest. "Let me go!" She screamed at the top of her lungs and was pleased when she noticed him wince in pain. Wildly, she beat at his chest with one hand and kicked her legs like a woman gone wild. That chest was even more firm then she thought it would be, and a tingle of something that wasn't fear seared through her.

The naked man released her, and she darted away. Facing him, she cast him a glare. "Thanks for saving me, but you could have put me down sooner. I'm not one for being pressed up against a man's naked chest when I have no clue who he is… or what he is."

Naked man moved in the blink of an eye and shoved her up against the rough bark of a tree.

"Eep." She exhaled as his naked muscled body flattened against hers. That flaccid member, well, it wasn't so flaccid anymore. It pressed urgently against her abdomen, demanding her attention.

Andrea raised her hands to his chest and immediately regretted the decision. The feel of his rock-hard tanned pecs under her hands had a tingle of awareness spearing through her body.

Naked man bent his head down, his mouth next to her cheek. Then he growled something next to her ear, and even though she didn't understand the words, a deeply hidden feminine part of her knew exactly what he was saying. He promised her pleasure beyond her wildest dreams.

Then his head drew back, and she glanced up at him, still too frozen in shock to move or protest their closeness. His lips curved up in a smile, and her eyes drifted down to them, and she tried to imagine what those lips would feel like on hers.

Emma had told Andrea that she must have read too many werewolf romance novels, and maybe she had. Maybe this was a dream made in part because of her job and because of her favorite romance novels.

Leaning up on her toes, Andrea captured his lips with her mouth as she made a decision. It appeared to be the invite he needed. His lips slanted over hers as his head bent, deepening their kiss. His lips worked hers right before the tip of his tongue slid against the crease of her lips, asking for entrance.

Andrea was more than happy to part her lips and allow his exploring tongue entrance into her mouth. He scraped his tongue across her front teeth before fighting with her tongue in a dueling dance.

Her hands scraped down his chest and then back up before she wrapped her arms around his strong neck. Her hands curled into his hair as her body thrummed in excitement. An excitement he was slowly stoking within her. An excitement she hadn't felt in years with a man.

His hot hands worked over her body as if he was trying to memorize her form. His lips disengaged from hers, and he nuzzled her neck as one of his hands slipped between her thighs.

Andrea eagerly parted her thighs as his fingers explored further. One finger slid between her folds, which were slick with her desire. She wasn't normally this easy to turn on, but it'd been years since a boyfriend had graced her life, and she refused to have sex with anyone on the dig sites she worked.

And here was a man who could only ever exist in her dreams, acting like he wanted to ravish her. It was too hard to pass up.

The tip of his erection pressed into her abdomen, and a moan escaped her lips as his exploring finger found her clit. The pad of his rough finger circled as her hips bucked against his hand. His finger felt great, but what she wanted was the thick hard cock pressing against her trembling abdomen.

Then he slipped a couple of fingers into her slicked entrance, sliding in with ease.

"Oh, yes." Andrea moaned as her eyes slid closed.

The naked man's head dipped lower, and he sucked a tight bud into his mouth. His tongue swirled around her nipple, and pleasure engulfed her. Her mind went blank, and all she could think about was getting off.

"Yes, yes! Harder!" She begged, unsure if he understood her, but hoping the desperation in her voice would translate her words for her.

A shudder rolled through her entire body, and if naked man's hand hadn't been on her ass, she would have melted and slumped onto the ground. Her pussy clamped down around his fingers, and stars shot across her vision until the tremors faded.

Andrea sighed in satisfaction.

Naked man's hands gripped her ass and yanked her up, then he pressed her against the tree trunk, grabbed his cock in one hand and...

"Hell, no!" Andrea barked as she yanked out of his arms and landed on her feet.

When she met his eyes, she could see the fire dancing in those golden eyes once more, and his dark eyebrows drew down over his eyes. He took a threatening step towards her, so she held out a hand and glared him down. Wasn't that what people were supposed to do with dogs and wolves? Meet their eyes and stare them down?

His eyes widened as he realized she wasn't going to let them go any further.

Poor guy. She had led him on a bit, but no was no in her world, and she was ready to enforce it here in the ice age.

"No more." Andrea's eyes lowered to his still proud and jutting cock. "As much as I want to have sex with a primal man against a tree or in the grass, we can't. I can't."

The naked man growled at her, the sound feral. It sent shivers of primitive fear running down her spine as a tiny voice in her head yelled at her to run, but she squashed it like a bug. If she ran, he would just turn into a wolf and chase her down, like he already had.

"We can't do this," Andrea explained despite the language barrier, "when this dream ends because this has to be a dream if there are werewolves, although to be honest, I guess werewolves are just as far-fetched as time travel… anyways," she shook her head as she realized she was rambling like an idiot, "I'm getting off topic here. If this is a dream," she restarted, "then I'm going to wake up someday, and you won't be real, and I'll be hot and needy, and all I'll have is a dildo and vibrator to satiate me. And as good as they are, I'm sure you'd be much better." Her gaze once more slid down to his pulsing member, which strained for her loving attentions.

He growled at her.

Andrea yanked her eyes from his cock and met his golden eyes. "Sorry. Hard not to stare. I don't mean to tease."

Naked man took another step towards her as he offered her a hand. A hand that had brought her so much delicious pleasure.

Andrea shook her head as she backed up. Her hand came up to fiddle with the wooden bracelet on her other wrist. It was time to end this. His eyes fell to the bracelet, and she removed it while she wished to be back in her hotel bed.

Chapter 7

Rokki blinked dumbly as he stared at the empty spot before him. One moment his mate was standing before him, and then the next she was gone, like the last time he'd seen her.

The shift ripped over him.

Lifting his head, he howled to the sun above in protest. She was gone, and Rokki had no idea when he would next see her, or if he would ever see her again. He hadn't understood a single word that she'd spoken, but her tone... he understood her tone. It had sounded like a goodbye to him.

His wolf howled in anger once again.

Raking his claws against a nearby tree, he ripped chunks clean off the trunk. His mate had fiddled with a wooden bracelet on her wrist before she'd disappeared, and he was sure that object was to blame. If he saw her again, he would rip it off her wrist and break the bloody thing.

Nothing.

Nothing would take his mate from him ever again.

Rokki's dire wolf refused to leave the area. The sun moved through the sky as it headed west, and as the sun finally began to sink below the horizon, he gave up hope of her coming back that day.

Shaking out his thick shaggy coat, Rokki sniffed the area, memorizing the area. His mate had reappeared near the same area where she'd disappeared the first time. If she came back, then he assumed it would be near here.

Once he was sure he had the area memorized, he loped off, back to his village. Until she came back, he didn't need any of his pack sniffing around or wondering where he kept going. No one needed to know he may have found his mate. There would be too many questions, and none he would be able to answer.

As Rokki broke into the village, he shifted back into his human form, never missing a step as he strolled between a couple of mammoth skin huts.

"Where have you been?"

Rokki turned to spot his one of his three sisters watching him with her intelligent brown eyes, a hand on her hip. "Taking a run through the forest and searching for any signs of Neanderthals." Partly true, he had been searching for Neanderthals before he'd heard the mammoth trumpeting in the forest and smelled the sweet scent of his mate.

"Did you find any sign of them?" Zuri asked as her hand dropped from her waist, and she walked past him.

Rokki followed her into the village, unconcerned with his nudity. Being unclothed was beneficial when one was a shifter. Now he could shift without shredding his clothing, which took time to make. Tanning hides and sewing them together was a long process. If he didn't watch how many he tore, the women in the clan wouldn't be shy about sharing their opinions with him.

"No."

"Good. Darc wouldn't like to hear that the Neanderthals were spotted in our territory again." Zuri said, referring to their brother. "He worries about them harming someone in the pack."

Rokki's brother liked to pretend that he was leader of the pack. Rokki suppressed a growl that threatened to rumble out of his throat. Their uncle was the leader until one of the brothers found their mate, but not just any mate, whichever brother found a witch as his mate would lead the clan. It had been foretold by a seer long ago.

Both brothers were alphas, and when one of them became leader, the other would be forced to leave. That was the way it was. There could only be one alpha, or they would continue to fight. They could barely tolerate each other as it was. Rokki wished his dire wolf could tolerate Darc's dire wolf, but the two alpha males couldn't.

"I think you meant to say that our uncle would be upset by the Neanderthals wandering into our territory since he is the pack leader." Rokki corrected his sister.

Zuri flashed him a smile over her shoulder. "Want to be pack leader, little brother?"

"What alpha wouldn't want to be pack leader?" Rokki asked as he ignored his sister's teasing of his age. Every alpha wanted to be a pack leader, and their pack was the perfect pack. It was a large pack with nearly forty dire wolves, and one of the largest in the area.

"You'll need your mate then."

He had found his mate, and he wanted to tell his sister, but he clamped his mouth shut. With his mate disappearing and reappearing, there was the chance she was using magic, which would mean that his mate was a witch. And if Darc found out he had a witch as a mate, her life would be in danger. He didn't want to believe his brother would kill her, but he couldn't be sure.

So, for now, his possible mate was going to stay a secret.

"I know some of the pack were thinking about hunting. You might want to join if Darc doesn't go." Zuri informed him. "The more time apart for you two would be best. The pack doesn't need to see you and Darc fight."

"He'll go. Darc can't resist leading a hunting party." Rokki wasn't too worried about getting into a brawl with Darc. Their dire wolves might be hard to control, but they were two brothers who wanted the best for the pack.

"Rokki!" Ode pranced into his arms and wrapped her long arms around him in a tight hug. Then she glanced up at him after he'd wrapped his arms around her. Her blue eyes shimmered with happiness.

"What has you so happy?" Rokki smiled as his youngest sister clung to him. She'd just come into age, and her dire wolf was gorgeous. Rokki would have a hard time keeping men away from her, but he would do it. He wasn't even sure he would let her mate get near her. This was his little sister. She was precious.

"I shifted today." She beamed up at him, nearly blinding him with her smile.

Rokki hugged her closer as her statement sank in. Not only was his little sister of age, but now she'd shifted, and soon werewolf males would come sniffing to see if she was their mate. His sister. If they didn't treat her carefully, he would eagerly rip out their throats.

"How did you enjoy your dire wolf form?" Rokki asked as he released her, and she took a couple of steps back.

"It was so freeing!" Ode's smile grew larger, and she swung her arms out as she spun in a tight circle. "My wolf and I went for a run in the forest, and all the scents and sounds…" she drifted off as her eyes hazed over as she recalled her run.

"She's a beautiful wolf." Zuri wrapped an arm around Ode's shoulders, bringing Ode back to the present. "A slender white wolf with blue eyes."

Rokki would have to seal Ode into her hut. Male wolves were sure to be attracted to her. White wolves were rarer than black, grey, and brown wolves, and males would be even more interested in knowing if she might be their mate.

"Don't even think about it, Rokki." Ode glared at him as her sky-blue eyes darkened.

"Do what?" He held up his hands innocently.

"Don't scare away the wolves who will come to see if I am their mate. I'm old enough and ready to be claimed as someone's mate."

"If they bother you, you will tell me?" Rokki asked.

Ode nodded her head eagerly, her long brown hair bouncing around her shoulders. "Don't scare them off, Rokki. Darc already gave his approval to males seeking me out."

Rokki smothered a growl at the mention of his brother, but he couldn't help the curl of his upper lip as his inner dire wolf begged to start a fight with his brother's wolf. How dare Darc act like the alpha of the pack while Rokki was out of the village. They should have discussed their sister's coming of age and releasing of her dire wolf.

"Don't kill him." Ode held out a hand as if she would be able to stop him if he did decide to seek out Darc. "I came to both of you with this, not just him."

His inner dire wolf settled down… a bit. She had come to both of them for approval. She wasn't choosing who she wanted to be alpha.

"I wish you luck in finding your mate." Rokki stepped forward and placed a kiss to Ode's forehead. Some werewolves could go years, sometimes even a lifetime without finding their mates. He would never wish that on his sweet sister. She deserved to have some pups.

Ode danced off, her steps light and giddy.

"She will be fine, Rokki. She has two alpha brothers. No wolf would think of hurting her and facing the wrath of the alpha dire wolf brothers." Zuri smiled. "The two of you may disagree on a lot, but I know you would join together to kill any man who hurts her."

"If a male does hurt her, you can be sure it will be the first time Darc and I work together to destroy him," Rokki growled low in the back of his throat.

Zuri patted his bareback with a hand. "Get some food, and I will see if Darc is heading out with the hunting party." His sister strode away. She wore an animal skin shirt and animal skin pants, not a dress like most of the other women.

When Zuri found her mate, Rokki would never have to worry about her. Zuri knew her place in this world, and her dire wolf would show anyone and everyone. He might actually pity any male who mated with her.

The last flickers of sunlight disappeared as the sun sank below the horizon. Darkness crept over the land, casting shadows for predators to lurk.

Rokki's mind shifted back to his mate… his human mate, who was somewhere out there. He prayed to the gods, whichever would listen, that his mate would be fine without him by her side. Their world was dangerous, and she seemed to attract danger.

The flickering orange light drew Rokki in as he weaved his way through the huts and towards the village fire. As he neared, he caught sight of a pack member passing out chunks of fresh meat, blood still running out of the piece.

His stomach let out a rumble of hunger, and his footsteps hastened towards the fresh meat. "I'll take a piece." He held out his hand.

The man cutting up the animal sent him a brief smile before slicing a slab off the animal with a stone blade and then handed it over to Rokki.

Taking his piece of meat, Rokki sat down in front of the fire, his back pressed to a log as he snarfed his raw piece of meat down. Some day soon, he would have to give his dire wolf some freedom and go on a hunt in his other form, but for now, he had enough to worry about, like his mate.

Ruub plopped down on one side of him, and Naab plopped down on the other side.

"I heard Darc left to go hunting with some of the men," Ruub commented.

Rokki arched a dark brow. "Why does this concern me?" He finished off his meat and licked the trickles of blood off his hand.

"One of you needs to find your mate, so this prophecy can be determined, and the other can leave." Ruub frowned at the leaping flames of the fire. "The whole pack is tense and worried about the two of you. We're waiting for one of you to rip out the other's throat. It's no good."

"Darc and I haven't had a fight in months, and it was barely anything the last time." They'd been hunting together, to try and bring them closer like when they'd been pups, but in the end, their dire wolves had decided that fighting each other would be better. It had been a small scrap, nothing more.

"Because the two of you haven't set eyes on each other since the last fight." Ruub countered.

That was true. He and Darc had kept their distance since the last scrap.

Rokki stretched out his long bare legs towards the fire until he could feel the warmth of the flames touching the bottoms of his feet. As the cold night air settled around them, his human skin was beginning to prickle in an effort to conserve heat.

"One of you needs to find their mate."

Rokki glared over at Ruub. "You've said that, and if you have any great ideas of where one of our mates might be, I'm sure we would listen to you."

Ruub shook his head of shoulder-length brown hair. "If I knew how to find mates, I'd have a bigger hut and my own mate!"

Naab and Rokki chuckled.

The men fell into silence as more pack members joined them at the fire, some in their dire wolf forms, and some naked, like himself. A few female pack members had animal skin skirts around their waists, but nothing covered their breasts, exposing them to anyone's view.

Rokki didn't stare at any of them, though. All he could think about was his mate. He still felt irritated with her disappearance. What bothered him was the fact that he couldn't do anything. He was useless.

Powerless. He'd never felt this way before, and he wasn't fond of the emotions.

A shadow fell over Rokki, and when he glanced up to see what was blocking the light from the fire, he saw a female pack member standing over his legs. Each of her small feet were on either side of his calves.

"Ira." Rokki greeted her.

"Rokki." She purred in a smooth voice that spoke volumes. Reaching up, she cupped the undersides of her breasts and lifted them slightly. "Want to see if we're mates?"

Rokki rolled his eyes. "My dire wolf doesn't respond to yours." They'd even tried sex to see if the wolves would respond to each other, but nothing had happened, except now Ira was determined to see them mated. It had been a mistake.

"Maybe we weren't mates back then, but our wolves could have changed. We could be mates now."

Oh, how he wished he could tell her, he'd found his mate, and it wasn't her. But he couldn't. Not now.

"I'd be willing to see if we are mates." Ruub sent Ira a saucy grin.

Ira's lips drew down in a scowl as her eyes slid over to him. "We'd know by now if we were mates." And then she walked off with a stiff back.

Rokki was thankful for the save by Ruub, whether the man had meant to or not.

"I wish I was an alpha sometimes," Ruub commented. "Then, females would flock to me like they do with you, and unlike you, I would enjoy every single one in my bed."

Naab leaned over so he could see Ruub past Rokki. "If you were alpha, your life would continuously be in danger. Other males would always be challenging you."

"True." Ruub nodded his head, then he patted Rokki's back. "Maybe I should be glad to be middle of the pack. No one wishes me dead."

Sometimes Rokki wished he was just a normal pack member, not an omega, not a beta and especially not an alpha. The position did come with its issues, like the lingering threat of death, but it also came with great moments, like leading his clan to success and seeing them through hard times.

Shoving himself to his feet, Rokki strode away from the fire and his pack mates. He needed to find some clothes. He strode over to his hut, pushed through the animal skin flap guarding the entrance. Some warm coals glowed in his personal fire pit, which meant someone in the clan was kind enough to keep his fire going so his hut didn't get cold.

Opening a basket made of dried reeds, he dug out a shirt and some pants. Then he found a pair of moccasins and slipped them around his feet. Now he just needed some female clothing for his mate. So far, she kept appearing naked. He didn't need his human mate catching a chill and dying on him.

Slipping out of his tent, and with a quick glance around to make sure most of the pack was around the village fire, Rokki loped over to the hut his sisters shared. With another quick glance, he made sure no one was around before sliding into the hut, which was empty.

Scrounging through the hut, Rokki dug around as he searched for some clothing that he thought would fit his mate. He'd felt her curvy body, and he knew none of Zuri's clothing would fit her, but maybe Ibi would have some clothing that would fit his mate. Ibi was his middle sister, younger than him, but older than Ode, and she had a few curves.

Once Rokki found a shirt and pants, he maneuvered over to the hut entrance. Slipping a finger through the entrance, he brought back the flap and peered out. There still wasn't anyone nearby to spot him, so he slid out of his sisters' hut and into the forest.

He needed to be careful with how much he left the village lest someone grow interested in his movements.

Rokki couldn't stop the hop in his steps as he wandered back to the spot where she'd disappeared. Soon, he would have her in his arms again, and this time he was removing that bracelet from her wrist.

Chapter 8

Andrea woke in her hotel bed, the sheets tangled around her legs. Her body was hot and soaked in sweat. The sweet spot between her thighs ached, and she groaned as she flipped onto her stomach and mumbled into her pillow. She beat her fists against the mattress in frustration.

Regret filled her, and she resisted the temptation to slip the wooden bracelet back on her wrist and go back to mister dreamy. His black shoulder-length hair and those piercing golden eyes that sent her heart skittering in delight. Oh, and those lips. They'd been so hard and demanding, but at the same time, soft and gentle.

These thoughts were the exact reason why she didn't want to get intimate with her dreamy werewolf friend. Now she was hot and bothered and wanted something more than what they'd already shared. She wanted that man between her thighs, penetrating her, sucking on her breasts, and bringing her the best god damn orgasm she'd ever experienced.

But now Andrea was alone in her bed.

The alarm next to the bed began screaming with a high-pitched buzzing noise like a banshee gone wild.

Screech! Screech! Screech!

"I'm up!" Andrea screamed back at the machine. A flailing hand tried in vain to find the snooze button, but eventually, she had to give up after she knocked a couple of items off the nightstand and onto the hotel bedroom floor.

"Fine!" Andrea scrambled to sit on the edge of the bed. She reached out and grabbed the alarm with two hands. The red numbers on the front of the screen blinked at her in annoyance. She smacked the off button.

It was time to get back to work, and she felt like she hadn't slept a wink. Great. This was yet another reason why she shouldn't be so eager to jump back into her dream world because it was a dream. There was no such thing as a werewolf. If there were, she figured she'd know of them in the twenty-first century.

Leaping from the bed, Andrea grabbed one of the many pairs of cargo pants that she owned and yanked them onto her legs. Then she grabbed her bra and a shirt and whipped them on. As she danced through the kitchenette area, she grabbed a power bar off the countertop and darted for her door.

She needed to talk to Emma about this.

The moment Andrea threw her car into park, she glanced down at her wrist and realized the wooden bracelet was still dangling there. She blinked dumbly for a couple of seconds, before ripping it off and stuffing it into her cargo pants pocket.

If she found a chance alone, she should return the object to the right table and never think about it again.

She'd almost worn it back into the dig site like a complete idiot. These dreams had her losing her mind, and if she wasn't careful, she might lose her job.

Emma strode past her car and waved at her. A smile always on her red-tinged lips. Her bouncy curls had been pulled into a tight ponytail behind her head.

Andrea popped the door open and stepped out. "Hey, Emma."

"Hey. You look tired." Emma's head tilted to the side as her light blue eyes skimmed over Andrea's face. "Still having some side effects from when you passed out? Should you be here working? Maybe you should get some rest. None of us want you to pass out again."

"No," Andrea waved it away even though she was touched by Emma's concern, "I just haven't been sleeping the best at night. I might buy some tea before I head back to my hotel room tonight, something to conk me out."

"Well, you let me know." Emma winked at her. "I have some wicked awesome pills that will put you right out if you end up needing something with a bigger punch."

"Uhhh, yeah, thanks for the offer." Andrea wasn't someone who was comfortable taking medications that her doctor hadn't prescribed for her. "But I think I'm good. I'll try to drink some tea before I go to bed tonight rather than wine."

"Any time."

"You know those dreams I told you about?" Andrea asked as they started towards the dig site. Her shows kicked up dust every time she took a step. The area they were digging was dry as a bone, and even though the sun had only just come up, it was already sweltering hot.

"The dreams with the werewolf?" Emma asked as they walked over to a tent and grabbed their supplies for another day of digging in the dirt and cleaning off artifacts.

"Yeah, that one." Andrea hefted her heavy bag of metal tools and brushes.

"What about it?" Emma asked.

"Well," Andrea tucked her tools under her arm, "I had them again last night."

"Ooo la la." Emma sang. "End in anything fun this time?" She sent Andrea a wink and a couple of wiggles of her eyebrows.

Andrea shrugged. "It was decent... didn't get as far as I would have liked, but I chickened out. My werewolf would have sealed the deal with me if I hadn't pushed him away." She still regretted her decision. There were so many things she should do, but she didn't want to do.

"You should talk to your dream self because if a hunky werewolf ever visited my dreams, I would jump him like he was a slice of chocolate cake and never look back."

Andrea's eyes skimmed over Emma's perfect frame. "When do you eat chocolate cake?"

"That's the point!" Emma laughed. "I don't eat cake, but if I ever decided to have a slice, watch out, because I would cramp it into my mouth by the fistfuls."

Andrea pealed into a bit of laughter at the image of Emma and her perfect hair and perfect makeup, slamming chocolate cake into her mouth. "Don't forget to enjoy the occasional slice, Emma."

"I enjoy a slice every birthday," Emma said with a solid nod of her head.

"Well, anyway, the werewolf and I had a lovely time, and right as we were about to do the nasty, I stopped him."

"Bet your dream man wasn't happy about that."

Andrea shook her head. His eyes had widened with shock at her refusal to go further, and she had to admit she was a bit confused why she hadn't gone further. It'd been a dream! There were no consequences in a dream.

"Was he in human form, or was he wolfed out?"

"Excuse me?" Andrea asked as she climbed the metal ladder into the dig site, which was below ground level.

Emma quickly followed her down the metal rungs before landing in the dirt.

"Was he in human form or wolf form when you two were getting frisky?" Emma wiggled her brows. "Was he hairy and scary?"

"What?" Andrea scowled. "No! He was human."

"Too bad. I think I'd prefer a slightly wolfed out version of the man myself. Maybe he could wolf out only halfway? Still a man, but with claws and canines?" Emma continued to wiggle her eyebrows, looking like a dumb dumb.

"I guess it would depend on how wolfed out he was," Andrea admitted. She wasn't sure she would want a fully wolfed man, but she supposed there was a certain appeal to a somewhat wolfed out man. As long as he wasn't covered in hair. Yuck! She wasn't sure she would be into that.

"You doing better?"

Andrea glanced up to see Clyde crouched at the top of the dig pit she and Emma were in. "I'm good." She gave him the thumbs-up signal.

"I don't need you fainting again." Clyde's steely blue eyes searched her as though he would be able to visibly assess her for any signs of possible fainting.

"I'm not going to faint." Andrea rolled her eyes. Not unless she put the wooden bracelet on her wrist again, but she wouldn't do that while she was at work.

"Maybe you should take a couple of days off or see a doctor. It could be low blood pressure or something."

"Clyde! You aren't a doctor."

"That's why I think you should set up an appointment. I'll pay for the visit." Clyde insisted.

Andrea cried out. "I'm fine! Leave us to work and stop worrying like my mother." Although, to be honest, her mother didn't worry about her all that much because she was a grown woman.

"How about this," Emma interjected, "I'll stay by her side all day, and if I notice anything weird, you'll be the first person I tell."

Clyde ran a hand through his dirty blonde hair as his eyes shifted between the two of them. "Fine. That will work." Standing up, he turned and left them to continue working in the dirt.

"He's worse than a mother bear." Emma rolled her eyes. "But at least our boss cares about us."

"He probably doesn't want to fill out an injury report, not that he cares." Andrea laughed as she took a small pick out of her tool kit and gently removed dirt in case there was anything lying underneath the ground. She'd hate to damage any submerged artifacts.

Emma rolled her eyes. "He worries about all of us. Anyways," she waved a manicured hand that shouldn't be anywhere near dirt, "anything more about this dream of yours?"

"Not really. Just the werewolf and a little," Andrea's cheeks heated as she recalled the vivid memory, "fooling around. It felt so real like it wasn't a dream. I have no idea how to explain it, but werewolves aren't real."

"Maybe you should join one of these dating apps, you know the ones where you swipe right or left. Get some of those urges dealt with a little fling that means nothing... get the urges itched."

"Yeah... no thanks." Andrea shook her head, causing her ponytail to bounce around as she continued to dig at the dirt with a pick. "I'm not into one-night stand situations... you don't know who those people are. They could be killers."

"True. That's why I don't do them."

Andrea's head popped up as she stared at Emma. "So, you suggest that I use apps that you wouldn't even consider?"

"What?" Emma shrugged as she laughed the word out. "Maybe you would be into this kind of thing. I don't know until I suggest something."

"We've found a mammoth skull!" Someone from another dig pit yelled excitedly.

"Did they just say mammoth skull?" Emma's head popped up, and her eyes sparkled excitedly.

"I think they did."

Both of the women dropped their tools and raced up the ladder to find where this fun discovery was located. Andrea loved the thrills of her job… and even more than that, she enjoyed her ice age dreams.

Andrea laid down on her hotel bed, ignoring the grumbling of her stomach. This bracelet was like an addiction, something that influenced her actions and flooded her mind with wishful thoughts. All she wanted to do was get another dose.

Slipping the cool wood around her hand and onto her wrist, Andrea shut her eyes and waited for sleep to overtake her. This bracelet was an addiction, and she was helpless to resist it.

It didn't take long until Andrea felt blades of grass under her naked back and tickling the sides of her arms. Cooler air puckered her skin as her body protested the sudden change in temperature from her hotel room to the outside air. She was back in the ice age. Her heart rate increased as excitement pumped through her.

Andrea couldn't wait to explore this world some more. There was a part of her that was slowly beginning to think this was time travel. As far-fetched as it might be with the werewolf. Everything was so real and vivid.

Opening her eyes, Andrea rose from her prone position and smiled. Trees soared high above her, the sun rays beamed down to warm her chilled flesh, and a slight breeze caused the grass to dance around like it was alive.

At first, Andrea thought she was alone, but then her eyes caught on a large fluffy black dire wolf with golden eyes staring straight at her.

She froze.

But her heart didn't get the memo and thundered away in her chest as it prepared her for a run for her life. She didn't leap to her feet, though. There was something familiar about this wolf. It looked like the dire wolf who changed into a sexy man and then ran his large skilled hands all over her body like she was the best-looking woman he'd ever set eyes on.

Wow.

Her thoughts were running away with her.

Andrea took a moment to take him in. The dire wolf was enormous, even though it was sitting on its haunches. The fur was about three or four inches thick, and she would bet it'd be super soft if she swiped a hand through it. And those ears! So pointy and tipped with fur. He was a magnificent wolf, she'd give him that.

"Is it you?" Andrea asked.

The dire wolf didn't give her a vocal response. Instead, he tilted his head to the side, allowing his large pink tongue to roll out of his mouth as he sent her a wolfy smirk. As a wolf, his smile came off a bit daunting because of his mouthful of sharp white teeth.

As Andrea stared at the dire wolf in front of her, it slowly shifted into the form of a man. The snout receded, and the fur slipped back into the tan skin, and within a second, a tall, well-built man stood before her.

"Oh my…" Andrea whispered under her breath as she stared up his impressive frame. He was so tall, but maybe that was because she was still sitting on her ass like a moron. Slowly, she pushed herself onto her feet and glanced back up at him… and up. Nope. He was still taller than her.

The man growled something to her in a guttural language.

It was Andrea's turn to cock her head at him. "Excuse me?" She shrugged her shoulders as she asked the question, knowing he wouldn't understand her but unable to stop herself.

The man lifted a hand and pointed to something lying next to a tree trunk.

Andrea glanced to her side and bent at the waist as she got a closer look. It was... clothing! Righting herself, she smiled over at him, "For me?" She pointed to her chest.

The man nodded his head of black hair. Taking a few steps over to the clothing, he grabbed a couple of articles and then turned to her presenting her with the animal skin clothing.

"Thanks." Her eager hands reached out for the clothing, but he withdrew them before she could get a hold of them. "Ummm...." She stared up at him in puzzlement. "Aren't those for me? They look too small for you."

Naked man sent her a wide grin as he tapped a finger to his lips.

Andrea's eyes narrowed to slits as she watched the gesture. "You want an exchange? A kiss for the clothes?" Her eyes slipped to the clothing that he held in a hand. She would like to cover her body while here, but was it worth a kiss?

With this handsome man, a kiss could turn into something more.

Andrea pursed her lips as her eyes slid back over to him. He was still smiling at her as he waited for her to come to a decision. Ugh. She had done some intimate things with him already, like coming in his arms, but still... she didn't know him, and she wasn't passion crazed right now. Right now, she would be making a level-headed decision, a choice, to kiss him.

Decision made then.

She couldn't kiss him again.

Eyeing the clothing again, she suddenly threw her body into motion and lunged for the clothing. Naked man moved quicker than she could have ever thought possible. In the blink of an eye, he had her pressed up against a tree trunk, the clothing landing at their feet.

Naked man's face got up in her personal space, and he growled guttural words at her. The smile was gone from his lips, and a glint of fire burned in his golden eyes. She'd angered him by lunging for the clothes.

"Sorry." Andrea murmured, but she never dropped her head or her gaze. Instead, she stared the wolf man down. She knew a bit about dogs and wolves. She might not be an alpha, but she definitely wasn't a woman who was going to back down and cower in front of him.

A corner of his mouth lifted. A hand came up, and he pointed to his lips.

"Fine." Andrea grumped as she rolled her eyes. Darting forward, she landed a peck on his lips, but before she could draw back her head, one of his hands plowed into her hair and pressed her lips firmly against his, deepening the kiss.

Instantly, she melted against him. She knew she should pull away and protest, but he tasted so good like the musky scent of earth and trees with a hint of warm spice. It drew her in and swamped her senses.

His cock jumped to attention and pressed into her abdomen, clearly showing her how much he was enjoying this kiss.

Naked man pulled away, breaking the kiss, a triumphant smile on his amazing lips.

"Yeah, yeah, you won." But so had she. That kiss had been one of a kind. Gentle and demanding, and it left her wishing for more. "Can I have the clothes now?" She asked as she pointed to the clothing lying on the ground.

He nodded his head.

Bending over, Andrea eagerly wrapped her fingers around the animal skin pants and slipped them over her legs before grabbing the shirt and slipping it over her head. Then she noticed a small pair of shoes, and a larger smile spread over her lips. Now she didn't have to worry about scraping up the bottoms of her feet.

When she finished dressing, she glanced back over at naked man to find him dressed as well. He'd brought clothing for the both of them.

Thank goodness!

It was hard to stop fantasizing about him when he was exposed to her view. His body was made of pure granite and shaped by the gods. He'd been molded and shaped into her fantasy man.

Another reason this was a dream.

Fantasy men didn't exist. He was too good to be true.

Andrea glanced down at the clothes she wore to find them decorated with small stones and bones from small animals. The designs were pretty, and she wished she could ask where he'd gotten the clothing. What she wore were clearly women's clothing, so had he gone back to a village? Was he going to bring her to a village?

Excitement pulsed through Andrea. She'd love to see a working ice age village... then again, if he was a werewolf, that might mean his village would consist of werewolves. Yeah, she wasn't too sure she was up for meeting so many werewolves when she was just a simple human.

Then her fully dressed werewolf was on her in a second, with a hand pressed to the small of her back he pushed her chest into his and his lips once more captured hers. Her eyes widened in shock before sliding shut in pleasure as she eagerly took his demands. Her tongue demanding its own pleasure.

One of his hands captured her wrist, and she wondered why they'd bothered to get dressed if he was just going to try and seduce her. Then he pulled back, and the wooden bracelet slipped off her wrist.

"Wait, what?" Andrea stumbled back a step as her brain processed what was going on. Glancing at his hand, she noticed he had her bracelet. "That's mine!" She barked as she darted forward, but she didn't get far before he snapped the wood with his hands.

She let out a scream of pain and astonishment. "Why... why would you break it?!" She stared dumbly at his hands, completely frozen in place.

Then Andrea reacted.

Leaping forward, she raised her hands, balled them into fists, and hammered away on his chest. Her werewolf stood there, taking her hits as she screamed at him like a hysterical woman. Then she backed off, and he continued to watch her silently with those golden eyes of his.

"If the bracelet is off my wrist, shouldn't I be waking up in my bed?" Andrea asked, perplexed. "Why am I still here?" She raised her hands in exasperation as the scenery stayed the same. Where were her hotel walls?

Wolf man dropped the two halves of her bracelet, and she scrambled forward to gather them up. Kneeling, she scooped them up and cradled them like they were her children. They were her ticket back to her world, which she was beginning to think was in the future, which meant she was in the ice age... with werewolves.

Chapter 9

Rokki watched his mate rush forward to gather up the bracelet. Wetness gathered in her eyes as she stared down at the wood. He hoped the bracelet wasn't precious to her. Still, he was sure of one thing – this bracelet was the cause of her disappearing and reappearing. If the bracelet was broken, then there'd be no more magic in the object. There'd be no more disappearing on his mate's part.

If she was a witch, she'd have to make another bracelet, and it wouldn't happen under his watch.

Now, if only he could speak with her and tell her why he would act so cruelly. It wasn't like he wanted to trap her, but he did want time to win her over so she would stop leaving him. He needed her to understand what she was to him.

Thankfully, Rokki knew of a woman who could help them. A seer who also happened to dabble in witchcraft. She would have some sort of spell or potion to allow them to speak, he was sure of it.

A spicy scent drifted through the air to his nose as his mate's anger drifted off of her in waves. When he glanced down, he found her glaring up from where she crouched on the ground. Gone were the unshed tears, replaced with a white-hot burning anger in her swirling green eyes.

Rokki wasn't entirely sure which emotion he preferred to see in his mate's eyes. He wasn't sure which emotion would make his task of winning her over would easier.

Good thing his mate was unarmed because he could see her trying to impale him... unless she was a skilled witch who could curse him with a spell. His eyes narrowed, but if she knew magic, then she would have used it rather than her fists.

"Stand up, mate. We have a witch to visit."

She stood, but Rokki doubted it was because she understood him. She growled something at him that he didn't understand, and then he watched her spin on a heel and storm away from him.

Rokki cocked his head to the side as he watched the angry sway of her intoxicating hips. "Where do you think you're going, mate?"

She didn't respond, and instead, she continued to walk away, shoving branches out of her way.

With a sigh, Rokki followed after her.

If there was one thing his sisters had taught him about females, it was to be patient and let them work their emotions out. If he ran up to his mate, grabbed her arm, and forced her to come with him, she would protest, and they would get nowhere. So, he followed after her.

The sun slowly shifted in the sky as he let his mate wander through the land. He could smell several predators roaming the area, but they could also smell him, and they steered clear. A werewolf was not a creature to mess with, especially when his mate was nearby, and those predators could smell it.

Then his mate stopped. He could see the tenseness in her shoulder muscles as she hunched over a bit.

She murmured something at him before spinning around and heaving a sigh.

If he had any sons, he would be sure to share this nugget of perspective with them. Patience was vital with females. Let them work out their thoughts and emotions.

"Aye em steel awgry wit du." She said as she pointed an accusing finger at him, the broken bracelet clutched in her other hand.

Rokki simply shrugged at her words but nodded his head. "You are angry." He held out a pleading hand. "I am sorry for that." He hoped she could hear the regret in his voice, even if she couldn't understand his words. "I've waited so long to find my mate, and here you are," he waved a hand up and down to encompass her before him, "I couldn't let you disappear."

"Oookae." She motioned for him to guide them.

Rokkie eyed her. The spicy scent still drifted off her, so she hadn't forgiven him, but she was allowing him to retake control. "Come mate. Let us seek out the witch who can help us."

After just a few hours of walking up and down rolling hills, through forests, and over streams, Rokki found his mate drifting further and further behind him. He slowed his pace, but when even that didn't help her, he came to the realization that where ever she came from, she wasn't used to walking for long periods of time.

Stopping for a little bit, he allowed her time to catch up. He didn't need a sabertooth jumping out of nowhere to take her down and him too far away to stop her death.

His mate trudged up to him, a hand pressing into her side.

"Aye downt tink aye can gow andy fudder." She heaved next to him as she lifted each foot with a wince.

Ah. Rokki glanced down at her small feet. They were sore from walking, and she was telling him she didn't want to continue. With a huff, he glanced in the direction they were headed. It was still about a day's walk to the witch's cave.

"Sit down."

She cocked her head at him as her eyes tried to understand what he had just said to her.

Rokki pointed a finger towards the ground.

His mate promptly fell flat on her butt. A sigh of relief parted her lips, and all he could think about was pressing her into the grass and claiming her with his mouth before he claimed her with a bite to her neck as he thrust his shaft deep into her.

Rokki shook his head to clear the thoughts. Now was not the time to be fantasizing about her. They needed to get to the witch so they could speak.

His dire wolf whimpered inside, begging to claim its mate. It didn't understand why Rokki wanted to speak with his mate when he claimed her, but Rokki wanted to be able to tell her how beautiful she was and how she would be the most precious thing in his life. He shoved the beast into the back of his mind. He would let it out to play later... at a better time.

Walking away, Rokki searched the immediate area for some plants. When he found a patch of the little yellow flowers, he plucked several of them. As he walked back over to his mate, he crushed them between the palm of one hand and the heel of the other.

"Vwats dat?" His mate asked as she pointed to the yellow flowers in his palm.

"To help your feet," Rokki said, knowing she wanted to know what he was doing. He continued to mash the flowers between his hands.

Once he had a paste, he bent down next to her and used one hand to remove her leather shoes from her dainty feet.

"Uh, vwat rrr du duing?" She asked as she tried to yank her feet out of his grasp.

"Calm." Rokki met her gaze and tried to communicate with his tone. He pointed to the paste, and then to her feet. "It will help the pain."

His mate hesitated one second and then nodded her head.

Then Rokki grabbed a hold of her feet and rubbed the mixture into the soles of her soft feet.

"Ooooh, yeeeaaah." His mate's eyes closed as a lazy smile spread across her face.

His dire wolf surged to the front, claws formed on his hands, and his canines sprang out of his gums. He fought for control, and thankfully won when he told the beast it would only scare their mate. The claws and canines receded. Good thing she had closed her eyes, or she would have seen his wolf coming out to play.

His thumb worked the yellow paste into her skin, dyeing the pale skin with the color.

"Du can doo dat furever." She murmured.

His mate enjoyed foot rubs? He could do that. Any chance to touch her.

Rokki pulled away after a few more minutes and stood. "Your feet should feel better now. We need to keep moving." He used a couple of fingers to mimic walking.

His mate sent him a pout with her lower lip.

He made the motion again.

"Fiene." She placed the animal skin shoes back on her feet and stood next to him.

Her scent wrapped around him, and for once, he couldn't seem to think straight. All he wanted to do was dive into her, and let her scent mix with his as they explored each other's bodies.

Ugh, she made it hard for him to think straight when she was around.

"Come, mate, before I ravish you here. My wolf wants you, and I am unsure how long I can keep him back."

Side by side, they walked together. Every step closer to the seer gave him hope that he would finally be able to speak with his mate, to learn everything about her and where she came from, and how many children she wanted to have because he wanted as many as she could give him.

It wasn't long before they spotted a herd of horses in a field. He would have walked straight past them without a second thought, but his mate seemed fascinated as she stopped to admire them.

"Oooo." She crept closer.

Rokki glanced at the stocky animals that drew her attention. They weren't anything special, a common animal to spot in the area. Her eyes seemed to take them in as though she were memorizing their colorings and sizes.

Wondering if he missed something, he glanced back at the herd, but they grazed like normal, and there was nothing strange. He sniffed the air, and none of them were shifters.

Rokki crouched beside her. "What fascinates you, mate?"

She met his eyes as she pointed to the horses. "Whoses."

His mate acted as though she'd never seen them before, which would be strange because horse herds were pretty common in the area. Then again, he had no idea where she went when she used her magic bracelet to disappear.

"One day, I will hunt one down for you, but we have no time for hunting right now. We need to get to the witch, and with how slow you walk, we will have to make camp tonight." Rokki hoped it wouldn't take her long to get into shape. His world was one built around alphas, and he couldn't expect his people to respect her if she couldn't even attempt to keep up.

Rokki eyed her as she stared in amazement at the horses. How was he going to bring her back to his village? If she wasn't a witch and a simple human, then she would stand no chance in his village. The male alpha controlled the males, and the female alpha kept the females in line… if she were a witch, she could use magic to even the odds against a werewolf, but a human… she wouldn't be able to control a single pup.

Then again, he might not have to worry about it because of the prophecy. If his mate was human, they would be expected to leave the clan, and then he would have to take care of a vulnerable human female while he found a new home for them.

Rokki's fingers shook as the future weighed down on him. It was a lot of pressure.

He glanced over at her. Her long auburn locks were curled at the ends and draped down her back about halfway. He wanted nothing more than to run his hands through the long strands and breath in the sweet, delicate scent that wafted off of her.

He was glad his sister's clothing had fit her. His mate seemed more comfortable being around him while clothed rather than naked. Her people must prefer clothing, which would make sense for humans since they didn't need to worry about a sudden need to shift.

"Come, mate." Rokki reached out and wrapped a hand around her upper arm. "It's time for us to leave."

With some gentle coaxing, he eventually led his mate away from the horse herd without bothering the grazing animals.

As the sun set, vibrant colors blazed across the sky, painting the clouds in oranges, pinks, blues, and reds. Andrea stared up at the sky in wonderment as she wished she had a camera. She wasn't sure why, but the colors were the best she'd ever seen, and she had to wonder if it was because there was no pollution in the skies. There was nothing between her and the big poofy clouds except normal clean air.

Naked man touched her arm with a gentle hand.

Andrea looked away from the sky and into his deep golden eyes, "Yes?"

He motioned to a small outcropping of rocks ahead. As they'd walked throughout the day, the terrain had begun to increase in severity, and they were entering some hills. She could see some mountain tips soaring into the low laying clouds off in the distance.

She wasn't entirely sure where he was taking her, but she was eager to see his village because she was sure he would be a part of a village. Living on his own in the ice age would be nearly impossible.

Andrea followed him over to the boulders. It was a good place to make camp for the night. With night approaching quickly, she was sure the predators would soon make their presence well known.

As the image of a sabertooth flew through her mind, a shiver overtook her. She'd already had too many close encounters with those scary creatures.

When Andrea noticed her not-so-naked man collecting sticks and branches, she jumped into action. She might not know much about how this world worked in real life, but she knew how to collect dry sticks off the ground.

Studying the ice age in a classroom and digging up sites in her world was distinctly different than actually living in the ice age.

Once Andrea had a decent sized armful of sticks, she walked back to the outcropping of boulders proudly. When she dumped her armful on the ground, wolf man sent her a thankful smile as he crouched by the sticks and began to organize them.

Andrea bent close as she watched what he did. How to create a fire was something she should know.

Her werewolf noticed her interest and slowed his movements so she could understand what to do.

Then he had a flicker of flames in a few more minutes, and in a couple of more minutes, she heard the happy crackle of the fire as night finally set in around them.

Plopping a seat by the fire, Andrea held out her hands to the warmth of the flames as night surrounded them with a cold blanket of dark.

Wolf man sat down next to her and pulled out a small pouch that she hadn't noticed before.

"What's that?" She asked with a pointed finger.

Wolf man opened the pouch by pulling a couple of leather strings, and when he presented the opened top, she leaned over to get a better view.

"Is that food?" It looked like dried meat to her, and her stomach let out a loud grumble of delight. "May I?" She looked up at wolf man and motioned eating to him.

Wolf man nodded his chiseled chin as he held the animal skin pouch out to her.

Slipping a hand into the pouch, Andrea grabbed a hold of a couple of strips of dried meat and pulled them out. "Thanks." She sent him a smile before munching down on the meat and watching the flames of the fire.

She was trying to keep her cool, but it was hard to stop her body from responding to his presence. She'd been intimate with this man, and now here she was sitting beside him next to a fire. One could say this was almost romantic in nature.

Andrea munched faster on the dried meat, but her eyes kept drifting over to her wolf man. The firelight danced across his face, and she noticed something about him that she'd never seen before. He had a couple of scars running down his face. One over his eyebrow and the other ran down the length of the side of his face.

He'd been in a fight, and the opponent had claws.

When his head turned, and he raised his eyebrows as he caught her staring, she blushed.

"I wish I could talk to you, even if you did break my bracelet. And I'm still pissed about that, but either way, this is an archeologist's wet dream right here. Although, as far as I'm aware, there weren't any werewolves in the ice age."

"Rokki." Wolf man suddenly said as he thumped a fist against his chest.

Andrea blinked dumbly for a couple of seconds, but when he repeated the word and the gesture, realization dawned. "Ah. You are Rokki." She pointed to him.

He nodded his head eagerly. Then he poked a finger into her chest, right between her breasts.

"Me?"

"Me." He echoed.

"No, no, no." Andrea shook her head as she waved her hands wildly in front of her before she pointed to herself, "Andrea."

"Andrea." Rokki echoed.

"Gosh, I know names are the right direction to knowing each other, but I really wish there was more we could communicate." Like how the hell he changed into a massive dire wolf.

As if the world around them could read her thoughts, an anguished howl echoed through the night air.

Andrea jumped out of her skin, nearly landing in Rokki's lap as she huddled closer to him. Then another howl responded to the first, and then a third and a fourth.

"Are we safe?" Panic coated each word as she pressed herself into him.

Rokki said something guttural to her before he gripped her upper arms and moved her away from him. Then he stood and backed away.

"What are you doing?" More panic surged through her as she thought he was about to leave her.

Rokki stripped down, yanking his decorated leather shirt up and over his head, and then he jerked off his pants and shoes.

"I don't think this is really the time for..." Andrea drifted off as black hair sprang out of his body, his face elongated into a snout, and before she even had time to blink, he was a large black dire wolf with golden eyes. "Oh my god..." She felt frozen in place, and she was sure her eyes were as wide as dinner plates.

The dire wolf chuffed at her, and she couldn't help the squeak of terror at the sight of the impressively long canines that peaked out at her. With one last chuff, the black dire wolf leaped into the night and disappeared.

Andrea huddled closer to the fire. Supposedly, wild animals were scared of fire, and she prayed that was true because she was now alone with some of the scariest predators that ever roamed the planet.

Another howl echoed through the nearby trees and into her protected rock outcropping. She was fairly certain the howling came from her wolf man, Rokki.

She hadn't been sure what he had said to her earlier, but now that she heard him howling, she'd put two and two together. He was out marking the territory and letting the other wolves know this space was occupied.

Andrea liked the name. Rokki. It was a rough and tough name and seemed to fit him. It also rolled off her tongue with ease and sent tingles of awareness racing up and down her spine.

It only took a few minutes before the massive dire wolf popped back into the circle boulders. Andrea screamed before recognition had her clamping a firm hand over her mouth.

In the blink of an eye, the dire wolf disappeared only to be replaced by Rokki.

"Andrea." He said, his voice soft and coaxing as he held out his hands.

"Sorry," she apologized, "you don't scare me. I was just surprised." She kept her voice calm and repositioned herself at the fire.

Rokki took a seat beside her.

The silence weighed heavily on her as they sat staring at the fire. If she had to take a guess, Rokki had shifted into his dire wolf form and marked the immediate area because the howls of the other wolves grew distant in the night. After he'd made sure they were safe, she'd screamed and pulled away from him.

"I wanted to thank you for saving," Andrea faced him, "my life so…" She trailed off when Rokki wrapped an arm of steel around her waist and drew her into his naked embrace. He placed her on his lap, facing him with her legs wrapped around him.

"Andrea." Rokki murmured as he leaned in.

His breath tickled her neck as he nuzzled her. He growled in her ear, and she knew he was speaking, but she had no idea what he said.

"Rokki... you sure we should do this?"

Rokki crushed his lips across hers. And she melted. Her arms encircled his neck as her hands ran up and down the backside of his head and through his shoulder-length black hair. He smelled like perfection, like moss and earth.

Repositioning them, slowly, Rokki tilted her back until she was lying with her back pressed into the ground, and Rokki laid on top of her. Her wolf man broke the kiss, and in the flickering firelight, she watched his fingers work under her waistband, and he slid them over her hips, down her thighs and calves until he could flip the article of clothing away. Then he grabbed the hem of her shirt, and when she leaned up and held her hands over her head, he yanked it up and over her head and discarded it as well.

Her wolf man leaned back on his heels, and his golden eyes skimmed over her naked form. It wasn't her first time being naked in front of him, but she still felt shy and nervous about her nakedness. She was exposed, and her emotions were vulnerable. She wanted all of this to be real. With everything in her heart, she wanted this to be real.

When Andrea glanced down, some of her nerves fled in a flutter of excitement as her gaze fell on his erection. If his jutting length could speak, she was sure it would tell her there was nothing to worry about, and her body was amazing.

A blush seared across her cheeks as desire flooded her body in a rush. Reaching out, she wrapped a hand around his thick length, and her mouth popped open when she felt the heat radiating off his length. She couldn't even fit the whole length in her hand. It was so large. His member stood proudly in front of him. It promised her pleasure.

Growing more confident, Andrea pumped his cock cautiously before sliding her palm over the tip of his cock. The bead of cum wet her hand, and she rubbed it over his sensitive length.

When she glanced up, she saw his eyes were slits, pleasure rolling over his face as his mouth opened slightly in desire. She smiled in response to his enjoyment.

"You've got a stunning body." Andrea's hands abandoned his bobbing cock, and instead, she ran the tips of her fingers over the ridges of his abdomen. If she was back in her time, she would say he worked out every day, but since they were in the ice age, this just proved how much he had to run and naturally work out in this environment.

Rokki sighed in pleasure as she continued to explore his body. His face had gone soft like there wasn't a care in the world. He wasn't the only one enjoying this. There wasn't a single inch that she didn't explore, and he let her explore her body at her own pace. He just sat back and enjoyed it.

When Andrea finished her explorations, she leaned back until she was lying on the short grass. "I think it's your turn to explore my body." She sent him her best alluring smile as she spread her legs slightly, communicating without words that she was ready for something more than simple kisses and caresses.

A wolfy grin spread across Rokki's face,

causing a small dimple to pop up on one side of his scarred face. He leaned over her as he placed a hand on either side of her chest. He planted a small peck of a kiss on her lips before kissing her jaw, the center of her neck, and then down to a breast. He placed gentle kisses around her nipple as one hand skimmed across her side, tickling her slightly, and she let out a small giggle.

Then his rough-skinned fingers tangled in the protective curls on top of her mound before slipping between her legs. His fingers nestled themselves in between her wet lips. A growl of pleasure parted his lips, his canines glinting in the firelight.

Andrea blinked. His canines had grown a bit, giving him a wolfier look and adding to her attraction to him. Golden eyes, shoulder-length black hair and canines. Emma had been right. This slightly wolfy look was appealing.

When the tip of Rokki's fingers found her clit, her mind refocused on what he was doing rather than his wolfy looks. His wicked fingers circled her clit, before pinching the sensitive nub between a couple of fingers, pulling lightly on it, before circling it once again.

"Yes, yes!" Andrea panted as her head thrashed a bit, and her hips bucked. At this very moment, she hoped this wasn't a dream, that her werewolf was real, because she wanted more moments like this.

Rokki's mind fought to hold back his wolf side, but his beast wanted to be a part of this as well. This was the first time their mate was letting them go further than kisses. He could read it in her eyes. There was a burning lust in her grass-green eyes.

His canines elongated, and he didn't miss her wide eyes and parted mouth as she spotted his growing teeth. If his beast wasn't careful, it would ruin what Rokki had done so hard to get started.

The firelight played over her soft features, and she looked absolutely gorgeous. Her auburn curls framed her face as she laid in the grass. Firelight reflected off her eyes, making it look like there was a fire of desire burning deep within her.

His cock swelled to a painful point as he admired his mate, and all he wanted to do was plunge into her welcoming heat, but he refrained. First, he was going to explore her fully and take his time with her.

Rokki straddled one of her thighs, so he could get easy access to her nub. She squirmed under his administrations, and her cheeks flushed pick as the pressure under her skin built. Soon he would send her crashing over the edge, not only giving her pleasure but himself. There was nothing better than pushing his mate over the edge and watching her ecstasy flashing over her face.

"I want to see you shatter under me." He growled low in his throat. "I want to see my mate filled with pleasure."

Her entrance grew even slicker as she came around his hand, and he growled in contentment. Andrea squirmed under him as the orgasm faded, but the pleasure continued to roll through her frame. He loved watching her come below him.

"Aye need ywur cok." She said, but he had no clue what it meant, and it frustrated him. He wanted to know what she said and have her understand him.

Then Andrea's hand shot out, and his mate took a firm hold of his member. She stroked her hand up and down his length as her body shuddered below him. His eyelids slid closed, and her lips opened on a breathy sigh. Her hips bucked, begging him for more than just his fingers, but he wasn't about to interrupt her pleasure.

Then Andrea came. A throaty moan tore up her throat as her hips bucked wildly under him. He circled his finger faster on her nub as her hand worked vigorously on his member. His balls tightened at the sight of his mate coming, and his inner wolf couldn't leave well enough alone.

Rokki felt the shift overcoming him.

If they didn't finish this soon, he'd be more wolf than man, and that was sure to scare her away. His human mate wouldn't want to see him with long claws and elongated canines. It would scare her. He was certain of that much.

The moment her shudders of pleasure ceased, Rokki wrapped his hands around her hips and paused when he noticed claws on his fingertips. He flipped her onto her hands and knees, the way he preferred to take a woman, and it would satiate his inner beast while making sure Andrea didn't see his beast joining in on their first time.

A startled gasp escaped his mate, but she wiggled her ass at him with a light giggle.

It was all he needed.

Wrapping a clawed hand around his member, Rokki slid the tip between her lips, the head of his cock pushing against her tight entrance. As he pushed further, her pleasured body welcomed him with a slick hug. It was perfect. They were under the stars in the forest while they enjoyed each other's bodies.

A rumble of pleasure flowed through him as she eagerly took his length. Once he had his full length deep inside her, he gripped her waist and pumped her over his cock.

Suddenly, Andrea rocked back and forth, leaving his hands free to explore her back. His hands slid up her spine as she rode his cock with eager thrusts. One of his hands dug into her long auburn locks, which looked like flames with the firelight flickering off of them. Grabbing a section, he yanked her head back, causing her back to arch.

Together they moaned as the pleasure increased.

His balls slapped against her wet flesh, and before he knew it, they both roared to the moon as they came. His cock pumped its hot load deep into her, and his wolf howled with happiness and begged him to lean over her and give her his bite, but he resisted. Clamping his jaw tight, Rokki refused to give in to his dire wolf.

Rokki wasn't going to scare his human mate with a jarring bite... not on their first time together. He should do it on the next full moon, which wasn't too far away. He could be patient. He had her in his arms, which was all he needed. By then, the seer who lived in the caves would have cast a spell over them, allowing them to speak so he could explain his desire to claim her under the moon with his bite.

Pulling out of her, Rokki wrapped his arms around her and laid them both down on the ground. He placed her between his hot body and the warmth of the fire so she wouldn't grow chilled as the night only grew colder.

"Aye whant du toh knohw aye awm stweel pissd at du." His mate mumbled to him as sleep washed over her.

Rokki stroked a hand through her hair as he massaged her scalp, loving the closeness with her. Someday, he would know what she was saying, and he couldn't wait.

Chapter 10

Rokki wanted nothing more than to speak with her... his mate. There was no doubt in his mind that they were built for each other. The gods were smiling down on him, and he wanted nothing more than to join with her under the full moon before tying their lives together in their village cave.

The evening had passed uneventfully, except for their passionate time in each other's arms. A memory he would never be able to forget. Ever. His Andrea was so passionate and responsive. He wished he could lay her down on the ground and dive in between her legs again.

Sadly, they had no time.

Rokki was determined to get to the seer before another night enveloped them in darkness. He'd much rather stay the night in a cave than under the trees. There were a lot of predators out there, and he didn't need a hungry animal challenging him to a fight so it could make an easy meal of his mate.

He had a mate to protect, and she made him vulnerable.

If two or more predators attacked, like a pack of wolves, there was no possible way for him to keep her safe from all those teeth and claws. He would end up dying trying to save her, and then she would be left to die on her own.

Rokki growled to himself as he and his dire wolf protested the thought of her dying.

He had to get them to the seer.

The terrain grew rougher the further they walked. Large grey boulders dotted the area, replacing the dark green pine trees. Despite looking like she wanted to quit, Andrea kept trudging on. It looked like her feet hurt her again, as she seemed to shift her weight on them. Rokki made a mental note of it. He would have to give her some more of the yellow flowers for her feet, or maybe the seer would have something stronger.

If he wasn't so anxious to speak with his mate, he wouldn't push them so hard, but there were things he needed to know about her, like if she was a witch or a human.

If she were a witch, it would mean he was the prophesized son who would take control of the pack as alpha, and if she were human, he would be the one to be kicked out of the clan once his brother found his mate.

Rokki wasn't entirely sure what he wanted her to be, or if he even wanted to lead the clan. His dire wolf wanted to be pack leader, it was ingrained in his alpha beast, but his human head knew a lot went into keeping his pack safe. It would be a lot of weight on his shoulders, a weight he wasn't sure he wanted or could lift.

Rokki's eyes slid over to where Andrea walked beside him. She caught him staring and sent him a wide smile.

"Hewwo." Andrea sent him a wave with one of her hands.

His brows drew down as they continued to walk up the hill. He wasn't completely sure why she was greeting him... they hadn't separated long enough for a greeting. He shrugged it off. His mate had some strange habits, but maybe among her clan, it was normal to randomly wave at someone who had never left.

By mid-day, Rokki spotted the caves up ahead of them. Just a couple of seconds, and they would be standing at the entrance of the cave. His heart sped up in his chest, like a herd of mammoths charging. Soon, he would understand his mate!

Caw!

Rokki tilted his head back until he spotted a black dot circling above them.

A black raven cawed above them. The large wings were stretched wide, and the bird circled above them, cawing their arrival.

The seer, who was also a witch, had raised this raven since it was a chick, and rumor in the clan gatherings was that it was another pair of eyes for her. No one could sneak up on her without that bird announcing their arrival, which meant she would be ready for them.

"We are here." Rokki took the lead as he led them up a small rocky trail to the entrance of the cave.

"Who comes to my cave?" A female voice called from the cave. It wasn't a booming voice. It was light and musical.

As Rokki and Andrea walked up to the dark entrance of the cave, he finally saw the witch's face. It'd been tattooed with red ink. Lines and dots crisscrossed over her young face, and long black hair curled around her shoulders like poisonous snakes that were ready to strike. She held a gnarled wood staff in one hand, and her breasts were bare to the world. She was a beauty, Rokki would give her that, but no one was more beautiful than his mate.

Andrea sucked in a scandalized breath.

Rokki glanced over to her with raised brows and saw that his mate stared openly at the seer's breasts.

Like he'd thought, her clan must believe in covering up more than the clans in this area. It wasn't uncommon to see men and women exposing their bodies to the world.

"We seek your help," Rokki said as he turned his attention back to the seer.

The seer's upper lip pulled back. "A wolf." Her hand went white on her staff as her green eyes glared daggers at him.

Rokki's hackles rose. Would she curse him and throw him out for being a werewolf? "I am."

"You've brought me your mate?" The seer eyed Andrea with less hostility. "Ah, I can see your dilemma, wolf. Your mate is unable to speak with you." She said when Andrea just glanced between them with a blank stare.

"She can speak, but I don't understand her." Rokki corrected the seer's words.

"It is the same." The seer waved a hand dismissively and strode back into her cave.

"Will you help us?" Rokki took a step forward as a bit of panic set in. It looked like the seer wasn't going to help them. If the seer didn't help, he would have to teach his mate how to speak his language, and he'd hate to know how long that would take her.

"I will help you." The seer called out as she walked further into her cave.

Rokki wasn't sure whether or not to follow the seer since she wasn't saying anything, but he chose to place a hand on the small of Andrea's back, and guided her into the cave beside him.

Darkness surrounded them as they walked over the rough entrance of the cave. The seer's cave hadn't been lived in long enough to form a smooth floor, and Rokki did his best to guide Andrea, who couldn't see as well in the dark. Thankfully, it wasn't long before they broke into a small chamber with a fire burning in the center. A hole in the ceiling of the cave allowed the smoke to vent without suffocating the occupants.

"Take a seat." The seer laid her staff on the floor and took a seat on some folded animal skins next to the fire.

Rokki sat and patted the spot on the stone floor next to him to indicate Andrea should also be seated. She complied, her eyes still stuck on the seer in front of them as she crisscrossed her legs. His eyes narrowed as he found his mate's gaze stuck on the seer's breasts. When Andrea set foot in his village, her eyes would surely pop out of her head when she saw all the half-naked women walking around.

The seer pulled some grass baskets, and some animal skin sacks to her, before grabbing a bowl made of wood. Taking different items out of each bag, she used a stick to make a paste, and then poured some water into the bowl to make a liquid, and then presented it to Andrea with two hands.

Andrea finally glanced away from the seer to him.

Rokki nodded his head and raised his hands to his mouth and tilted his head back, mimicking drinking from the bowl. He couldn't tell her it was safe with words, but he could still tell her that this was something she should do, and he hoped she trusted him enough to do it.

Andrea turned back to the bowl, held out her hands, and took the small wooden bowl from the seer. She raised it to her nose, which automatically crinkled, and she held the bowl away from her face. "Du espect meh to drwink dis?"

He mimicked drinking the bowl again.

"Oh, gawd." Andrea grimaced, but she raised the lip of the bowl to her mouth, squeezed her eyes shut, and chugged the contents of the bowl. "Gah!" Her tongue leaped out of her mouth, and she shook it a little as she grimaced.

Once she recovered, Andrea handed the bowl back to the seer. "That was horrible."

Shock widened Rokki's eyes before a pleased smile crossed his lips. "I can understand you."

Andrea's head of auburn locks nearly spun off her neck as she twisted to set her green eyes on him. "I can… understand you, but how?" She glanced between him and the seer like they'd both suddenly sprouted wings.

"I asked the seer to use her magic to allow us to speak," Rokki explained with awe in his voice. It had worked! The potion had worked on Andrea!

"Magic?" Andrea asked as she continued to glance between them.

"Yes, magic," Rokki confirmed.

"You fucking asshole."

Rokki's head shot back like she'd slapped him. Those had not been the words he'd expected out of her mouth.

"How dare you!" Andrea grabbed the bowl, which sat on the ground near her and threw the object at him.

Rokki ducked, and the bowl soared over his head before clattering against the rock wall behind him. "Andrea?" He asked as he righted himself.

"You broke my bracelet." She pulled the bracelet out, which he hadn't known she still had on her, and she shoved it into his face. "You took my freedom from me!"

Andrea couldn't help her white-hot anger. She'd been waiting to vent to him and thought she would never get the chance. Last night when she'd closed her eyes, she'd expected to wake back up in her hotel room, but she hadn't. And now she firmly believed the bracelet was magic and brought her back to the ice age.

Rokki had literally crushed her chance at going home!

"I'm stuck here because of you." She hissed.

Rokki appeared speechless at her venomous tone. His golden eyes grew stormy as he suddenly flung himself to his feet, nearly conking his head on the stone ceiling of the cave. "I need to go back to my village before my pack wonders where I've gone. She needs something for her feet." He motioned to Andrea while addressing the seer.

Then he stormed away before she could utter a single word. His black hair swung around his face as he turned on a heel and strode towards the entrance of the cave.

"Where's he going?" Andrea asked the seer as her eyes drifted over to the woman. "Is he leaving me here?" Panic set into her chest.

"Let the wolf go," the woman waved a hand dismissively, "No one needs a wolf around. Troublesome and easy to anger those beasts." The woman began to put her supplies away.

Andrea's heart thundered in her chest as she debated running after Rokki, but she willed herself to calm. Closing her eyes, she asked, "He called you a seer?"

"Witch. Seer. I dabble in both."

"Is this a dream?" Now that Andrea could speak with people, they were going to have a hard time shutting her up. There were so many questions swirling around her head.

"Dream?" The seer laughed as her green eyes danced with amusement. "This is no dream." The seer cocked her head to the side, and her green eyes grew hazy as she stared at Andrea.

"Hello?" Andrea waved a hand in the air.

A few seconds later, and after thoroughly creeping out Andrea, the seer righted her head.

"You are from the future, and your world is strange to me, but you are meant to be here. You belong here. This is your destiny."

"Uh, yeah." What was a twenty-first century woman supposed to say to that? "Well, as much as I would love to stay, I was hoping you might be able to fix this for me?" She held out the bracelet that Rokki had snapped in half.

"Hmmm." The seer studied it before plucking the two halves out of Andrea's hand. "Very beautiful. Does it have meaning to you?"

"Yes. A lot." Andrea said, truthfully. "It can bring me back to my world."

"You don't need it." The seer said as her green eyes studied Andrea.

"I need it fixed," Andrea assured the woman. "I need to get home. People, my people, will wonder where I am."

The seer shrugged with a sigh. "I can build you another, but you will need to wait. This takes time."

"Of course." Andrea wasn't going to place any time constraints on the woman when the seer was willing to fix her bracelet.

Andrea looked towards the entrance of the cave, wondering if and when Rokki would make his reappearance.

"He won't be back for a while."

"How do you know that?" Andrea faced the woman again. When the woman sent her a quirked eyebrow, Andrea held up a hand, "Yeah, I should have known. You're a seer. You can see the future."

As the seer put her pouches and baskets away in the cave, Andrea cleared her throat. "What should I call you?"

"My name is Elvira and yours?"

"Andrea."

A caw echoed down the cave entrance as a large black blob flew across Andrea's line of sight.

"Ack!" Andrea scrambled back until her back bumped into the pokey cave wall. When she found the source of the movement with her eyes, she found the raven from outside was now inside the cave, sitting on a root that protruded from a cave wall. "Is," she pointed at the raven, "that your pet?"

Elvira glanced over at her black feathered companion. "I don't know what pet is, but he is my companion. I found him on the forest floor a long time ago when he was a chick and raised him as my own. Perhaps you could call him my child."

The raven cawed like he understood the seer. Then again, if Elvira was a witch as well as a seer, she could have cast a spell on the raven so she could understand the animal.

"So, he's kind of like your familiar."

"You speak strange words," Elvira said with a chuckle. "My potion allows us to speak, but there are still words that I don't understand."

Andrea skipped the assumption. It didn't matter what the raven was to Elvira. "Are you sure this isn't a dream?"

"I am," Elvira said with a firm nod of her head. "Rokki, Jepriz, and I are all real."

Putting two and two together, Andrea figured Jepriz must be Elvira's raven. The beady black eyes of the raven followed her every moment. Jepriz would turn his head to fix Andrea with an eye. He was an intelligent little bird.

"So, how long until the bracelet is fixed? I wouldn't mind going home." Soon. But she didn't say the word out loud. She figured it was implied.

"Be patient. Magic takes time, and magic that's rushed always goes bad. You wouldn't want to keep going further back in time, would you?" Elvira's green eyes studied her as she waited for a response.

"I guess not," Andrea admitted. Although seeing even more of the past would hold interest, she'd hate to get stuck there. "I have another question."

"I will do my best to answer your question." Elvira held out her arm, and her raven flew to her. When he landed, he floofed his wings, poofing out before his glossy black feathers fell flat on his body.

"Is this my real body, or is my body still in my time… rotting away." It was a real worry. She didn't want her twenty-first century self rotting in her hotel bed. That would disturb the hotel's housekeeper.

A smile cracked across Elvira's lips. "Your bed is empty. You are you. There is no need to worry about another body."

Well, that was good, at least. She'd hate for someone at the hotel to wander across her body and think she was in a coma or worse, dead, when really she wasn't... or bury her because they thought was dead.

Andrea cringed at the thought of waking up in a coffin in the ground. Nightmares of all nightmares. To be surrounded by dark in a tiny space under six feet of heavy, suffocating dirt. Shudders rolled through her at the image her mind had created.

"I can see you're worried about being here," the seer interrupted Andrea's thoughts, "but your wolf will take care of you."

Elvira's words calmed Andrea a bit, but still, "I don't know him."

"Don't you?" Elvira raised a dark eyebrow with a knowing smile.

A blush sprang across Andrea's face in a flood of heat, and it had nothing to do with the warmth pumping off the fire in front of her. She was speaking with a seer. This woman may have seen her night in Rokki's arms long before it had happened. "Sleeping with him doesn't mean I know him."

Elvira shrugged her exposed shoulders, jostling her naked breasts with the sudden movement. "Although a wolf wouldn't be my first choice in a man, I can see why he would attract you." Her green eyes twinkled in the firelight.

"Wait," Andrea held up a hand, "I think we're getting ahead of ourselves here. I slept with him, I didn't proclaim my love." She wouldn't mind some more nights with him, even if she were pissed about his actions. He was an attractive man and so far very gentle with her. And someday, she would get her apology out of him for breaking her way home.

"He is a werewolf, Andrea," Elvira said as though she should know what that meant.

"So?" Andrea scrunched up her face in confusion.

"Wolves mate for life." Elvira offered a tid bit to her raven, Jepriz. The bird's long black beak snatched up the offered food, and he quickly guzzled it.

Andrea blinked as the information settled in, and her brain had time to process the words. "Are you saying... he thinks we are mates?!"

"I can't say what he thinks since I am not him, but he is a werewolf." Elvira lifted her arm, and Jepriz flew back to his perch on the tree root. "If you aren't his mate, I don't know why he would bother with you."

Eeep!

Andrea wasn't sure she could commit to being in a dedicated relationship with Rokki. She didn't even know his mom or dad, or what his favorite animal to eat was, or how many siblings he had... which brought her to another strange thought.

"Do werewolves birth puppies?"

Elvira snorted as she cackled, completely disturbing Jepriz as he cawed at them to stop their loud noises.

"What's so funny?" Andrea folded her arms in front of her chest, the animal shirt bunching up in front of her at the movement.

"Please ask Rokki that question when he comes back," Elvira begged as she wiped tears off her cheeks. "In front of me. I wouldn't want to miss seeing his face."

Andrea pursed one side of her mouth in annoyance. "I'm going to assume that means no."

Elvira shook her head. "The children are born in human form and can't shift until they are of age. A werewolf heavy with child might not be able to shift. They do usually have multiple offspring when they deliver."

Yeah, no. Andrea wasn't about to deliver any babies in the ice age. Talk about horrible medical care, and multiple babies at once? Talk about risky. "No, thanks."

Elvira rolled her eyes. "Then you shouldn't bed the wolf."

"True." Andrea nodded her head. They'd already had one moment of unprotected sex, which could be enough to get her pregnant. Double yikes! "I won't have to worry about it if you would fix that bracelet." At the raised eyebrow sent her way, Andrea quickly changed her tone, "Sorry, that came out ruder than I meant."

"I can't blame you," Elvira confessed. "I wouldn't be thrilled about mating a wolf, either."

"Any particular reason?" Andrea hadn't missed the glares and crinkled nose when Rokki was around.

"I saw my future."

Vague, but intriguing. "Bad?"

"Very," Elvira confirmed. "A werewolf will be the end of me."

"I'm," what did someone say to that? "sorry to hear that."

Elvira shrugged. "We all die someday. Most of us don't see it coming, but I intend to avoid the werewolf for as long as I can."

Chapter 11

Andrea swung her legs in slow back and forth motions as she sat on a large boulder right outside the mouth of the cave. Night was creeping up on the land, and the sky was once again ablaze in brilliant colors as the sun set over the horizon.

Paste dried on her feet as she swung them through the air. After Rokki's burst of anger, the seer had inspected Andrea's feet and created some cream out of some of those tiny yellow flowers.

She could have sat there all day watching the scenery. She had a sneaky suspicion that Elvira had chosen this cave on purpose. From this exact spot, Andrea could see over the forest below, and there were some distant mountains out there. She squinted as she attempted to figure out where she may be. She knew when, but where was a whole other story.

She had to wonder what Emma was up to at this exact moment, or her mom. Did they even know she was missing? Maybe no time had passed since she was in the past, and they were in the future… which meant they hadn't been born yet, which really hurt her head to think about.

Andrea shook it off. She wasn't about to think about it too hard. It was magic. That was all she needed to know.

Any parts of her exposed skin puckered as the temperature of the air slowly dropped as the last rays of sunlight disappeared.

"You'll want to spend the night in the cave."

Elvira walked up beside her. Her gnarled wood staff was in one hand with Jepriz sitting on the top.

Jepriz speared Andrea with a beady eye, and her eyes narrowed on the bird. She felt like there was some sort of intelligence in the raven. More than a normal raven. Like a human intelligence.

"Thanks for not tossing me out." Andrea smiled over at the other woman. "I wouldn't survive a single night on my own."

"You'll be safe here. Animals and people are scared of me. I'm considered almost evil, but they need my magic, so they visit me."

Andrea eyed the other woman. She was tattooed pretty heavily, but there was nothing that screamed evil to her. Elvira's green eyes danced with an easy light, and there was always a bit of a smile curling her lips, as though she was sure of what life held and had no worries.

"You don't seem evil to me."

"Thank you." Elvira ducked her head as a slight blush decorated her cheeks in the dark. "Now, let's head in before any snow falls."

"Snow?" Andrea turned her eyes up to the sky above them. It was a bit cloudy, but snow?

"A few flakes will fall, but it won't stick to the ground." Elvira turned and strode back into the cave.

Hopping off the boulder, Andrea was quick to follow after Elvira. She didn't want to be outside the cave when dark finished blanketing the land. No need to tempt fate when the predators come out to play.

After a dinner of dried meat and silence, Elvira gave her a couple of furs to sleep on. Andrea unrolled the furs with a flick of her wrist and picked a spot that was clear of grass baskets and animal pouches. Then she laid down, wrapped the second fur around her, and closed her eyes.

She wasn't sure if she would wake up back in her hotel bed, or find herself still in the ice age… and a small part of her hoped she never saw the inside of that hotel ever again. Nothing was more exciting than this. Not that she wanted to stay around forever. At some point, she had to return home, back to her world and time.

Every time she thought about going home, Rokki's dashing face would appear in her mind. She'd barely known the man, the werewolf, and just the thought of him had some jitters fluttering through her… though that could be the anger she felt towards him after he trapped her in the ice age.

Andrea tossed and turned as echoes of animal noises from outside penetrated the cave, and her inner primitive side shivered in fear.

After what felt like a few minutes of sleeping, Andrea cracked her eyelids as chanting filled her ears. Peeking over at Elvira, she found the seer chanting, her lips barely moving. Her hands were raised above her head, and some sort of black substance was scrubbed all over her face, neck, and chest. Elvira grabbed a bowl… made of an animal skull and drank the contents, and when the seer opened her eyes, they were glazed over, appearing almost white. It was like she was in a trance.

Another shiver raced down Andrea's spine. Magic was definitely real in this world.

As Elvira's voice rose in volume, so did the

flames of the fire in front of her.

Andrea squeezed her eyes shut and waited for sleep to pull her back into a peaceful oblivion. There was only so much her mind could take in for one day.

"Andrea." A warm hand lightly shook her shoulder.

Eyes cracking opening, she raised a hand to her eyes to scrape away the sleep that covered her eyelids. "What?" She croaked. The previous night had been restless, and her mind had to work double-time to figure where and when and what had happened the past few days.

"I have come back for you." Rokki's deep voice wrapped her in a warm embrace.

"Rokki? You came back?" Andrea couldn't stop the smile from spreading over her lips as she blinked away the sleep and saw his handsome face in her line of sight.

"I will always come for you, my Andrea." His voice was a possessive growl that sent her stomach trembling as a million butterflies fluttered around inside her.

His Andrea.

His.

Wasn't it just last night that Elvira had told her that wolves mated for life? At some point, she might have to broach the subject with Rokki, but she didn't want to do it with an audience.

"How was your village doing?" She asked as she remembered his reason for leaving last night. Other than being frustrated with her calling him nasty names that he probably didn't understand. Her tone, however. That had been crystal clear.

A smile spread across Rokki's dangerously sexy lips, seeming pleased that she had bothered to inquire about his people. "They are well. Our meat hut is stocked, and everyone is happy."

"Are you taking me there?"

Rokki grew silent as his golden eyes moved over her. "Not yet."

"Why not?" Andrea's eyes narrowed at the cautious tone of his voice.

"I want to make sure you will be accepted. You will be the first human to join our pack, and I am an… alpha. They may test you."

"Test?" She wasn't keen on that idea. The image of claws and teeth entered her mind, and she cringed inwardly.

Rokki stood and faced Elvira, who watched them from the other side of the cave. The fire had died down, and there were now just hot embers burning brightly in the fire pit. "Can I leave her with you longer?"

"No." Elvira shook her head. Her pitch-black locks bouncing around her shoulders like they were alive. "I like your female, wolf, but this is my cave, and I will have it back now."

Rokki glanced back at Andrea as she slowly stood and stretched out her limps. It looked like he was trying to figure out what to do with her.

"I will find a place for her to stay then." He motioned for Andrea to come with him, "Come, we need to be moving."

As he walked back towards the entrance, Andrea faced Elvira, "Thank you for everything."

"Of course." Elvira inclined her head. "I will send Jepriz to you when your bracelet is finished."

"Thank you." Then Andrea rushed down the tunnel of the cave to catch up to Rokki and his ling strides. There was a bit of a bounce to her step as she felt hope soar through her. With Elvira's help, Andrea might actually have a chance at going home!

"Where are we headed?" Andrea asked as she sidled up beside Rokki.

"I'm not sure yet."

Rokki wished Elvira would let his mate stay longer with her. He knew Andrea would be safe with the witch, but now he would have to find another place to stash his mate until he could introduce her to his pack.

As they walked down the hill and away from the seer's cave, he ran through all the spots that might be safe for her in his mind. There was one spot he knew of that might have some relative safety.

There was a small hunting hut out in the woods. It was a place where his pack would stay when going out for a long hunt, and he couldn't see his clan mates using it any time soon. They were currently hunting the east side of their territory, and Andrea would be on the west side. Unless something changed, she would be safe.

"How was your night with the seer?" Rokki's eyes slid over to Andrea, who was doing her best to keep up with his longer strides. Slowing down slightly, he allowed her an easier pace. The hut wasn't too far from here, and he'd already pushed her yesterday, so there was no need to rush them to the hut.

"Interesting." Andrea supplied. "Elvira did a... spell, I guess," she shrugged, "last night. It kept me awake for a bit, but overall it was good."

"She performed a spell on you?" Rokki stopped, turned, gripped her upper arms, and looked into her green eyes as he searched for anything... off. "Are you well?"

What he was really asking was if he needed to march back to the seer and threaten her. If the seer had performed a spell on his mate without his permission...

"No, not on me." Andrea shook off his grip as she shook her head vehemently. "She just casted a spell in general, or maybe she was seeing into the future. It was crazy to watch, but it had nothing to do with me."

Rokki searched his mate's eyes for a second longer before smiling with relief. "As long as she didn't try to cast a spell on you."

"I don't think she's that kind of witch. She seems very nice."

Rokki continued their walk since he was satisfied with Andrea's answer, but he wasn't going to argue with Andrea about the seer being a slightly evil witch. Elvira had cursed a few people in her life, and it had not turned out well for them. The woman wasn't entirely evil, but she dealt with people who disrespected her with swift justice.

"Does it hurt to shift?"

He rotated his head to see Andrea focused on the ground below their feet since the terrain was littered with rocks that threatened to trip anyone who didn't pay attention to where they walked. Her question was sudden and without warning, but he was willing to switch topics and felt a bit pleased she wanted to know more about him.

"The first shift can be painful and alarming, but after years of shifting, it doesn't bother me anymore," Rokki said as he thought back to his very first shift when he'd been introduced to his alpha dire wolf. That night had been one of excitement and hope for the future, and it had been the night he began to search for his mate.

"Are you in control of the wolf?"

"You are curious about my dire wolf?"

"Yes." Andrea looked over at him, and he could see her green eyes swirled with curiosity. "I haven't known a werewolf before. I never thought I would know a werewolf. I've heard plenty of stories, but I'm not sure if any of them are true."

Rokki felt a bit of surprise that she hadn't come in contact with a werewolf before him. Although the human clans preferred to stay away from weres, they still knew about weres and dealt with them on occasion.

"Your clan must be very isolated."

"Ummm," Andrea seemed to consider his words, "I suppose we can say that since I have no idea how to explain my people to you."

"Any more questions?" Rokki asked as he skirted past a decent sized boulder.

"Yes, I have more. Do you know how werewolves came to be?"

Rokki nodded his head as he closed his eyes briefly, "I do, but you should allow our pack shaman to tell you the story. He is the best storyteller in the clan, and I will only ruin it." He had fond memories of the old shaman telling the stories of how werewolves became when he was a child sitting in front of a fire with other children. He would hate to take that feeling from Andrea.

"I look forward to hearing it."

They fell back into a comfortable silence as they traveled through meadows, over hills, and through thick forests. Andrea insisted on stopping several times to examine things like plants and animals. He found himself enjoying her sense of curiosity rather than being frustrated by the sudden stops.

The day grew colder, and a few flakes of snow drifted through the air as they traveled.

It wasn't winter, but the snow always lingered over the land. Threatening them. It wouldn't let them forget about its presence. Soon, winter would be on them once again, driving away prey and making their lives a little more difficult.

Rokki cast his eyes up to the skies and glared. Like his clan didn't have enough to worry about with the Neanderthal's invading their territory. The gods threw them too many trials, and he wished they would see fit to give his clan some respite from all these troubles.

"If I ask too many questions, let me know," Andrea said as she broke the silence.

"You are curious about me and the land around us. I like it." And it gave him hope. She wasn't running from him in terror. To see fear on her face because she was scared of him, would ruin his day. His beast would never intentionally cause her harm. A mate was something to be treasured and protected.

"Can you change to half beast and half human?" Her green eyes surveyed him openly.

"Like this?" Rokki asked as he held out a hand and let the beast show itself in the form of claws on his hands.

"Wow." Andrea breathed out in amazement as her eyes went wide. "Scary."

Rokki let the claws melt back into his hand, returning it to a normal human hand. "There is nothing to fear. My inner beast would never use his claws against you."

"I'll have to take your word on it."

"Take my word?"

"Trust you."

"Ah," Rokki nodded his head as he finally understood the phrasing of her words. For the most part, he understood her way of speaking, but there were some words she liked to put together that didn't make much sense to him. "You can always trust me," he reassured her.

"Can you shift any more? Like, can you have the body of a man but hairy with the face of a wolf?"

Rokki chuckled heartily as he shook his head. "I can show my canines and claws, but that is all unless I shift fully." He scratched his chin, noticing for the first time, that his beard was growing back. During the warmer months, he did his best to keep it shaved down with a sharp stone blade. "I don't know of any dire wolves who can shift like you described."

"Are there other kinds of shifters?"

Rokki nodded his head. "There are all kinds. Sabertooths, rabbits, horses, dire wolves, even more dangerous people like demons, but those don't shift."

"Demons?" Andrea halted, and Rokki had to pause and turn to see her eyes widen. "With horns and what not?"

"And wings." He told her honestly. There were all sorts of creatures running around their land. "Demons and bloodsuckers tend to stay to the south where it is warmer, but we get them up here every now and then."

"Bloodsuckers? You mean vampires?"

Rokki shrugged. "I don't know this word… vamp… ires?"

"They have fangs," Andrea pointed to her teeth, "that come down and penetrate the neck, or I guess any part of the body, and drink the blood of another living creature."

"Ah," he nodded his head, "those would be bloodsuckers."

"Wow. I couldn't imagine seeing all these things in my life."

"I have not seen a bloodsucker, but I have heard many stories about them. You would never want to encounter one, Andrea, and if you do, you should immediately find me."

He'd never realized how dangerous this land was until he met Andrea. Anything and everything could take her from him, and it had his heart thundering around in his chest. Grabbing her hand, he rushed them towards their destination. The sooner he had her stashed somewhere safe, the better, in his opinion.

The rest of their journey went about the same. There were moments of silence as his mate gathered her thoughts, and then she would ask more questions like she'd never lived in this world before. Which caused him to wonder where exactly she'd gone when she'd disappeared on him.

Rokki supposed he might never know, and that was fine with him, as long as he knew where she would be from now on. He had until the seer fixed Andrea's bracelet to convince his mate that life without him would be less enjoyable.

Chapter 12

Andrea's feet ached more than she wished for them to ache. She wouldn't be entirely surprised if she developed some blisters on the bottoms of her feet from all this walking. It was nice of Rokki to have given her some moccasins, but they didn't provide a lot of arch support and weren't thick enough to prevent rocks from poking her.

As they rounded a small hill covered in tall grass, she spotted a small hut built between two massive trees. It wasn't large. A simple hut made of tanned animal skin, sinew, and animal bones.

"This will be a safe area for you while I figure out how to introduce you to my pack." Rokki pressed a warm hand to the small of her back as he propelled her towards the hut.

Her archeologist side came out, and she didn't need the push of encouragement. Striding over to the hut, her aching feet completely forgotten, she ran a hand over the animal skin sides of the hut and over a mammoth bone that helped to support the entrance of the hut. It appeared that whoever had built the hut used deer skin as the sides of the hut, and a small hole was cut in at the top.

"May I go inside?" Andrea asked as she glanced over her shoulder at Rokki.

"Go in." Rokki pulled a skin flap aside and waved for her to go in.

Eagerly, Andrea walked inside, having to duck slightly to get in through the low entrance. It was a small hut, smaller than some huts she'd seen reconstructions of in her time at museums. It wasn't someone's home. Just a place to stay for a short time. There was a fire pit in the center, but no coals or flames. As she looked around, Rokki walked inside, crowding the small space with his large frame.

"I will get a fire started for you. Just feed it while I'm gone."

"How long will you be gone?" She asked as she unfolded some furs that had been stacked inside the hut and laid them out on the ground.

"I'm not sure. My pack is having trouble with Neanderthals invading our territory, so I might have to help my pack, but I will be back as soon as I can." Rokki crouched beside the pit and began to stack sticks and kindling. Then, with a skill, she was sure she lacked, got the fire started within a few minutes. Flames licked to life as they greedily ate at the wood. "There are some packs of dried meat over here." Rokki pointed to some pouches in the corner. "You may eat as much as you like."

Andrea twisted her hands in front of her as her eyes darted to the entrance of the hut. She wasn't keen on the idea of staying here alone. Especially for an unknown amount of time. She may not know Rokki that well, but she knew she was safe with him. He'd proven that several times already.

With a couple of strides, Rokki stepped up in front of her and grabbed her hands in his large warm ones. "You will be fine here." His golden eyes met hers, and she could see he was doing his best to will away any of her fears. "I would never let anything happen to you." He promised as he leaned in and placed a hot kiss against her lips.

Eager for the connection, Andrea met his kisses with her own eagerness. Now that she was in the ice age, he was her only friend and companion. He was the only person who made her feel safe in such an unpredictable world.

Rokki's hands gently roamed over her sides, and even through her thick animal pelt clothing, his body heat warmed her to the core.

If he was determined to leave her here at the hut, then she was going to draw out every single moment before he left.

Breaking away from her addicting lips and honey-sweet taste, Rokki's lips left hers, and he ran the fingertips of a hand down her brow and over the side of her face. She was beautiful. Her face was round and full, and her lips were bruised by his deep kisses.

"You pull me in." He said on a heated whisper. His mate was a sweet addiction that he wanted for the rest of his life. "Don't disappear on me again."

"I'll do my best," Andrea promised.

It wasn't the answer he'd been hoping for, but he would take it for now... but later, his dire wolf would want a better, more reassuring answer.

"I want you to kiss me again, Rokki," Andrea said, her pink lips parted, and her green eyes had gone pine tree dark with her lust.

"I should get back to my clan." Rokki's hand

continued to stroke the side of her face as his feet remained in place despite his words.

"I think your clan can wait a little bit longer." Andrea purred as she placed her hands on his shirt and dug in her nails, bunching up the material. "I need you right now."

His inner dire wolf whimpered as it pleaded him to stay in the hut and fulfill their mate's desire. She was right. If his clan had noticed his disappearance, then a few more minutes wouldn't matter.

Rokki's nostrils flared as he scented the air inside the hut. He could smell the heat drifting off her as her body warmed to his touches. There was no way he could leave now, not until he pleased her, or she would haunt him while he was gone… or maybe that was simply an excuse for him to stay.

As instinct pushed rational thoughts out of his mind. All he could focus on was the mate before him. A mate who was filling the hut with the scent of her desire. His nostrils flared as he sucked in her flowery fragrance with greedy intakes.

His head bent, and his lips slanted over hers. She moaned into his mouth, and he growled lightly with his desire. Tugging on her long auburn locks, he forced her head back so he could get better access to her mouth. A sigh of pleasure parted her lips, and he took full advantage of it. Slipping his tongue into her mouth, he teased her, tasted her. The tips of his fingers elongated a bit as claws began to form on his hands.

Breaking the kiss with an audible pop, Andrea drew back as her hands frantically clawed at the front of his shirt. "We need to get this off of you." She panted breathlessly. "I want to touch you without it in the way."

Chuckling, Rokki grabbed each of her dainty wrists in his large lands and drew them away from his chest. "Let me."

Andrea sucked in a harsh breath as she gasped.

Rokki froze, knowing she'd just spotted his clawed hands. Would she push him away? Waiting for her reaction, he didn't even dare breathe. He'd shown them to her once without her drawing away, but now that those hands were on her? He feared her reaction.

"Oh... wow." Andrea didn't pull back, and she seemed unable to look away from his hands. Holding them up closer to her face, she studied his clawed fingers.

"Do I scare you?" Rokki finally asked when he couldn't bear her silence anymore.

Shaking her head no, Andrea raised her eyes and met him square on. "You don't scare me... confuse me, maybe, but if you meant me any harm, you would have done something long ago, like when we first met." She sent him a cautious smile.

"I would never harm you." Rokki yanked her into his arms so he could wrap them around her and crush her against his chest. Even the thought of harming her caused his stomach to roll in distaste. "And I will never let anything harm you if I can do anything about it." He would throw himself in front of a charging woolly rhinoceros if it would save her life.

"Make love to me," Andrea whispered up at him, her green orbs fixing him with a lust clouded gaze.

There was no need for her to ask him twice. Breaking away from her, Rokki shed his clothing with quick and eager jerks of his hands, and when he straightened, he found his mate's gaze pinned on his jutting cock. A smug smile adorned his lips as he stood there proudly, allowing her to take her fill. Let her admire him.

Tensing the muscle in his member, it bobbed in front of Andrea, and the tip of her pink tongue darted out to wet her mouth.

Before he could even move, Andrea dropped to her knees and sent him a naughty smile before focusing her attention back on his cock. Her fingers wrapped around his hard length, and she slowly pumped his member with eager and sure strokes.

"Yes," Rokki murmured as he let his eyes slide closed and enjoyed the feel of his mate pleasuring him. Something hot and wet surrounded his cock, and when his eyes shot open to glance down, he found Andrea's tight mouth wrapped firmly around his cock. Her head bobbed on his cock, sending her auburn locks bouncing around. "Andrea." He growled as pressure built within him. He enjoyed this view of her as she pleasured his cock with her mouth. The gods had granted him a lusty mate, and it pleased him.

When she pulled her head back, he thought she was going to stop sucking on him with her need, but she didn't. Instead, she left the head of his cock in her mouth and swirled her tongue around the peak. "Mmmmm." She purred, which sent vibrations coursing through him.

"Gods, Andrea. You will make me come in your mouth." His dire wolf howled inside him with pleasure but at the same time growled at Rokki to push her onto all fours and take her from behind. Rokki yanked in the beast. His mate wanted to pleasure him, and he wanted to let her do it her way.

"Mmmhmmm." She agreed as she hungrily sucked on his cock, her cheeks caving in with the pressure. One of her hands worked the base of his cock while her other hand fondled his balls.

Eyes shutting once more, Rokki did his best not to let his legs buckle, but his mate possessed a talented tongue. She knew exactly which spots to tease and draw on.

"You want me to come in your mouth?" He asked as stars, and bright lights flashed across his closed eyelids.

"Mmmhmmm." Andrea purred again, never letting up as she greedily sucked on his cock, even increasing the pleasure with her mouth and hand.

Digging his fingers deep into her soft hair, he helped to guide her head over his cock. Within minutes, the pressure grew, and right before he came, he uttered, "Take me." He growled with almost a howl to his words.

Andrea wasn't usually a person who liked the taste of cum, but she couldn't resist the urge to suck him off. She could taste the saltiness as pre-cum leaked out of the slit in his cock, but she refused to release her hold.

Pumping her hand and sucking as much of his cock as she could, she felt him tense under her hands, and she took him deeper until the head of his cock bumped the back of her throat. And then he came. Hot seed coursed down her throat as she continued to work him, and he let out a pleasured groaned as he slumped a bit.

Once he was done, Andrea leaned back, releasing his cock and balls.

"You enjoyed?" Rokki asked as he opened his eyes and watched her lick her lips.

"I did, and you?"

"Very much," He nodded his head enthusiastically. His black hair swung around his shoulders. "Remove your clothing." He commanded as his golden eyes heated with desire. "It is my turn to pleasure you."

Standing up with a flutter of her heart, she slowly peeled off her shirt. She wasn't sure why, but her hands shook a bit. She wasn't used to a man as chiseled and good looking as Rokki showing interest in her. It wasn't like she was ugly, at least, she didn't think so, but back in her world, she was fairly certain he would have been out of her league.

She was his mate, which meant he had no option but to like her, and that thought had her desire tamping down. Mentally, she shook off her doubts. Who cared why he showed her this kind of attention. Who was she to look a gift horse in the mouth?

The shirt hit the dirt floor, and her pants and moccasins soon joined the discarded shirt.

"You are perfect." Rokki's deep voice wrapped around her, sending thrills of excitement racing over her.

Andrea figured she could lose a couple of pounds off her thighs and waist, but who was she to argue with an attractive man, especially when his golden eyes were filled to the brim with desire as he stared at her.

"Lie down," Rokki commanded her.

Andrea obeyed him eagerly. Sitting down on the furs she'd spread earlier, she laid down on the fur that was spread out over the dirt floor of the hut. Rokki stood above her, unmoving as his golden eyes roamed up and down her. As he studied her, she allowed her eyes to roam over him in return. His cock was semi-hard, still jutting out from between his legs, reluctant to go down when the promise of more pleasure was hanging in the air. His taste was still on her lips, and she didn't mind it as much as she used to, maybe because her head was so fuzzy with desire.

"Spread your thighs." He once more commanded her. There was a fire burning bright in his golden eyes as he stared at the hair guarding her feminine center.

Biting the inside of her cheek with her teeth, Andrea inched open her legs, leaving herself exposed as his eyes lazily drifted down to the area between her thighs. A blush crept up her cheeks as she laid there under his scrutiny. Here she was, spread to his view, and she had no idea what he thought! Butterflies zoomed around in her stomach as she waited for his reaction.

A low rumbling growl vibrated through the air of the hut.

Rokki moved faster than her mind could process. When she blinked, she found her werewolf kneeling between her legs. His hair roughened legs brushed her calves and then her thighs as he positioned himself. Leaning over her, one hand braced by her side, he grabbed his cock and brushed the tip over her engorged folds. "So wet for me." He growled with approval.

"Enter me." Andrea panted, her voice gone soft and wanton with the need to come that coursed through her. She didn't need him to tease or play with her. Her body was hot and ready.

"Do you enjoy my cock?" He asked as he teased her, rubbing the tip of his cock against her nub, which was slicked with her own juices.

"Yes." Andrea panted as she bucked her hips in an attempt to get his cock inside her. To feel it fill her.

"Eager mate?" Rokki chuckled as he pulled back, slightly taking his cock away from her aching center.

Andrea glanced up at him to see a teasing smile on his lips, his canines popped below his upper lip, reminding her he was half beast and half human. "I need to feel you fill me." She pleaded with him.

As their eyes connected, he leaned forward and sank into her heat, using his hips to push his cock into her. His other hand came to land on the fur on her other side. Raising her legs, she wrapped them around his waist, connecting her ankles, locking him in place so he could choose to pull away from her again.

Andrea was so tight and went. Her body welcomed Rokki's hard length wrapping his hard spear in her soft flesh, coaxing, tempting him to slide deeper. His dire wolf growled in approval at their mate's arousal.

Her sweet scent filled the hut, driving his animalistic side insane with the flowery pull.

His dire wolf growled to be let loose, to show itself, but Rokki pushed it back. It already had its opportunity to show itself to their mate. With a grumble, the beast retreated to the back of Rokki's mind, still there but not showing itself physically.

Unconsciously, Andrea's hips moved, and Rokki's mind went blank. His hips thrust forward as their bodies slapped together with the force of their joining.

Andrea moaned her pleasure as her own hips bucked and thrust along with him, driving his shaft as deep as it could go. The sounds of her rapture rang in the chilly air as a slight glisten to her skin shone in the dancing firelight.

"Oh, yes, Rokki!" She panted under him.

Satisfaction rolled through him that he could bring her such pleasure.

Bending his head, Rokki captured her lips with his. Her moans poured into his mouth as her hands desperately clung to his back, to his shoulder, and to his arms. Giving a hearty growl, Rokki slid his tongue against the seam of her lips until she opened them to him. Then he slid his tongue into her mouth, penetrating her with more than just his member.

Lowering his body, he let his chest rub up against her pert nipples, causing a sensational friction between them as their bodies thrust against each other.

"Mmmmm." Andrea groaned.

Pulling his head back, Rokki glanced down at his mate, who's green eyes were swirling pools of desire. All sanity had been replaced with lust as her mind and body strived for one thing. Climax.

Pulling back even further, but never ceasing in his fast and deep thrusts, Rokki smiled as he watched her breasts bounce with their enthusiasm. The smooth orbs tempted him as her rosy nipples bounced back and forth.

His mate was perfection. The gods must have taken pleasure in creating her. Just as much as he was enjoying it right now.

"Oh, yes." Andrea rocked her hips with his movements driving his cock as deep as it could go within her. Her eyes slid shut as his cock hit every sensitive part inside her. She was so riled up. Could barely think.

"Open your eyes." Rokki's deep voice sliced through the air. "I love seeing the desire flickering within."

Andrea's eyes popped open at his throaty command.

"I want to see your eyes as you take my shaft and come around me." His arms bulged as he thrust into her, jostling her breasts with the ferocity of his thrusts and sending a whole new sensation rolling through her. "I want to feel you come around me. Coax my seed deep inside you, mate." The last of his words faded into a growl.

Andrea's hands ran up and down his arms, feeling the tense muscles under her touch as he drove into her with wild thrusts. Her legs shook as pleasure seared through her, and she felt as though she was on a fluffy cloud. Just floating. Ready to drop into the vibrant abyss of ecstasy.

"Oh, yes." She began to pant as her entrance began to clamp down around his cock. "Oh, yes!" She shook as pleasure vibrated through her. Her pussy clamped down around his length.

Rokki's head drooped before he let out a guttural growl, and hot cum seared through her. His claws dug into the tender flesh of her hips as he pumped into her. His back ramrod straight as his golden eyes refused to leave hers. She saw her passion reflected back at her in his swirling golden eyes.

When Rokki finally slumped against her, pumping lightly with his hips, he said, "You tempt me to stay between your legs for the rest of my life."

Andrea chuckled as she rolled out from under him. Before she could get too far, one of his arms wrapped around her waist and drew her back into his chest as he laid down on the fur behind her.

"Don't you have to get back to your village?" Andrea hoped she had tired him out enough to spend the night with her. She wanted to delay his leaving her alone for as long as she could. There were so many dangers out there in the unpredictable ice age. She hated to sound like a weakling, but she needed him.

"They can wait a little longer," Rokki growled in her ear before rubbing the side of his face against her cheek in a lovely animalistic gesture. "I need time to hold you."

Andrea's heart fluttered wildly in her chest as she processed his words. When she saw her discarded clothing, she spotted the chunks of her wooden bracelet.

Gritting her teeth, she refused to give voice to her still hot anger about his actions. She was still pissed about it, but she didn't want angry words forcing him from the hut any sooner than he had to leave.

Andrea wasn't even sure she knew how to voice her anger. On one hand, she was peeved he'd so heartlessly shattered her ticket back home, but at the same time, she also was enjoying her time here. The two emotions warred inside her. She wanted to hate him for his actions, but after their intimate moment, she wasn't about to randomly lash out and ruin this. She was so warm and safe in his arms.

"How do you know I'll be safe here while you're gone?" Andrea wasn't too certain about being alone. She shifted on her feet nervously. The urge to scream that she couldn't be alone overwhelmed her, but she kept the trembling voice quiet.

After a few minutes of after sex cuddling, Rokki had unwrapped himself from around her and told her of his intention to leave.

"The area is well marked by my pack, and before I leave, I will change into my dire wolf form and make sure no animal feels comfortable sniffing around this hut," Rokki assured her.

Her hands shook a bit at the thought of being alone, but she plastered a smile on her lips. If he thought she'd be fine, then she would trust him... for now. He seemed to think she would be safer here rather than meeting his pack, and he knew this world better than she did.

"May I watch you shift?" Andrea asked, curious to see his wolf form now that she knew it wouldn't suddenly rip out her throat.

A pleased smile decorated his face, softening his scarred face. Andrea's eyes drifted over the scars, but in truth, she barely noticed them now.

"My dire wolf would love for you to watch. He also enjoys scratches behind his ears." Rokki advised.

"Are you joking?" Andrea asked as she cocked her head to the side, and her eyes narrowed. He said it with such a straight face that she had no idea if he jested or spoke the truth.

"Not at all." He laughed as he ducked under the entrance and exited the hut.

Jumping into action, Andrea followed after him. When she exited the hut, she found his golden eyes staring straight at her. Then he shifted. It only took a single blink of her eyes, and then a massive black dire wolf stood on four paws in front of her. It was a large beast, and a part of her mind told her not to trust the beast, but another reasoned that it was Rokki, and he would never harm her.

The wolf opened its massive mouth and sent her a wolfy grin as a large pink tongue rolled out the side of its mouth.

"Hi." Andrea waved a hand at the wolf.

The dire wolf gave her a growly woof, before slowly walking over to her. She held absolutely still as she waited to see what it would do. The dire wolf nuzzled its snout into her hand until her palm rested on its head.

"So soft." She murmured as her hand ran over his furry head. Remembering Rokki's words, she scratched a couple of fingers behind one of his ears, and the dire wolf chuffed in pleasure. She'd never owned a pet, and she wouldn't call Rokki's dire wolf a pet, but she did enjoy running her hands through his fur. It felt therapeutic and relaxed her.

Rokki's dire wolf form bumped his head into her waist.

"What do you want?"

He thumped a front paw on the ground.

"Kneel?"

He thumped his paw again.

"Okay." Andrea sank to her knees, and he licked her cheek as the large wolf's head nuzzled her. "Rokki!" She laughed.

He pressed his wet black nose against her face before backing away. With a small nod from his massive head, he bounded into the forest, disappearing in a matter of seconds.

Heaving a sigh, Andrea glanced around. Alone again. In the ice age. Damn. And knowing her luck, this wouldn't end well.

Chapter 13

Andrea had sat down in the entrance of the hut after Rokki left, but as night had fallen around her and the noises of nocturnal animals grew louder, she'd headed inside the hut. She placed any baskets and extra furs against the hut entrance to keep the flap closed and hopefully, any curious animals out.

Throwing a couple of sticks onto the fire, she watched the flames chew through the wood, putting off waves of welcome heat. She wrapped a fur firmly around her shoulders, finding comfort in being wrapped up.

She'd really hoped Rokki would be back by now, but it seemed he might not be coming for her tonight. Right now, she'd rather face a village full of werewolves than be alone in the forest. When Rokki came back, she was going to voice her preference.

Distant howls echoed through the trees outside of her hut, but it was far away from her. Reaching out, she snatched a pouch and pulled a piece of dried meat out. Absently, she munched on the meat as something skittered through the fallen leaves near the hut.

Jumping out of her skin, Andrea bolted to her feet, the fur slipping from around her shoulders and landing on the ground. Whatever it had been was small, but her nerves were frayed, and every little sound outside the hut sounded ten times louder, causing her to think something huge was outside.

Grabbing a few more logs of wood, she

placed them over the fire, and when they lit, warmth washed through the hut. Rokki should have left her with a weapon. She wouldn't have known how to use it, but at least she would have a chance at defending herself from the animals out there.

Andrea settled back down on the floor of the hut, and she wrapped the fur firmly around her shoulders once more. Once she was done with her dinner of dried meat, and she was done missing greasy, cheesy, deep-dish pizza, she huddled closer to the fire.

If she remained in the ice age, she would have to get used to simplistic meals. There'd be no more ramen, pizza, ice cream, or sushi for her. Was Rokki yummier than all those delicious foods?

She pursed her lips. She wasn't quite sure yet.

It wasn't long until Andrea dozed off next to the warmth of the dancing orange flames. The crackle of the flames relaxed her and caused her eyelids to slide shut with tiredness.

A growl nearby had her shooting back to her feet. Turning in a tight circle, Andrea tried to pinpoint where the noise had come from. Stopping, she waited as her eyes darted around the inside of the hut.

It wasn't long until the growl vibrated through the air around her once more.

That was it.

She was done.

Dashing to the opposite side of the hut, she lifted a side flap, glanced around, saw the immediate area was clear and scrambled out under the animal hide side. With frantic wiggles of her body, she popped loose from the tent, dashed to her feet, and bolted into the dark forest.

Andrea wasn't sure what had been sniffing around the hut, and she wasn't about to wait to find out. With her mind blank, except for fear, she let the moonlight guide her through the trees. She brushed back bushes as she let nothing stand in her way.

As she ran through the forest, she could barely see everything around her as she plunged forward. When she placed a foot on the ground and launched into another step, her other foot came down, and nothing met it… no ground, just air.

With a squeak, she tumbled to the ground and rolled in a heap down a hill. Dirt flew around her, and every time she sucked in a breath, the loose dirt would fill her nose. Raising her arms, she wrapped them like a shield around her head as she tumbled uncontrollably.

Something in the dark caught on her foot, and her momentum yanked it. Letting out an ear-piercing scream, she continued to tumble through the dirt until she landed on solid ground once more.

Groaning, Andrea braced her hands on the ground and heaved herself into a sitting position. Her head hurt, her legs and arms hurt from where they'd bumped into debris, and most of all, her ankle drove her nuts.

Gripping her ankle in both of her hands, she wished with all her might that it would feel better. As she rocked back and forth on her butt, she squeezed her eyes shut and wished it better.

After a couple of seconds, the slight ache emanating from her ankle slowly dissipated. Cracking her eyes open, Andrea glanced down at her foot.

Moonlight streamed through the leaves above her, allowing her the ability to examine her ankle.

The pain was gone, and she could easily move her foot without a single wince.

Andrea cautiously stood, and when her foot gave her zero issues, she put her full weight on the ankle and smiled. It was fine. The fall had probably caused her to think her injuries were worse than they were.

Something in the forest cracked, sending Andrea back into a frantic sprint. The moment she ran across a tree with low enough branches, she frantically began climbing the tree. She had no idea if staying the night in a tree would be better than the ground, but she was already halfway up.

Once she got to a large enough branch, she wrapped herself around it and settled down for the night. When the sun lighted the area in the morning, she would try to find her way back to the hut. Otherwise, she would have to hope Rokki could find her when he found her missing.

Rokki faced Ruub and Naab, his foot tapping the ground impatiently as he waited for them to tell him why he was needed in the village. He was eager to get back to Andrea and to make sure he kept his promise of keeping her safe.

"There are signs Neanderthals have once again encroached on our territory last night," Ruub commented with a growl of frustration and a clenched fist. "The hunting party saw signs of old campfires and smelled them in the area."

Frowning, Rokki was only able to think about getting back to his mate. He didn't want to stay away from her any longer than he had to lest she run into any predators. Raising a hand to his face, he used a couple of fingers to massage his temple. "Why didn't the hunting party go after them?"

Silence greeted him before Naab explained, "They had prey to bring back. They didn't want the meat to spoil before they got it to the smoking hut."

Rokki shook his head. He wasn't thinking clearly, of course, they'd have prey to bring back if they'd been hunting. It was rare for their hunters not to catch something. It was one of the reasons their clan was able to grow so large.

"And Darc is still out with his own hunting party. Your uncle may run the pack until one of you finds your witch mate," Naab said, referring to the pack's prophecy, "but he wants the both of you to be involved in the pack before one of you take over the pack. While Darc is gone, it falls to you to find the Neanderthal threat."

As much as Rokki wanted to use his newly found mate as an excuse, he couldn't risk telling anyone about her. Not yet. Not until he was sure what she was, otherwise, there would be many questions, and he didn't need to introduce a human mate to his pack until she was fully prepared.

"Do we have any idea as to how big this Neanderthal group is?" Rokki asked, wondering how many men he would need to get rid of the threat. If a group of Neanderthals ran into one of their lone females, it might not matter if she could turn into a wolf, they might still be able to capture or kill her, like they'd done in the past.

"No bigger than four men from what the hunting party reported smelling."

"Where were they?"

"By the gnarled tree to the west," Ruub said as he raised a hand to point a finger to the other side of the village. His animal skin shirt pulled back with his movement exposing his wrist.

"Then you two will come with me." Rokki headed towards the edge of the village, knowing the two men would follow him. If he ever became alpha of this pack, he knew Ruub would end up being his beta. The three of them were closer than he was to his own brother… and if he was forced to leave one day because his mate was human, he knew they would follow him.

Stripping off his clothing, Rokki placed it beside a moss-covered rock before letting the shift overcome him. His beast eagerly jumped at the chance to show itself to the world. It was never one for being cooped up inside for too long.

Once freed, it stretched its long front black legs out in front of it, as its back arched up and its tail raised up behind it for a full-body stretch. Then his dire wolf shook out its large frame in a full-body shudder.

When his beast finished enjoying its freedom, he turned to glance back at Ruub and Naab. Both men were now in their wolf forms. Each wolf was impressive in size, and his wolf felt the need to snap its teeth and snarl at them to assert its dominance.

Their wolves immediately crouched low to the ground, and their ears flicked backward as they showed their submissiveness. Satisfied, Rokki's dire wolf turned and trotted off into the forest.

A massive amount of scents smacked him in the face. Off to his left, he knew there was a rabbit cowering in fear at the sight of three dire wolves, he could smell the decaying leaves under his paws, and his wolf could smell Ruub and Naab trailing after him.

His dire wolf wanted to seek out their mate, but he kept the beast's nose firmly pointed towards the west. They were going to find Neanderthals and drive them away, and if it came to it, they would kill them.

It didn't take Rokki, Ruub, and Naab long to sniff out the Neanderthal intruders. Their scent was distinctive – like a mix of feces and sweat. It always curled Rokki's upper lip when he caught a whiff. Loping through the thinly wooded forest, he slowed down as the scent grew stronger.

Then his triangular ears zipped forward on his dire wolf's head as guttural words could be heard in the distance. Slowing down, he trotted up behind a thickly leafed bush and peered around the edge.

Rokki spotted four Neanderthals in front of them. They had a couple of dead rabbits slung over their shoulders and were walking away, further into their pack's territory.

He ran out from behind the bush, not making a single noise as his soft padded feet muffled any noise from the leaves littering the ground. His men followed behind him, and with a flick of his tail, he signaled his men to pick a Neanderthal to attack.

Picking up speed, Rokki bunched his back legs and launched at the Neanderthal back that was closest to him. The man had no idea what hit him when Rokki landed on the Neanderthal's back, throwing him to the ground.

Rokki stretched his wolf's jaw wide and wrapped his sharp teeth around the man's neck. Then he latched on, and a flood of hot blood coated his tongue as the Neanderthal stayed down with a gurgling cry.

A couple more cries went up as Naab and Ruub attacked the Neanderthals.

When Rokki's golden dire wolf eyes glanced around, he saw the fourth Neanderthal swinging a wooden club aimed right for Rokki's head. Leaping back, he let go of the first Neanderthal's neck since the man wasn't alive, and if he was, he wouldn't be for much longer and was no threat now.

The second Neanderthal ran towards him with a guttural war cry as he pulled the club back and tried again to smack Rokki in the side of the face. Jumping to the side, Rokki dodged the attacked and ran behind the man, but the Neanderthal was faster on his feet and spun, nailing Rokki in a back thigh.

Letting out a yelp of pain, Rokki gritted his sharp teeth as he pushed through the pain. Thankfully, it was nothing serious and hadn't been hard enough to break his bones, but he had to be careful. These Neanderthals had strength, and one good swing of that club would shatter any of Rokki's bones.

The Neanderthal charged with another guttural war cry, but Naab's grey form flew out of nowhere and laid the Neanderthal flat on his side with a grunt of surprise.

Leaping back into action, Rokki joined Naab in the attack. When he noticed the Neanderthal had lifted a stone dagger, Rokki launched himself at the man's arm. He sank his teeth into the Neanderthal's forearm, causing the man to scream and drop the dagger. If Rokki hadn't noticed, Naab would have been stabbed in the side, and the wound would have most likely been fatal.

Rokki's heart thundered under his ribcage as the thought of losing a clan mate to a Neanderthal had his blood boiling. Thrashing his head, Rokki heard the disturbing sound of the Neanderthal's arm breaking.

The Neanderthal's scream was cut short as Naab chomped down on the man's throat, ending his life swiftly with a sudden gush of blood.

Releasing his hold on the Neanderthal's arm, Rokki glanced over to where Ruub stood over the body of his Neanderthal. They'd taken out the Neanderthal threat without anyone being harmed. Rokki would call it a good day.

Ruub shifted into his human form, blood-streaked across his chest, but from here, Rokki's nose could tell it was just the Neanderthal's, and Ruub wasn't injured.

"No need to let these rabbits go to waste." Ruub quickly ran around the area and gathered up the rabbits that had been discarded during the fight. "I'll walk back to the village with these." Ruub hefted the rabbits into the air with a wide grin.

Rokki rolled his eyes and huffed through his black snout as he presented his side to Ruub.

"We could do that." Ruub tossed the strung-up rabbits across Rokki's back. Then Ruub shifted back into his dire wolf form.

Now they could head back to the village at a brisker pace, and Rokki would take the first chance to get back to his mate. His skin prickled with uneasiness being away from her for this long.

Andrea had been wandering around the forest, meadows, and rivers for most of the next day while she attempted to find her way back to the hut Rokki had stashed her at, but it seemed she was more lost than she'd thought. Her wild dash through the forest last night had been that, a wild dash, and she hadn't paid any attention to possible landmarks.

Every tree and rock she passed looked the same as the last. With a huff, she folded her arms in front of her chest and leaned back against a tree trunk as she studied the area around her. In good news, she hadn't come across any predators.

Glancing down at her foot, Andrea thanked her lucky stars that her foot didn't appear to be twisted. Last night, it had caused her so much searing pain, and now it was perfectly fine. It was a pleasant twist of her fate.

Huffing and puffing, Andrea pushed off the tree trunk and began walking once more. She was so lost, it probably didn't matter if she got more lost. Rokki was a werewolf after all, as impossible as it seemed, and it meant his sense of smell should be impeccable. If he got back to the hut and found her missing, she was sure he would search the entire planet for her. There was something shining in those golden eyes... almost love, but not quite. Maybe obsession would be the better word for the look in those mesmerizing eyes. She was his obsession.

Birds scattered from a nearby bush in a frantic flapping of wings sensing her... or so she thought until a growl pierced the air behind her.

Startling her, Andrea spun to spy a pack of dire wolves melting out of thin air. Her breath left her chest in a whoosh as she stared at the large predators. The lead dire wolf's golden eyes looked so familiar, but the anger churning in its eyes and the growl on its curled mouth told her it wasn't Rokki. Then her eyes drifted up to its ears, and she noticed there was a bite missing out of one of the tips. It wasn't her dire wolf then.

When the black dire wolf darted forward, Andrea let out a squeak and flew through the forest in the opposite direction. She wasn't sure she could out run a dire wolf, but she had to do something. Thank goodness her ankle wasn't causing her any more pain! Her legs ate up the ground under her as her heart thundered in desperation.

Suddenly, something smacked into her back, throwing her off balance and slamming her back into the trunk of a tree. The rough bark caught on the fur of her shirt and jerked her to a sudden stop.

A man stood in front of her, gripping her shirt in both of his fists as he forced her between him and the tree trunk. "Who are you?" He growled down at her. Shoulder length black hair framed his face. It was just like Rokki's, but this wasn't Rokki.

Did he have an evil twin?

Andrea gulped. It was another werewolf, and his enlarged canines glinted in the sunlight filtering through the branches high above their heads. "I'm... I'm... Andrea." She trembled in his grasp.

The man was butt ass naked and pressed so close to her, but unlike Rokki, he didn't excite her, just made her fear for her life.

His golden eyes were hard, like the rocks that dotted the landscape around them. "What clan do you come from, and why are you in our territory?" The man growled down at her.

Her head barely came up to his shoulders, and his massive frame had her trembling with fear for her life.

"I...I have no clan."

The man's head dipped down, and he sucked in a deep breath next to her face. "You smell like… Rokki?" The man's head shot back up as his golden eyes bored into her very soul. "Why do you smell like my brother?" The man's eyes narrowed on her.

"You- you're brother?" Hope flooded through Andrea. No wonder the eyes looked so familiar, and his wolf wasn't too different from Rokki's either.

"You're his mate?" The brother's eyes raked over her and turned a shade darker as a curl of disgust had his lips pulling back to expose his canines some more. "Are you a witch?"

"What?! No!" Andrea shook her head. "I'm not a witch, and I'm not his mate."

Rokki's brother growled between his clenched teeth, "You're lying to me."

"No, I'm not!" Andrea glared at the man who had her pressed up against the rough bark of a tree. "I know I am not a witch, and Rokki never said I was his mate." All of that was true.

"Darc, if she is Rokki's mate, we need to bring her back to the village." Another naked man strode up to them and placed a hand on Darc's shoulder.

"I'm not his mate!" Andrea yelled at the men in front of her. It was like they couldn't hear the words coming out of her mouth.

"There's no other reason why my brother's scent would be all over a human." The man's golden eyes narrowed on her once more. "If you weren't his mate, he would never have approached you…" Darc inhaled another hefty breath. "He never would have bedded you and given his seed to a woman who wasn't his mate.

Andrea's cheeks heated as she realized he'd smelled sex on her, and worse than that, this was Rokki's brother. She was mortified.

Not noticing her discomfort, or ignoring it, Darc said, "Deny it all you want, human, but you are his mate. The only question left is, are you a witch?"

"No." Andrea shook her head.

"We will see." Darc pushed away from her, releasing her shirt at the same time. "Walk, human." He held out a hand, guiding her in a particular direction.

As much as Andrea wanted to run in the opposite direction, she knew it wouldn't do her any good. "Okay." She shoved herself off the tree and strode into the forest with her back straight. She'd read enough books about wolves and werewolves. She needed to assert herself and not appear too submissive but also not challenge this Darc, who claimed to be Rokki's brother.

"Not too fast." Dark strode up beside her and clamped a controlling hand around her upper arm as he guided their small group through the woods.

Glancing around, Andrea found there were about four dire wolves trailing behind and around them as they walked, and there were two men, Darc and the other man who'd tried to calm their leader in their human form.

Darc and the other man were butt naked, and it was hard for her not to take side glances at their bodies. Each man was well-toned probably because they lived in the rough and tough ice age, a time where there were no cars, and they had to walk or run everywhere. They also had to chop wood and hunt animals. Animals that she could only imagine since she'd only begun to see them since she'd arrived here. Seeing the bones and reconstructions in museums had nothing on seeing these animals first hand.

"You're Rokki's brother, then?" Andrea asked, trying to start up some sort of conversation.

Darc's dark gold eyes flickered over to her, and she shivered at their intensity and hostility. He didn't know her, and he'd clearly decided he didn't like her, and she had no idea why.

Okay then. No conversation.

No wonder Rokki hadn't wanted to introduce her to his pack. If they were all as welcoming as Darc, she wasn't sure she wanted to set foot in their village.

If she read the movement of the sun correctly, it only took them a couple of hours walking in the forest to break free of the trees and into a small meadow where an ice age village resided.

Andrea's eyes widened as her archeologist dream suddenly came to life.

Chapter 14

There were some large animal skin huts and some smaller ones that dotted the meadow in front of them. Each hut had brown animal hides covering the sides, but Andrea could see where sinew had been used to tie each fur to some massive bones, which she assumed were mammoth bones.

Butterflies danced around inside her stomach as she realized she would be the first archeologist to see a real-life working ice age village! If she ever got back to her time, she'd have to share this with Emma... no... she couldn't do that, and that put a slight downer on her mood. There still wasn't anyone she could tell about this without sounding like a crazy person living in a delusional fantasy.

Andrea shook her head. It didn't matter what other people thought of her, as long as she knew what the truth was.

Turning her gaze once more to the village, she watched grey smoke trickled out of each hut and swirl up into the sky to slowly disperse and disappear into the air.

Glancing back down, she caught sight of several people walking around within the village of huts. A couple of them were women, and they only wore small skirts with the tops of their bodies exposed.

It wasn't shocking for Andrea to see them striding around with bared breasts. She'd studied enough history to know most historians believed clothing hadn't been such a huge deal back in the ice age then it would be in the twenty-first century.

Darc shoved her arm when her feet stalled, "Keep moving, human."

Andrea quickly got her feet moving once more. She couldn't keep her eyes from wandering over everything, though. Her wide eyes took in everything, and even though she had a menacing werewolf at her side, she couldn't help the smile on her lips.

As they passed by a hut, she reached out her free hand and brushed her fingertips over the coarse fur that acted like walls for the hut. To think how far humans had gone. From living under the stars to fur huts to wood shacks to stone houses, and now people had a choice of materials to build their homes with.

"What do you have?" A female voice asked.

Darc paused, and since his hand was firmly clamped on her arm, Andrea had no choice but to stop with him.

A woman strode around them, her eyes scanning over Andrea before shifting to Darc. "Why do you have a human?" Then the woman's eyes widened. "Is this... is this your mate?"

"What?!" Darc's head flew backward like an invisible hand had punched him in the nose. "She isn't my mate." He spat the words like the idea of being mated to Andrea was the most distasteful thing in the world.

Andrea glared at him as her lips thinned into a straight line. Well, he wasn't a catch either. With this grumpy attitude of his, he would need luck keeping any mate around.

"Oh." The woman glanced between them. "Then why do you have a human?"

"I could smell Rokki on her, so I brought her back to ask him the very same question." Darc's hand tightened slightly on her upper arm, and Andrea winced at the pressure.

The woman's eyes lit up. "Rokki found his mate?"

"I'm not Rokki's mate," Andrea grumbled under her breath. She was done being ignored, and she refused to give up on telling everyone her thoughts. Someone was bound to listen to her at some point.

"What did she say?" The woman leaned in, her brown eyes piercing into Andrea, and Andrea got the feeling the woman found her fascinating.

"She says she isn't Rokki's mate, but that wouldn't make sense… Rokki's scent is all over her… and he's bedded her."

Andrea's face flamed as Darc blurted those last words. Great. Soon everyone in the entire village would know Rokki, and she had slept together.

"Does she have his bite?" The woman took a couple of steps closer as her eyes fell to Andrea's neck and shoulder area. "I don't see one." Her eyes squinted as she examined Andrea's skin.

"She doesn't have a bite."

"Hmmm." The woman's lips pursed as she looked undecided on this mate discussion. "I will take her." The woman's hand snapped out and clasped Andrea's other arm.

"This doesn't concern you, Zuri," Darc growled low in his throat, a fire sparking in his golden depths as he tugged Andrea closer.

Zuri tugged Andrea back to her. "If she is Rokki's mate, then she belongs with the women of the clan." Zuri's brown eyes flashed with her own inner fire.

Darc's upper lip pulled back as he snarled at her.

A shiver of fear speared through Andrea, but Zuri didn't back down.

"Don't challenge me, brother, unless you're willing to use those canines on me." Zuri threatened him.

Andrea had to give this other woman credit for having a steel backbone against Darc. His dire wolf was massive, and Zuri was basically challenging him to morph and attack.

"If you see Rokki first, let him know I have more questions about this human woman." His grip released Andrea's arm before he strode further into the village.

"You will have to excuse his gruffness with you." Zuri apologized for her brother.

Andrea turned to face the woman. "He seems tense."

Zuri rolled her eyes. "Sometimes, I wish the gods hadn't given me brothers. They're a handful, and their beasts don't help. Alpha males are the worst kind of wolf."

Andrea chuckled as the tenseness in her shoulders eased off of her. "I don't have any siblings, but I could imagine having brothers." And werewolf brothers at that, which brought her to another thought. "You are also a… werewolf?"

"Yes. Everyone in this clan can shift into a dire wolf." Zuri waved a hand to encompass the entire village.

Another shaft of fear speared through her. Everyone in this clan could shift into a dangerous beast, except for her. Andrea just had this one form.

"There's no need to fear any of us. Although I would give Darc some distance." Zuri commented as she tugged on Andrea's arm and slowly guided them through the village.

"I'll do my best not to fear anyone, but you will have to give me time. A human among a clan of werewolves can be a bit… overwhelming." Andrea could still barely believe her eyes. If werewolves were a part of her world, they must have hidden themselves well from the modern world.

"Once Rokki comes back from his hunt, he will let us know what is between the two of you because I too can smell his scent all over you." Zuri's eyes drifted over to Andrea as she raised her nose and gave an audible sniff of the air. "Are you a witch?"

"No, I am not a witch." Andrea sighed. She felt like a robot on repeat around these people.

"Are you sure you aren't a witch? Perhaps your parents were witches? An aunt?"

Andrea shook her head. "I am sure. I think I would know if I was a witch, or if anyone in my family had magical powers."

Zuri turned back to the direction in which they were walking, but Andrea didn't miss the disappointment that shown in her dark brown eyes.

"Does this have to do with the prophecy Rokki told me earlier?" Andrea asked, needing to know more about the importance of this prophecy.

Zuri nodded her head as they wandered over to a large firepit in the middle of the village. Andrea could imagine large bonfires burning in there, but right now, there were only small trickles of smoke drifting off blackened logs as red-hot coals burned under them.

"When Darc and Rokki were born, a shaman read their futures in a ceremony. One brother would find a human mate and leave the clan, and one brother would find a witch as a mate and lead the clan. If this prophecy is followed, the clan won't have to worry about disease or shortages of food." Zuri took a seat and patted a spot next to her on the ground. "But if we do not honor what the gods have shown us, then our clan will be doomed to fall to disease and hunger."

Folding her legs under her bottom, Andrea plopped down beside the other woman. "So... Darc is worried about me being a witch because he could be cast out while Rokki remains."

"Yes." Zuri nodded her head. "Both brothers are alpha dire wolves, and only one can lead the clan."

"What happens to the brother who is cast out? Does he… start a new clan or what?" It seemed kind of cruel of them to cast out one of their own. To force a brother out only because some shaman long ago had foreseen two possible outcomes. Then again, she had to remember when and where she was right now. These people might be shifters, but they still had gods they feared and respected, like gods of fertility, gods of the weather, and gods of the seasons.

"We fear what the gods might do to us if we don't obey them." Zuri turned her eyes to the dead fire. "What the cast-out brother does is up to him. The prophecy says nothing about what will become of him."

Andrea stopped herself from saying anything else without first thinking. She was now living in a world where people firmly believed in gods and prophecies, and she didn't want to be on the wrong side of a prophecy.

To the people of the ice age, everything around them was scary and could take their life as suddenly as it had been given to them at birth. Anything they didn't understand was easily explained by gods being happy or unhappy with them.

Andrea stared at the glowing coals. She felt bad for Rokki. She was just a simple human, which meant he was going to get kicked out of this clan. Thanks to her. No wonder he hadn't wanted to introduce her to the clan. This prophecy meant they'd be forced out into the wilderness with just each other, and she didn't even know how to live here without help. It must seem like a daunting challenge to him.

She hated feeling useless, but if they were cast out, she would do her best to learn how to live in this world as quickly as she could. Rokki had kept her safe when he didn't have to. He'd made a choice. She was a smart woman. If she applied herself, she had no doubt she could learn tasks to ease his load.

"I suppose that explains why Rokki kept me hidden in the forest rather than bringing me here."

Zuri sent her a smile. "Don't be insulted." She placed a hand on Andrea's. "I am sure my brother only wanted to make sure it was the right time. With the prophecy, he wasn't sure how we might react, but we've had years to prepare for this time." Zuri's smile turned sad as her brown eyes drifted back to the firepit. "I wish it wasn't so soon, but I am also glad one of my brothers have found their mate. Mates are to be treasured."

"How long until he and I are kicked out of the clan?" Andrea asked as she fiddled with a rock bead that's been sewed onto her shirt.

"That will be decided by the current leader of the clan, our uncle."

Now Andrea just had to hope the uncle liked Rokki enough to postpone their being kicked out of the clan… at least long enough for her bracelet to be repaired. Then she could get back to her time… and leave Rokki to get kicked out of the clan by himself.

Andrea cringed as she watched a coal flicker back to life and glitter with an inner fire like it was angry with the direction of her thoughts.

"Where is Rokki?" Andrea asked as her eyes skimmed over the huts that surrounded them and found several curious glances cast her way as clanmates went about their daily activities. It was a bustling medium-sized village. Their clan was doing very well, and she could see why they would like to continue to please the gods. It would be a shame to have all this taken away.

"He is on a hunt for the Neanderthals who have trespassed on our pack territory. We aren't sure why, but they've been wandering across our territory, taking our prey and causing our men to worry about our women hunting alone."

"Oh, yes. Sorry. I forgot you said he was on a hunt." Like the night when Andrea had first seen Rokki in his dire wolf form. He had been hunting the Neanderthals, and in the process, had saved her.

"Is this her?" Another woman skipped into view, a long brunette braid bouncing behind her. Then the young woman squatted in front of Andrea as she peered into Andrea's face. "Are you Rokki's mate?"

"I'm not his mate." Andrea tried once more, hoping someone in this clan of dire wolves would listen to her.

The young woman took an audible whiff of the air. "You smell of Rokki," she cocked her head to the side, causing her braid to shift to the other shoulder, "almost more than your own scent... and if I'm smelling it correctly, the two of you have been under the furs together."

"Wait, what?" Andrea scooted back on her butt. "Can everyone in this village smell this on me?"

The new woman shrugged. "There's nothing wrong about joining Rokki under the furs." She winked over at Zuri. "There are many women who wish to be joined with him."

"He's a womanizer?"

Silence greeted her question. Zuri shrugged, and the other woman squinted her eyes at Andrea as she tried to process the words. Ah, womanizer probably wasn't in their vocabulary.

"He's with a lot of women?" Andrea clarified.

"No," the new woman shook her head vigorously. "If he does lay with women, then he does it outside the clan."

"So, you haven't slept with him?" Andrea wasn't sure how this woman knew Rokki, and she couldn't stop herself from asking.

"Her?" Zuri laughed. "He's our brother."

"Oh." Andrea looked between the two of them. The new woman didn't look horribly similar to Rokki or Darc, but she knew genetics could be funny sometimes with how it blended from two parents. And now that she looked at Zuri, she didn't look similar to either of her brothers as well.

"I'm Ode, and the youngest of the siblings." Ode smiled over at Andrea. "It's good to have another sister in our family, even if you aren't a dire wolf."

Andrea smiled at Ode. Other than Darc, the rest of Rokki's pack seemed to be welcoming.

"She won't be here with us for long," Zuri said. "She isn't the witch."

"Oh." The smile slipped off Ode's face. "I love Darc, but I was hoping that out of both of them, Rokki would be staying with us."

Andrea wished she could change who she was for them, but she couldn't. She just hoped Rokki wouldn't hold it against her. She was forcing him out of his own clan because of who she was.

Her heart went out to him. She'd just left her mother in another time. Her heart ached about that, but at the same time, it wasn't like she saw her mother all that much. An archeologist went where the jobs were, and usually, that wasn't anywhere near one's home town. To be frank, it was usually in another country. Which made her think she was only experiencing a fraction of what Ode and Zuri felt.

Andrea let the women draw her into conversation, as she hoped for Rokki's return. Hopefully, he wouldn't be much longer. He was her one rock in this world of large beasts and unknowns.

Chapter 15

Rokki loped into the village in his dire wolf form, his men hot on his heels. He shrugged off the strung-up rabbits they'd stripped off the Neanderthals and shifted back into his human form. Fur melted into tanned skin, and his paws elongated into long, strong fingers, and his snout receded back into his face.

"Take the rabbits over to Vor's hut. He will spread them out among our pack mates or have them smoked into strips of meat." Rokki instructed his men. "I have other things to do." And then he strode away knowing his men would follow his instructions.

It was time to head back to his hut, get some supplies for Andrea, and get back to her. He could only imagine how she felt being left alone in the middle of a forest, but he'd needed to take care of the Neanderthals.

As he strode among the huts and said his hellos to fellow pack members, a sweet scent drifted on the air, right past his nose. His inner dire wolf demanded that he take a better whiff, and something about it was familiar, comforting.

Pausing mid-step, Rokki sucked in another whiff of the appealing scent. Then his eyes popped wide as it finally hit him how he knew the scent.

"Andrea?" He whispered as he suddenly spun in a tight circle, all the while sniffing the air. Once he pinpointed the direction from where it came, he marched off, determined to find the source of his mate's scent.

As he neared the village fire, he spotted her. Andrea sat on the ground, speaking with his two sisters. There was a light smile on her lips, so she was happy, and he couldn't smell any fear or worry coming off of her. She seemed comfortable.

How had Andrea found her way here? He supposed he might never know unless he walked over and asked her.

Rokki relaxed a bit as he took in the scene in front of him with pleasure. He hadn't been sure his sisters would welcome his mate, but it was nice to see they were accepting her.

"Where have you been?" A voice growled from behind him.

Spinning, Rokki growled in kind, a snarl curling one side of his lips. "What do you want, Darc?"

"Where have you been?" Darc repeated as he folded his arms in front of his chest, showing off his impressive display of muscles. Unfortunately for him, Rokki was just as muscled.

"I dealt with some Neanderthals in our territory."

"I found your mate wandering around lost in the woods."

"She wasn't in the hunting hut?"

Darc shook his head. "You should take better care of your mate, little brother. Leaving her alone in the forest was foolish. Anything could have ended her life before your return."

"I can handle my own mate," Rokki growled low in his throat. His beast wasn't pleased someone else would criticize decisions they made about their mate.

Darc's golden eyes narrowed on him. "You should have brought her back to the clan when you found her."

"I was going to once I was sure she would be safe here." Rokki didn't bother to hide his meaning from Darc as he stared his brother in the eyes.

"Is she a witch?" Darc throat bobbed as he swallowed, waiting impatiently for Rokki's answer.

Now it was Rokki's time to narrow his eyes on his brother. "She says she is a human, and so far, I haven't seen her use any magic." He wasn't about to tell Darc that he'd seen her disappear and appear. There was still the possibility she was a witch and didn't know. Maybe she hadn't grown up in a coven and had no idea she had magic coursing through her blood. It was possible, and it gave him hope.

Darc's eyes left him and glanced over Rokki's shoulder to where Andrea sat with their sisters. "If she ends up being human, our uncle will cast you out. I'll make sure of it."

Rokki chuckled, and Darc's eyes landed back on him as he scowled. "That could be years, brother. If you want me kicked out, you must find your witch mate to prove mine is just a human. The prophecy doesn't say when I have to be kicked out, it just says the brother with a human mate must leave when the other finds their witch mate."

And Rokki prayed to the gods it ended up being Darc who left the clan, not him. He loved Darc, despite the tension between them, but it hadn't always been like this. When they were children, and their dire wolves had yet to show themselves, they'd been inseparable. Only when their dire wolves showed themselves to be alpha wolves had the problems developed.

Darc grumbled something under his breath before striding away. Rokki would take it as a win, and his inner dire wolf wanted to howl in triumph, but he refrained. There was no need to provoke Darc and wind up rolling around on the ground in a fight... in front of the whole clan.

"Rokki?"

Spinning on a foot, he found his sisters and Andrea staring over at him.

"What did Darc want from you?" Zuri asked as he walked over to them.

"Nothing." Rokki wasn't about to bring up the issue right now. Right now, he wanted to enjoy having his mate in his pack village. "I heard Darc found you wandering around the forest. Why didn't you stay in the hunting hut?" He folded his arms over his bare chest as he raised a dark eyebrow and stared down at Andrea, who still sat on the ground.

"Well," Andrea blushed as she looked to the other women, "something came sniffing around the hut... I got scared and ran."

"What was it?" Ode asked breathlessly. "A sabertooth? A male mammoth on a rampage?"

"I have no idea." Andrea's face colored even more.

"Probably a squirrel." Rokki shook his head. His loose black hair swirled around his shoulders. "Everything sounds larger in the dark."

Andrea glared up at him. Her green eyes churned with anger at his words. "It was large. It wasn't a squirrel." She blustered.

Zuri glared up at him. "You weren't there, Rokki. And she is human. You can't blame her for running when something comes sniffing around. You are the one at fault. You should have brought her to the pack the moment you found her."

"I needed to make sure she was safe here."

Zuri scoffed. "You and Darc may fight, but there is no way he would harm your mate. He would never do such a thing. It goes against everything we believe. Mates are life. If he harmed her, he would be shunned by the pack, whether or not his mate turns out to be a witch."

Rokki shook his head. "None of us know what he would and still could do to Andrea if she were a witch." He didn't like the idea, but if his brother ever threatened Andrea's life, he would rip his brother's throat out.

"If she were a witch, she would be able to hold her own against Darc." Zuri reasoned. "And if she is a human, she has nothing to fear from Darc, because you'll be banished with her soon enough."

"Enough of this pointless discussion. She is here, and so far, everything is fine." Rokki wasn't going to keep discussing this with them. "Come," he held out his hand to Andrea, "we need to bring you to the shaman."

"Why?" Andrea questioned, but she still slipped her hand into his and allowed him to pull her up. Trust glistened brightly in her eyes.

"We need to get you tattooed."

"Wait, what?" Andrea asked as she suddenly tried to yank back her hand. Rokki's grip was like iron, tough, unyielding.

"You are a part of this pack now, and we must get you the tattoos. If you ever encounter another dire wolf pack, they will know where you belong." Rokki explained as though this should be a simple matter.

"I've never had a tattoo, and I'm not sure I want one." Andrea didn't believe twenty-first century tattoo parlors were sanitary, and she knew for sure that ice age tattooing couldn't be any more sanitary.

"You are now a part of the pack, and you must fit in, Andrea." Rokki motioned to his chest and upper arms, at the reddish tattoos that decorated his skin.

The tattoos added a dangerous and sexy appeal to his already well-muscled body. The swirls and dots were mesmerizing, and someday she would ask him what every single one of them meant to him and his people.

"Do I have to get a tattoo?" Andrea turned her eyes up to him and batted her lashes. She wasn't sure it would work, but she was willing to give it a try.

"I will delay it, but you will need to get your tattoo someday." Rokki squeezed her hand. "Are you afraid of the pain?"

She nodded her head.

"I won't lie. It is uncomfortable, but the shaman has plenty of herbs for you to smoke or drink that will dull it." Rokki promised.

Andrea sighed in relief that she had been able to postpone the tattoos. When he tugged on her hand, she allowed him to pull her along as he guided her to a large hut on the edge of the village.

"Does it even matter?" Andrea asked. "I'm human, and if we are kicked out of the pack, then why would it matter that I get the tattoo?"

"If we are forced to leave, it is important you get the tattoo." Rokki pulled up and brought her into his bare chest, and she felt his cock between their bodies. "If something happens to me out there, and you wander across a clan gathering or another dire wolf pack, they will bring you back to this pack, and this pack will protect you." Every word held such conviction that she found herself believing him.

Andrea could only nod her head. "I understand." If she did end up here for the rest of her life, she would be sure to get the tattoo.

"Now, come, I am sure the shaman is expecting us. He knows all." Rokki sent her a wink, before turning and ducking under the fur covering the entrance of the hut. Andrea followed after him.

The moment she stepped inside the hut, a thick layer of smoke smacked her in the face, and she coughed a bit. Raising a hand to her mouth and nose, she sucked in tentative breathes until her lungs grew used to all the smoke hanging in the air.

"I have been waiting for both of you." A strong male voice said somewhere inside the hut, but the smoke hid the speaker from her view.

"Sit here," Rokki commanded her.

Andrea could barely see the ground under her, but she sank to the ground and found a folded up fur below her. She sank onto it and enjoyed its softness under her butt.

Rokki sat beside her on another folded up fur.

As if on cue, the smoke dissipated, and Andrea finally got her first look at the man sitting across from them, a fire pit between them. Small orange flames licked across the wood logs and cackled in delight.

"I am the pack shaman."

"I am Andrea."

"I know who you are." A smile spread across the shaman's face, causing wrinkles to spread across his age softened skin. "Rokki has waited a long time for his mate."

There was that mate thing again, but she wasn't about to argue it with anyone else. It went in one ear and out the other. She had finally given up. Instead, she said, "I don't want a tattoo."

The old man chuckled. "When you are ready, you will get one. For now, Rokki believes it is important that I tell you the story of our people and how we came to be a part of this land."

Andrea's shoulders slumped in relief. She'd at least gotten the tattoo topic pushed off, and maybe if she was lucky, everyone would forget about it with time. When she knew she was stuck here forever or they were banished, then she would get the tattoo.

"You are the best storyteller in the pack." Rokki nodded his head.

Andrea glanced over at Rokki, where she saw admiration and respect shining bright in his golden eyes. He looked like an eager child waiting for his favorite bed time story… this mountain of a man who could turn into a menacing dire wolf liked to hear stories from the clan shaman.

A small smile upturned one side of her mouth. It was cute.

"I would love to hear the story of your people," Andrea said as she rotated her head and looked back at the old man sitting across the fire from her. She folded her hands in her lap as she readied herself for the tale.

The shaman picked up a long wooden pipe. One end was slightly raised, and as he pressed his lips to the other end, she saw a flicker of something catching fire inside the pipe. Then the shaman brought the pipe away from his mouth and sent a puff of smoke spiraling out of his nose. The smoke lazily trickled up to join the rest of the smoke inside the large hut. He passed the pipe to Rokki with two hands, and Rokki accepted it with a couple of hands and a slight incline of his head.

Rokki took a puff, tilted his head back, and slowly let the smoke out of his mouth in a stream of grey. Then he presented the wooden pipe to Andrea.

"Oh, no, thanks." She waved her hands in front of her.

Rokki's eyes narrowed on her. "You will not refuse the pipe in the shaman's hut, Andrea."

A small heat crept up her cheeks. She felt like a child being scolded about a rule she had no idea about.

"Here." Andrea held out her hands and accepted the pipe. This would be the very first time she ever smoked something. Images from her high school health class floated through her mind of blackened lungs. Sucking in a deep breath, she raised the tip of the pipe to her mouth and sucked in.

Immediately, she began to sputter and choke as she handed the pipe back to Rokki. A blush stained her cheeks. Clearly, she didn't know how to smoke, because neither of them had choked on the smoke like her.

Andrea blinked as she watched the flames of the fire flicker in front of her. She could swear she saw shapes within the flames. Squinting at the flames, she tried to make sense of what her eyes were attempting to tell her brain.

Then the shaman's strong voice carried through the hut. "A long time ago, there was a witch who fell in love with a man."

Andrea saw the flames play out the scene in front of her. Whatever had been in the pipe had been some good stuff. The flame woman wrapped her arms around the man who was also made of flames. Their feet were on a burning log in the fire pit.

"They had many lovely years together, and their union produced a couple of offspring." The shaman continued the story.

The flame woman and man were joined by a couple of flame children. They looked happy. The man scooped one of the flame children up and swung it around. The child's legs flung wildly in the air.

"Then, one day, the man came home with another wife."

Andrea felt a lump grow in the pit of her stomach. This story was about to take a turn. She'd read enough books and seen enough movies to know that there was also a climax or problem that arose for all the characters.

The flame man walked over with his second wife to where the first flame wife waited with the two children by her side.

"The first wife demanded that he get rid of the second wife, but he refused." The shaman's eyes were glazed over, and he stared at the figures in the fire like he was transfixed. "His second wife was with child, and he refused to turn her out of his hut."

Andrea's heart ached in her chest. It broke for the first wife. Life had been perfect until her husband had thrown a wrench in the plans by bringing home a second woman. But the second wife could also be a victim in this story. Maybe the man hadn't told her about the first wife and children he already had.

One of Rokki's hands wrapped around hers, and he squeezed it lightly.

"The first wife, angered with her man with his betrayal of their love, revealed that she wasn't just a human woman... she was a witch." The shaman's voice went a couple tones dark, giving his voice an ominous sound, "The woman cursed him to be a werewolf, a creature who only had one fated mate, and was bound by faithfulness."

Andrea watched the flame man slowly shift into a wolf.

"But the witch's anger was so strong that her magic went beyond just the man, and she cursed several human clans."

The flames changed to show entire villages turning into werewolves.

"And the werewolves were born." The shaman said. "We do not see it as a curse anymore. We see it as a sure way of finding the one person who the gods made for us."

Andrea looked up when the flames returned to normal long flickering flames of fire. The shaman's wise eyes peered directly at her as if he knew something about her that she didn't know.

She cocked her head to the side. "What happened to the witch and her werewolf?"

The shaman smiled at her. "Neither of the women were his true mate, and his dire wolf refused to stay with either. In the end, he roamed the land alone, searching for his mate and never finding her. That was his curse from the gods for being faithless."

So not a happy ending. Not that she thought the man really deserved a happy ending for putting the women and children through that, but she'd been hoping for more... more justice... more love? Something more.

"And the women?"

The shaman shrugged under the layers of fur he wore. "No one knows what happened to them."

"Did I not say he was the best storyteller in the pack? He knows how to draw in his listeners." Rokki said with a smile.

"Yes, he is." Andrea faced the shaman. "Thank you for sharing your origin story with me."

"Anyone in the pack is welcome to join me in my hut. Now leave me, I am old and require some sleep." The old shaman raised his wrinkled and freckled hands as he waved them away.

Rokki rose, and Andrea followed his lead, and when he walked out of the hut, she quickly left as well. She took her cues from him on how to behave in this foreign world.

"Your people believe a witch cursed you?" She asked the moment they broke free into the fresh air outside. She hadn't realized how much smoke had been in the hut. Her lungs jumped in happiness that they were out.

"She cursed our ancestors, yes, but like the shaman said, we don't think of it as a curse anymore." Rokki spun around and took her hands in his. Then he yanked her into his chest. "Now, we love and listen to our beast sides. It never fails to guide us right, especially where our mates are concerned."

His golden eyes bored into her, and she swallowed harshly. There was so much emotion in his gentle caresses and swirling golden eyes. It was so intense. He thought she was the last woman for him... and she kind of hoped he was right.

Ugh.

But then there was her life back in the twenty-first century. Could she really let go of all those things? Goodbye tv. Goodbye ice cream. Goodbye fast food.

His head descended, and his lips captured hers in a demanding kiss that spoke volumes and pushed all negative thoughts from her mind. He was claiming her with his kiss.

"No," Andrea laid her hands on his chest and pushed. She wasn't saying no to the kiss, the kiss was great, she was saying no to the meaning behind the kiss.

"Don't deny what is between us, Andrea," Rokki whispered the words against her cheek. His breath feather-light against her skin. "You are my mate. The gods created us for each other."

"I can't stay here, Rokki." Andrea saw hurt and confusion flash behind his eyes as he shook his head, as though he wished he could shake her words from his ears.

"I don't understand, Andrea." His eyes closed as he rested his forehead against hers. "Where would you go? Back to your clan?"

Andrea heaved a sigh as she ran a hand through his silky black hair. "I'm not exactly sure how to get back to my clan, but I can't stay here. I'm human, and you're a werewolf. A werewolf!"

"Stranger matches have been deemed by the gods." Rokki pulled back and met her eyes. "A human and a werewolf are not so strange."

She placed a hand on his bare chest. "Because of me, you will lose your clan."

Rokki smirked down at her as she tried in vain to pull away from his chest, but he kept his arms firmly around her. "Andrea. I am an alpha, and my brother is an alpha. One of us will have to leave, even if the prophecy didn't exist. We can't both live in the same clan. Neither of our dire wolves could tolerate the other leading the pack."

"I…" But she had no counter arguments for this or did she?

Rokki shook his head, and his black hair swooshed over his shoulders. "You can't blame yourself, Andrea. Darc and I grew up knowing about the prophecy. One of us would leave the clan, and we have come to accept it."

"Your brother doesn't seem to like the idea of leaving the clan."

"Darc just wants to be alpha, like I do. It's easier to take over a pack that already exists, rather than venturing out and taking another pack or creating a pack."

"Still—"

"Enough!" Rokki barked, and she clamped her mouth shut in surprise. "Come." Rokki tugged on her hand and guided her through the village. She was too stunned by his outburst to complain. He'd never raised his voice at her since they met.

He pulled her into a hut and released her hand the moment they entered.

"Is this your hut?" Andrea asked as she glanced about. There wasn't too much inside. There were some furs on one side of the hut and several weapons on the other with a fire pit in the middle.

"It is." Rokki plopped down and stretched out on his bed of furs. "Do you like it?"

"Bigger than I would have thought." By twenty-first century standards, it was smaller than most studio apartments, but by ice age standards, it was a mansion.

"Come join me," Rokki waved her over, a sly smile on his lips.

Andrea didn't think this was wise. Her mother had always told her that sex led to heightened emotions like love. They couldn't afford to fall in love only to have her return to her time. Then they both would end up with broken hearts.

"I don't think we should."

"We already have." He wiggled his eyebrows at her before his expression went more serious. "Why are you nervous?"

"Nervous?" Andrea shook her head as she laughed a bit. "I'm not nervous. Rokki, you have to face the fact that I will go back to my home someday. I don't belong here."

The smile slipped from his face, and she knew he wasn't pleased with her words.

"Come join me." He repeated with less cheeriness in his tone.

Andrea sighed as she approached the furs. "The seer is fixing my bracelet. When it's done, I will return home." She didn't have a choice. This wasn't her time, and she had no idea what she was doing here. Book knowledge wasn't the same as growing up in the ice age. Mammoths and sabertooths were out of her experience, and werewolves? Definitely out of her realm of knowledge.

"Come lay beside me." Rokki instructed as he scooted over on the furs, leaving her room on the fur.

Andrea's eyes skimmed over his naked form. He hadn't gotten dressed since he'd arrived in the village. Nakedness wasn't a problem back in the ice age. It was kind of freeing. She wasn't sure she was willing to strip down and run around outside the hut, but it was nice to know she didn't actually have to get dressed in the morning if she ever wanted a lazy day.

Rokki's cock was rock hard and jutting out from between his thighs. She raised an eyebrow. She felt like he was always hard when he was around her. Ready to go at a moment's notice.

Then there were those red tattoos strewn across his upper body. Someone had painstakingly put them there, and someday soon, she would ask him what they meant.

"Lay down." There was a growl to the end of each word. He was losing patience with her.

Maybe he had already fallen in love with her. If this mate thing was true, then he thought they were destined, and who was she to tell him he was wrong. It wasn't like she knew what the universe had decided for their lives. Just because she had been born in the twenty-first century didn't mean the ice age couldn't be where she should be.

Her mom was right. Sex led to feelings. Intense feelings. But the pull. Rokki had such a pull over her.

Gradually, Andrea knelt and then laid her head down on the arm he had outstretched.

"How can you deny us?" He asked as he turned his golden eyes on her. Rising up slightly, he stared down at her. "Can you not feel the fire when we touch?" As though to demonstrate, he bent his head and brushed his lips over hers.

Involuntarily, Andrea leaned up and brushed her lips over his when he leaned away from her. It was hard to deny the fire. An attraction burned between them. White hot and searing. It was like her every nerve ending was on fire when he was around her.

"We'll develop feelings." She protested, but the protest was weak and nothing more than words she felt obligated to utter.

"We are mates. Of course, we would have feelings for each other." Rokki rolled over her until his hips were straddling hers. "It's time we take these clothes off of you." His hands reached up to her collar, and he tugged the material off of her, exposing her breasts to his view. "So perfect and plump." He used his hands to push her breasts together and smothered himself between the warm mounds of flesh.

Chuckling Andrea playfully swatted at his shoulders. "Don't suffocate yourself between my breasts."

"It would be a lovely way to die." Rokki teased as he smiled up from between the mountains of her breasts. His hands massaged her flesh, his fingers pinching her hard nipples. He teased them with a brief pinch of pain and then a soothing rub from a pad of his finger. "I should taste them." He bent his head and sucked a peak into his mouth. The tip of his tongue danced around the rock-hard nipple before nipping it with his sharp teeth.

Andrea gasped as a spark of desire shot through her, and her hands clamped down around his biceps. "Mmm."

"Does my mate want me?"

"Who could resist you?" Andrea muttered. The man was built for every woman's dream, and here he was seeing to her every need.

Rokki chuckled in answer, the noise vibrated through her already sensitive nipple, and she sucked in another harsh breath. He released her nipple with a small pop, and then he shuffled back on his knees until he could draw her fur pants down her legs and threw them away from where they laid.

Reaching a hand between her creamy thighs, Rokki knocked them apart with the flick of his wrist. "So perfect for me." He growled, his canines growing slightly and claws forming on the tips of his fingers.

Andrea was sure she was insane because the thought of him being more than just a man... a werewolf... it turned her on! His golden eyes were on fire with lust as he raked his eyes over her body, his eyes landing on the curls of her sex the longest.

Smiling, she wiggled her butt and spread her thighs even wider. "Like what you see?"

A growl of appreciation was all that he was able to utter in response, and her smile grew.

Rokki felt like the luckiest werewolf alive. His mate was well built. She had flesh and curves in all the right places, and she was lusty. Her leaf green eyes were glazed over, and her pupils were dilated with her desire.

In the flickering light of his hut's fire, he could see a shimmer between her thighs. She was wet… for him. Another growl ripped up his throat as he smiled down at her.

"It looks like you need my cock," Rokki whispered harshly as he swiped a finger through her shimmering juices. "Oh, gods." He shuddered at the feel of her desire all over his fingertips.

"Yes." Andrea purred, and then she grabbed his wrist, raised his fingers to her lips, and once their eyes connected, her tongue flicked out from between her pink lips, and she licked her own wetness of his fingers.

"Mate." He growled as his cock jumped in eagerness, and his body trembled with his desire. "You will suck my cock." He stood to his full height, drawing his hand back.

Flipping onto her knees, Andrea wiggled towards him, her breasts jiggling wildly. "Whatever you want." She whispered wantonly. Then she wrapped a hand around his long length and placed a cool kiss against the head of his cock. It jerked eagerly at her attentions.

When Rokki glanced down at her, her green eyes stared up at him, reading his every reaction. Her tongue licked around the tip of his cock, and he groaned as his eyelids slid closed.

"Don't close your eyes," Andrea commanded him. "I want to see your desire."

Rokki's eyes flew open as she used his words right back at him. A smile curved the side of his mouth. "And I want to watch you moving on my shaft."

Her hot mouth felt so good as she slowly drew his length into her, and then she sucked in her cheeks, drawing on his cock like one would suck marrow out of a bone. An instinctual growl rumbled out of his mouth as he dug his hands into her head of thick hair, pushing her closer to his cock. And to his amazement, she didn't protest, she just took more of him until his cock was brushing the back of her throat.

One of her hands fondled his balls, finding a sensitive spot right behind them. The gods had given him a skilled mate. Perfection.

After a few more pumps with her mouth, Andrea drew back with a smile on her lips. "I think it's my turn."

"I think you're right, mate."

With a saucy smile, Andrea flipped around onto her hands and knees and presented him with her smooth and shapely ass. She wiggled the pale orbs at him, firelight flickering off of them.

His wolf took over. Instinct took over. No werewolf could resist a mate when she shook her pert ass at him and asked him to take her. In a second, his massive frame covered her back, the tip of his cock prodding her soaking wet entrance. He could feel her juices dampen the tip of his cock, prepping him to enter her. With his hands on the ground beside hers, he thrust his hips and his cock deep into her center.

Andrea's moan rocked through him, and he was sure anyone in the nearby huts would hear her cries of ecstasy as his cock filled and stretched her wide. He didn't give her body any time though, as he drew his cock out and then thrust it back in. His hips moved in fast deep strokes as he sought to bring them both pleasure.

Her gasps of desire blended with his guttural groans as he thrust deeper into her. Rokki ground his teeth as he held himself back. He wanted this to last forever. His mate was threatening to leave him the moment she could, and he needed to take every moment with her.

Reaching a hand up, he leaned back, and grabbed a fistful of her auburn locks. Yanking her head back, he forced her back to arch, allowing him to hit different spots within her.

Andrea cried out, but her words were too jumbled for him to make out. Otherwise, he was so delirious with passion that he couldn't understand her, but he could hear the pleasure in every note.

Rokki's eyes drifted to the section of her neck that was exposed to his view, the soft spot between her neck and shoulder, and the perfect place for his bite. His canines grew as his dire wolf begged him, whimpered for him, to bite her. To claim her.

Not yet!

No!

He wouldn't claim her. Now wasn't the time for him to place his mark on her.

Andrea threw her weight back as she thrust against him, making the pace fast and hard. He'd caught her body on fire, and now she wanted to be pushed over the edge.

Yanking her head back some more, Rokki forced her onto her knees, her back against his chest, never breaking contact. His shaft pumped into her as he took back control of the speed and rhythm. His hands worked their way to her hips, and he lifted her slightly.

"Oh my god, Rokki." Andrea panted. "Maybe you're a god." She groaned as her head fell forward.

His biceps corded as he lifted her and then plummeted her down on his shaft. She took him. All of him.

"If I am a god," he whispered in her ear with a gentle nip, "then you are my goddess." Hopefully, his goddess of fertility. He wanted a hut full of pups running around. There would never be enough.

"Oh! Oh!" She panted as her body grew close to climax.

Rokki was ready to throw them both over the edge of the cliff.

"Andrea." He uttered as they both shattered and shook around each other.

They flew off the cliff, and when they finally got off their high, he rested his head on her shoulder, his semi-hard shaft inside her. He licked a tongue across her skin and tasted the salt from her sweat.

"Rokki. I… that was amazing."

She still used weird words, but thankfully her words were communicated through her voice. She had enjoyed their moment together.

"Are you going to let me down?" Andrea giggled as she turned her head and met his gaze.

Rokki's shaft twitched inside her, rising back to life. "A werewolf can go more than once with his mate." He whispered seductively in her ear. "Let me shower you in pleasure."

"Yes, please."

It was all he needed to hear.

Chapter 16

Andrea sat before the village fire a few days later and wondered when the seer would send word about her bracelet. She enjoyed her time with Rokki, but people in her time had to be worrying about her. Then again, she wasn't sure how time travel worked. Technically, none of the people she knew had been born yet, so was there anyone to notice her missing?

Raising a hand, Andrea rubbed a couple of fingers against her temple. Time travel hurt her mind. She wasn't quite sure how it worked. She wasn't sure anyone knew how it worked... because it shouldn't be real. She'd read several articles, and she thought it shouldn't be possible. Then again, neither should magic.

Andrea jerked forward as someone's hand worked its way into her hair. Turning her head back, she found Ode sitting behind her on a log.

"I didn't mean to startle you." Ode apologized as she held up her hands. "I was talking when I sat down, did you not hear me?"

"No, sorry." Andrea settled back against the log, Ode's long legs on either side of her.

"I was asking if you would like me to braid your hair. Braided hair is much easier to take care of when there are so many twigs and such."

"Yes, that'd be nice. Thank you." Andrea nearly purred as Ode's fingers sifted through her long auburn hair. Then she felt something like a comb. "What are you using?"

Ode's hand popped in front of Andrea's face. She held a comb made of bone.

"It's pretty."

"Thank you." Ode went back to combing out the knots in Andrea's hair. "I was told it was my mother's."

"Where is she?"

"She and my father have gone to the Eternal Hunting Grounds."

"I'm sorry to hear that." Andrea murmured. She wasn't entirely sure what the Eternal Hunting Grounds were, but she got the idea. It was an afterlife for these people.

"What has you gazing into the fire?" Ode asked as she lightly pulled on the strands of hair in her hands, sending shivers of delight racing over Andrea's skin.

"Thinking of my family and friends."

"Are they far away? Maybe we could send someone to tell them you are now a part of our pack and well cared for here?"

Andrea shook her head lightly, not wanting to pull any of her hair out. "That wouldn't be possible. My... clan is too far away." Like thousands of years in the future. The only way for her to get back was that bracelet, so she doubted anyone here would be able to get a message back to her friends and family.

"Maybe you can find a place here with our pack." Ode continued, ever the optimist.

"Maybe," Andrea said. She wasn't willing to get into a discussion of why she couldn't or shouldn't. Ode wouldn't understand. The only thing a werewolf seemed to think was that mates were meant to spend eternity together.

"In a few days, the pack will run in their dire wolf forms." Ode's hands sectioned off Andrea's hair as she prepared to braid the auburn locks.

"Why?" Andrea asked. She knew nothing about werewolves or why they would do anything that they did, and Ode seemed like the best person in the pack to ask. She was honest and sweet.

Ode began to fold the sections into a braid. "Every full moon, we shift into our dire wolf forms and howl at the moon. It's also a time for wolves to frolic in the woods with their mates."

"You are forced to shift by the moonlight?"

Ode laughed, her voice light and musical. "No, no. No such thing. The moonlight doesn't cause us to shift. It's just a…" Ode searched for the right word, "sacred night where we let our dire wolves free."

"Is there anything I should do to prepare?" Like hide under her covers and wait for it to be over.

"Prepare for what?" A masculine voice asked, sending thrills racing over Andrea's skin.

Looking over to one side, Andrea glanced up and up. She craned her neck back as far as it would go until she met Rokki's golden eyes. "Ode was telling me about what you werewolves do on the full moon."

"All done!" Ode announced before leaping to her feet and walking around Andrea. "Do you like it?"

Andrea reached back behind her head with a hand and felt the length of the braided hair. Once she got to the end, she flung it over her shoulder and glanced down at the rawhide string Ode had used to tie off the braid. "It's lovely." She said truthfully.

"I will have some time with my mate." Rokki

addressed Ode, but his golden eyes never left Andrea.

"Yes, I will see you later, Andrea," Ode promised as she walked off to find something else to do.

Rokki walked behind Andrea and took Ode's seat, his thighs on either side of her. "We should speak of the full moon hunt."

"Hunt?" Andrea asked. Ode hadn't called it a hunt.

One of Rokki's hands came up to caress her jawline with the back of his fingers. "The pack will change into their dire wolf forms, and mated pairs will chase each other down, while others who have yet to find their mates frolic under the moon or hunt prey."

"Sounds interesting," Andrea said.

Rokki's hand retreated, and he tugged lightly at the braid, sending chills of pleasure through her. She loved it when someone played with her hair. It was part of the reason why she loved going to the hairdresser. There was something nice about someone brushing or pulling lightly on the strands of hair.

"As my mate, you would be expected to run into the woods with all of us."

"Me?" Andrea spun around, and Rokki's hands flew open, so he didn't yank on her braid accidentally. "I'm not a werewolf though. I can't shift." Her eyes widened. "Are you going to change me into a werewolf?" All those horror movies of the twenty-first century flew through her mind. All the blood and biting and horrible transforming.

"Change you?" Rokki's dark eyebrows drew together as he shook his head.

"By biting me. Would your bite change me

into a werewolf?"

Rokki burst into laughter as he shook his head, the strands of his black hair brushing over the shoulders of his animal skin shirt. "You must be born a dire wolf. My bite will not change you into a werewolf. I know of nothing that will change someone from human to werewolf." He kicked out his long legs and folded his ankles, trapping her in his embrace.

"That's good to know."

"My bite will claim you, however." He leaned into her ear once she'd faced forward again. "Once I bite your neck, you will be mine, and I will be yours. There will be no others."

A shiver ran through her. His words sounded so primitive, and she loved every possessive one of them. "If I run though." She challenged.

"You'll run. You will find it hard to resist when the howls fill the air." Rokki leaned back, and his hands fell on her shoulders, and he lovingly rubbed them. "You will find my sisters hard to resist. They will make sure you are a part of the run."

Andrea nodded her head in agreement. Zuri and Ode would be difficult to say no to that was for sure. Both of them were eager to introduce her to pack ways. "If I am to join the run through the woods, is there anything else to know?" She couldn't believe she was agreeing to this. She'd be the only human out there… defenseless while werewolves romped in the trees around her.

"There will be some painting on your skin, but other than that, no."

"On my skin?" Andrea's eyes narrowed on the fire burning in front of them. "Wait, will I be naked?"

"We all will be naked."

"No," she waved a finger in the air, "you all will be covered with fur."

"Ashamed to walk around naked, mate?" Rokki rubbed her shoulders some more, deepening his thumb strokes across her shoulder blades. "Trust me, there is no reason to hide your body. The gods blessed you with a wonderful body."

Andrea's cheeks flushed hot with color. "Rokki."

"They did."

Darc chose that moment to walk by. His golden eyes glared over at the pair of them, and Andrea knew he wished her gone. Even though everyone assured him she was a human, he still didn't believe them fully. If she were a witch, she'd know.

"Your brother still doesn't like me."

"Darc doesn't like anyone." Without even looking at Rokki's eyes, she knew he was rolling them.

"I just wish he would believe me when I say I'm not a witch."

"I don't know."

"What don't you know?" Andrea asked as she spun around between his legs and met his eyes.

"You kept disappearing and reappearing. Was that not magic?"

It was Andrea's turn to roll her eyes as she scoffed, "Have you forgotten about the bracelet? It was magic, not me."

Rokki pursed his lips as he thought about her words. "You haven't disappeared since it was taken off your wrist." He conceded.

"Since you broke it, you mean." Andrea scowled at him as her irritation finally reared its head.

"You would have disappeared on me again." Rokki accused. "I couldn't let you go, not when my dire wolf demanded to know you."

"I'm still angry with you." But there was no conviction behind her words. Darn it all. It was hard to stay mad at him. He was always doing something to make her fall in... love? Yeah, love.

"And I hope you can forgive me someday."

Andrea was pissed he'd taken her choice away. Now she was stuck here in the ice age. Was it interesting? Yes, but that didn't take away her fear. A simple cold or childbirth could kill her.

When Rokki reached down and tried to turn her so he could massage her shoulders again, she darted to her feet and strode away. Her anger had been renewed, and she needed some space from Rokki to let herself cool down.

Chapter 17

A few days later, as the sun began to set and cast a wildfire of colors into the sky, Andrea found herself surrounded by all the women in the clan. It was time to prepare for the full moon romp in the woods, and her heart hammered inside her chest. She had no idea what to expect, and with the glares Darc kept throwing her way all day, she was a bit worried about her safety.

"Are you excited?" Ode came up on one side.

"She smells of fear and sweat." Zuri came up on the other side and leaned in while she sniffed the air around Andrea.

"Don't smell me." Andrea scowled as she raised her hands and pushed Zuri away from her.

"I will smell you from here then." Zuri shrugged. "Your fear is filling the air around you."

"This will be my first time running naked under the moon." And Rokki had promised to hunt her down and claim her. Whatever that meant. Her stomach jumped with excitement at the idea of him hunting her down in his dire wolf form.

"There's nothing to fear." Ode threaded one of her arms with Andrea's. "I know we can look scary in our dire wolf forms, but we are still us. No one here will harm you, and nothing in the woods will come close to our village, not with a pack of werewolves hunting."

Great. She hadn't even thought about other predators that could be lurking out there.

"You must have said the wrong words, Ode because I can smell her fear even more clearly. It's so pungent. I could probably smell it from a valley away."

Ugh. How did anyone put up with werewolves?

Andrea might be able to keep her thoughts secret, but they would always be able to smell her emotions.

"Once she takes a puff from the wood pipe, all her fears will disappear." Ode said to Zuri like Andrea wasn't even there.

"A pipe?"

Ode nodded her head, her blue eyes sparkling as she finally glanced at Andrea and acknowledged her presence. "I believe you already saw the shaman. The women's hut has a pipe as well. We place dried leaves in one end, light it, and smoke it. It enhances our ceremonies and allows communication with the gods."

"Ah." Andrea nodded her head.

Hallucinatory drugs would definitely allow some communication with gods. Whether those gods were real or not… well, she wasn't going to say that out loud and debate it with them. These people believed what they believed. It wasn't like they were harming anyone by smoking a pipe and having some fun. If she ended up stuck here, she would have to just get used to the idea of smoking pipes every once in a while, and being a part of the ceremonies.

They walked up to a large hut that Andrea had never entered before. The hut didn't just have brown furs stretched over its frame, there were a few white pelts blended into the other furs. A dire wolf skull was tied above the entrance.

Zuri stepped to the side and, with one hand, opened the skin flap entrance and ushered the both of them inside.

Warm air smacked Andrea in the face as she entered the hut and found a roaring fire inside. Raising a finger to the collar of her fur shirt, she tugged at the material, trying to get some air to circulate around her breasts, which she could feel perspiring.

"You should take off your clothes." Ode said as she ripped her shirt up and over her head and discarded the shirt in a pile nearby. Then she bent over and did the same with her pants. "You will be asked to remove them when the ceremony starts anyway." Ode straightened and sent Andrea a warm smile.

"Okay." Andrea cast a quick glance around her and found the entire hut filled with already naked women, but there were no men inside, so... why not strip down. Shrugging out of her shirt, she cast it aside and then wiggled her butt out of her leather pants. Immediately, her body thanked her as her sweat met the air and cooled her body.

"Come," Zuri instructed as she strode by already in the nude.

When they joined the group of women near the firepit, an older woman walked over to them with a wooden bowl in her hand. She dipped a couple of her fingers into the bowl, and when she raised them, they were coated with some sort of red clay liquid. Then she reached out and drew over Andrea's exposed skin.

Watching in fascination, Andrea followed the lines as the woman drew them. She drew two red clay lines from Andrea's collar bone to her belly button, then she placed a couple of dots above each breast, and then she drew a few lines down Andrea's arms before finally decorating Andrea's face. Once she finished with Andrea, the woman moved on to Zuri.

"Do these mean anything?" Andrea asked as her archeologist side kicked into gear.

"These–" Ode said but was cut off as the women in the hut began to chant loudly.

Another woman lifted a long wooden pipe to her mouth, and with a couple of quick puffs of her cheeks, she had grey smoke streaming out of her nostrils. Then the pipe was passed with a small bag.

"What is in the pouch?" Andrea asked, leaning over to Ode's ear so she could be heard over the chanting women.

"More dried leaves for smoking." Ode said with a smile before joining in on the chanting.

Andrea felt compelled to move her mouth even though she didn't know the words. It was like when she went over to someone's house, and they said grace, she would move her lips, but she didn't know the words. This was the same kind of situation.

Ode took the pipe when it was offered and took a few pulls off the end before handing it over to Andrea. There went her smoke free lungs now that she was living in the ice age. Taking the pipe, she raised it to her lips and managed a couple of pulls on the end without coughing like a maniac. Then she passed it to the woman closest to her.

It only took moments for those dried leaves to take effect on her brain. The colors around her grew brighter, and any apprehension about tonight's hunt lifted off her shoulders. It was like she was living in a hazy carefree life. No worry would bring her down now.

After the pipe had been passed around the hut several more times, the women ceased their chanting, and Andrea's ears rang with the sudden silence.

"We shall now shift and run through the forests in our dire wolf forms." An older woman addressed them all before shifting into a tan furred dire wolf who then bounded out of the hut with an excited yip.

"Come." Ode said before she shifted in front of Andrea. It only took a split second, and when she blinked, she found a pure white dire wolf with blue eyes standing in front of her. The dire wolf licked her hand and flicked its massive head towards the hut entrance.

"You lead." Andrea motioned towards the wolf with a hand.

The white dire wolf who was Ode bounded to the entrance and disappeared on the other side of the animal skin flap.

For one second, Andrea hesitated, but when a dire wolf bumped her with its massive head, she stumbled forward and left the overly warm hut. The night air wrapped around her, spreading goosebumps all over her skin as it cooled the sweat on her body. When she turned her head up to the black sky, she found it littered with shining dots. With barely any light pollution, the sky was striking.

Another dire wolf brushed past her, and Andrea returned her attention to all the female dire wolves around her. They bounded into the forest, and

Andrea didn't hesitate to follow their lead. Kicking her feet into gear, she ran into the forest alongside some of them.

When a familiar white dire wolf trotted beside her, Andrea let out a hoot of laughter as a smile split her lips. It felt good to be running alongside all these other women, and for a fleeting moment, she wished with all her heart she could shift into a wolf to experience this with all of them, but she was just a human.

The deeper they ran into the forest, the more the dire wolves began to separate and pick different paths. And within minutes, Andrea was by herself. Slowing her pace, so she didn't tire herself out too early, Andrea listened carefully to the forest around her. With everything she'd experienced since arriving here, she thought she would be more scared of being alone in the dark forest, but she also knew one scream from her would have a whole pack of female dire wolves running straight for her.

As Andrea slowed to a walk, she took time to enjoy the scent of crushed leaves that wafted up to her nose with every step she took. It felt strange for her to walk around the forest without shoes. She came from a time and place where wearing shoes outside was like second nature, but this felt so natural to her. Pausing, she dug her toes into the grass under her bare feet. The cool shoots wrapped around her toes like a cool hug as they welcomed her into the forest.

A long lonely howl went up, ringing through the trees.

Spinning around, Andrea glanced back towards the village, but all she could see in the moonlight were trees.

When the howl ended, several more dire wolves howled into the dark night, and then more and more until she was sure the howls could be heard from several miles away. The men had shifted, which meant Rokki would soon be chasing her down.

Her heart skipped in excitement. She wasn't going to make it easy on him. Sprinting further into the forest, she couldn't help the smile that spread across her lips once more.

The moment he finished his howl, Rokki set his golden eyes on the forest in front of him. The women in the clan had already finished their ceremony, which meant his mate was out running free in the forest, waiting for him to join her.

His dire wolf growled in excitement of the chase.

His strong back legs bunched before sending him off into a run, spraying the wolves behind him with a shower of dirt. He heard some growls of displeasure but ignored them. This would be the night he claimed Andrea for his and only his. This would be the night he placed his bite on her neck.

When Rokki broke into the trees, a river of scents overwhelmed his sensitive nose. There was one scent his dire wolf wanted to pick out of all the scents floating around. After a few seconds, Rokki began to wonder if Andrea had decided to stay back at the village rather than join in the run. Disappointment soared through him when that thought drifted through his mind.

Running back and forth through the dense trees, he refused to give up. Andrea would have run with the women in the pack. Ode and Zuri would have made sure of it.

He picked up on a couple more scents and then... there it was! Andrea's spicy excited scent wrapped pleasantly around his dire wolf's nose.

His four legs carried him swiftly through the forest and whipped his black fur around his body. He felt so powerful and in tune with the land around him while in this dire wolf form.

With his mind on his mate, Rokki didn't notice the object flying through the air towards him. Before he could dodge, another black dire wolf smacked into him. The force knocked the breath out of his chest, and his head cracked up against the side of an unyielding tree. As his vision faded, he saw a black dire wolf with golden eyes and a chunk out of one ear standing above him.

Damn his brother.

What was Darc doing?

Then Rokki's world went black.

When the crunch of a stick sounded beside her, Andrea paused mid-step and spun around to see golden eyes gleaming at her through the inky darkness. Nighttime was even darker in the ice age, where light pollution wasn't a thing.

"Rokki?" Andrea asked, not sure if this might be another clan mate from the village. She squinted into the darkness, but all she could tell was that it was a massive black dire wolf. "Rokki?" She tried again.

With a growl that ripped through the air and sent a spark of fear racing through her, Andrea dodged to the left when the large animal flew at her. It passed by so close, she could feel the fur brush past her skin. When she landed back on her feet, she spun around to see the black dire wolf snarling at her. Its lips were drawn back, exposing massive canines.

Her heart leaped into her throat as her mind raced through options. None of them seemed good to her, and she definitely couldn't think of a scenario where she won against the clearly pissed off dire wolf.

When its back legs bent, and it looked ready to pounce, Andrea raised her hands like that would save her against the sharp claws and teeth. A blur of motion skidded in front of her, and when she blinked, she found two black dire wolves squaring off in front of her.

It was Rokki and Darc.

Darc, Rokki's brother, had attacked her?! She knew he didn't like her, but would he really attempt to end her life?

"Rokki?" Andrea asked cautiously.

The bushy black tail in front of her wagged slightly before going ramrod straight. Her ears swam with the noise of them growling at each other.

Deciding the fight wasn't worth his time, Darc backed up, and when she saw Rokki's dire wolf walk forward to continue the square off, she reached out and yanked... hard on his tail.

With a snarl, Rokki flipped around, his canines biting the air in front of her face in warning.

"Sorry," Andrea apologized, "but don't continue the fight. I want you and your brother to get along, and he didn't harm me." She held out her arms so he could see for himself.

Andrea had the feeling Darc could have killed her but had simply wanted to scare her.

Rokki's dire wolf turned to glance behind, but Darc's dark shape had faded into the shadows of the night. He was gone.

"Too bad he interrupted the hunt under the moon." Andrea wiggled her brows at Rokki in the dark as she tried to distract him. "I was looking forward to being chased." By the right dire wolf of course.

Seeming to forget the rude interruption, Rokki's wolf sent her a toothy grin. He barked lightly, seeming to encourage her to run off.

Andrea glanced into the dark woods. Darc was out there, but it wasn't like she'd get far... not with Rokki chasing her down. She was safe now.

With it all decided, Andrea spun on a bare heel and sprinted off into the woods.

As she ran, she listened behind her but didn't hear Rokki following her. He was giving her a head start, and she would take full advantage of it. She pushed her legs as fast as she could run.

Then a howl echoed through the forest, and she knew the chase was on.

Hearing the trickle of a stream, Andrea smirked as she darted to her right, and after testing a tentative foot in the water to make sure of its depth, she walked in and scuttled her feet over the smooth river rocks. She had to be quiet if she wanted to do her best to fool Rokki's super sensitive wolf nose and ears.

After a few minutes, Andrea leaped out of the stream and dart back into the forest. Every once in awhile, she heard wolf howls, but they didn't scare her. It was just the pack enjoying their run under the moon. Some were off hunting, and any that were lucky enough had a mate to play chase within the forest.

When Andrea came across a large bush, she ducked behind it. Breathing heavily, she waited, crouched behind the bush, and when what felt like several minutes went by without any sign of Rokki, she began to wonder if she'd done too good of a job in losing him.

Rising from her crouched position, Andrea walked around the bush and surveyed the dark forest around her. Placing her hands on her hips, she pursed her lips while she debated whether or not to whistle for Rokki like a dog so he could find her.

"And here I thought a wolf would have a better sense of smell than this." Andrea tapped a bare foot on the ground.

A snarl ripped through the air, and when she spun around, she found a black dire wolf with golden eyes flying towards her.

Chapter 18

Rokki shifted back into his human form as he wrapped his arms around Andrea and took the brunt of the fall as they landed on the ground.

"Ooomph." Rokki's breath was knocked out of his lungs as they landed. He might have a bruise in the morning, but it was worth it. His dire wolf growled in pleasure at hunting down their mate, and now the fun could begin.

"Thought you lost me, mate?" Rokkie growled into her ear.

Andrea laughed, a light and musical noise. "I thought I had. I was worried I made it too hard to follow my scent."

"I'll never let you go now that I have you." He nipped her earlobe with his teeth and pulled lightly on the flexible flesh. "Where ever you go, I won't be far behind."

She let out a squeak as she giggled and playfully slapped him away. "Rokki!"

"Yes?" He asked as his hands skimmed over her body, worshipping her curves with loving strokes. Her skin was so soft and supple, and he wasn't sure he could ever get enough of touching her. His wolf growled in agreement. Never enough.

Andrea might disagree with the possibility of being a witch, but he wasn't so sure because she definitely had him bewitched. He supposed only time would tell if he was right or if she was right.

Rokki dug his nose into the juncture of her

neck and shoulder and inhaled her intoxicating scent. "I've always dreamed of taking my mate under the light of the moon." He flipped over her, so her back was on the ground, and he kneeled over her.

The moonlight filtered through the leaves high above them and lit up her green eyes. It was an eye color he hadn't seen much of before, and he loved it. And he hoped beyond hope that any children they had possessed her striking eyes.

"Your eyes are beautiful."

He watched a slight blush creep up her face in the moonlight.

"Thank you."

Andrea's small hand reached out and gripped his cock. He sucked in a sharp breath, and within a few pumps of her hand, his shaft raged with need.

This pleased him. She had initiated this encounter, and he couldn't even sense indecision coming off of her. When he met her eyes, he saw desire pooled within those luminous green eyes.

Leaning up, Andrea parted her lips slightly, and Rokki dipped his head. Their lips met in a rush of exhaled breathes. She was soft and yielding under him. A few days ago, he would have said he was afraid she would leave him to go... wherever she went. But right now? Now, he would say she was happy with where she was. With who she was with.

Her lips quivered under him, and he felt her body tremble with need as she continued to stroke his hard length. Her strokes were gentle, sure, and warm. He loved the feeling of being in the palm of her hand.

"Rokki."

"Yes, mate?" Rokki groaned as he felt the seed rising in his shaft. Pulling out of her grasp and away from her kiss, Rokki reached out and stroked a finger across her jawline.

"I want… you… to take me." Andrea laid back on the grass and spread her thighs.

"I will." He promised. "But first, I want to taste you."

He caught one of her pert nipples in his mouth as one of his hands cupped the side of the perfect swell. Pushing lightly on her breast, he caused it to rise, allowing him better access to her nipple. His tongue lolled over the nipple, enjoying the tight bud against the tip of his tongue.

Andrea sucked in harsh breathes as her back arched, and her hands dug into his long hair. Her nails scraped against his scalp. Then she pushed on his head, breaking him free of her nipple, and then pushing him lower until he found his head between her creamy thighs.

"You said you wanted to taste me." She purred.

Rokki chuckled. "I did."

Flicking out his tongue, he licked her from the base to the top, enjoying her wetness on his tongue.

Andrea shuddered around him. "Yes." She purred.

He swept the flat side of his tongue across her sensitive nub, and her hips bucked under him in response. His mate liked being eaten. A growl ripped out of his throat as he stroked his tongue across her, using his spit and her juices to keep her nub moist.

Then he stroked lower, between her plump

folds to her wet entrance, and he stuck his tongue in. Raising a hand to her mound, he used a thumb to circle her nub as he sucked and licked her plump folds.

Her spicy scent filled his nostrils and sucked him in. He was mindless with their desire.

When he raised his eyes, he watched her breasts fall and rise with her pants, as she sucked in desperate breaths. Moonlight shafted between the leaves above and highlighted her face as her head thrashed while he played with her.

Then she shattered.

Andrea's thighs tightened around Rokki's face as her hips bucked. Pressing his hand down on her mound, he prevented her from bucking his face off while he sought her pleasure. When she ceased thrusting her hips, he released his hold and pulled away from her deliciously hot center.

Stars flew across her vision as Andrea came around Rokki's face. Her werewolf had to be part devil because he possessed a wicked tongue. "Your tongue…" She could even finish her sentence as the climax rolled through her like a tornado.

"Yes!" She screamed into the cold night air right before she collapsed back down on the cool grass. She could feel a light sheen of sweat beading on her skin after her intense orgasm.

Rokki pulled away, and she took a moment to enjoy the bliss as it rolled through her. One of Rokki's hands massaged her thigh, and she reveled in his touch as her body calmed.

"Oh, Rokki." Andrea rose, and before he had a chance to blink, she shoved a hand against his chest and sent him flying backward. The moment his back hit the ground, she jumped on top of him, placing her hands on his spread hair-roughened thighs. "I want to taste you now."

His mouth opened, "Andrea, I was…" His words faded into a groan as she licked the length of his cock, from the base to the tip, where she placed a gentle kiss.

"I'm so close," Rokki warned her. "Hearing you… it has… I'm close." He seemed to have an issue constructing a full sentence as her mouth worked on his hard length.

Andrea figured after giving her oral, he would be close to coming, and she him close. She couldn't get enough of him. Of holding him in her hand. Wrapping her mouth around the tip of his cock, she slowly went down on his shaft, taking him all the way… or as much of his cock as she could fit in her mouth.

"Andrea." Rokki groaned.

Andrea smiled as she moved up and down over his cock, using her hand to help guide his shaft in and out of her mouth. Every once in awhile, she would raise her eyes as she pumped him in and out of her mouth. His chest rose in uneven breaths, and his hips would slightly buck.

As he grew closer, she saw his hands clench into fists by his side. Rokki was attempting not to jerk his hips in excitement as the pressure grew within his body.

"Enough!" Rokki reached for her shoulders and dragged her up his body until their lips met once more. "I want to claim you." He gasped before entwining a hand into her hair and pushing her lips against his. The tip of his tongue licked the seam of her lips before diving into her mouth and entangling with her tongue.

A gasp escaped her when his hands wrapped around her hips, and he flung her onto her hands and knees and kneeled behind her.

Andrea moaned when he rubbed the tip of his shaft against her aching entrance. When she glanced over her shoulder, she saw a god poised behind her, his hard shaft gripped in one hand. Moonlight glinted over his toned body highlighting his biceps and pecs.

"I'm going to claim you, mate," Rokki growled, his golden eyes glinting in the night before his canines sank into her neck.

For a brief second, Andrea experienced pain as his teeth sank into her tender skin, and she had the urge to pull away. Then his cock thrust into her. Deep.

"Yes!" Andrea let her head fall to the side, allowing him better access to her neck as the most intense pleasure seared through her. The pain of his bite faded quickly as his hips worked, driving himself in and out of her.

She was his.

Andrea's heart skipped a beat at the idea of being his and only his. She loved her time and her family, but she still wished with all her heart that she could remain her with Rokki.

Satisfaction rolled through Rokki as he held onto his mate's neck. Andrea was his, and he was hers. His dire wolf would howl to the moon in happiness later this night.

"Rokki... it feels... so good." Andrea purred a bit of awe in her voice.

Releasing his hold on her neck, he raised himself on to his knees and pounded into her, his hands on her hips. He didn't hold on too tight, because his beast had come out in the form of claws and enlarged canines, and he had no desire to harm his mate.

With his beasts satisfied with the bite mark on her neck, Rokki withdrew his cock from within her warm shaft.

"What?" Andrea gasped as her wide eyes glanced over her shoulder at him. "Rokki?"

At hearing her lust-filled voice, he almost thrust his shaft back into her, but he refrained. Laying down on the ground, Rokki smiled over at his mate, her face scrunched up in confusion.

"Come, mate, I want you on top of me."

Realization dawned in her eyes, and Andrea crawled on all fours towards him, her hips swaying behind her, and her breasts swaying below her chest. Her pert nipples pointed towards the ground, and he licked his lips.

"You are perfection, mate."

Andrea laughed quietly. "I was thinking the same about you." She lifted a leg and straddled his waist. "Every part of you was sculpted by the gods."

Rokki placed his palms on the front of her thighs and ran his hands up to her waist. Moving her, he rubbed her sensitive spot against the length of his cock.

"Oh!" Andrea gasped. "I'd rather have you inside me, though." Raising up, she reached between them, gripped his cock, and then she sank down onto his length, easing herself slowly down. "Yes." She purred.

His mate's eyes sank closed as she seated herself fully on his shaft. Then she worked her hips back and forth, and his mind went blank as he watched her breasts bounce.

Rokki groaned. Pressure grew in the base of his cock. He wouldn't be able to hold on for long. Her sweet center held him perfectly.

"I want to see you fondle your breasts." His voice went raspy.

Andrea's eyes slid open again as she used her legs to pump herself on his cock while her hands cupped each alabaster orb. Her fingers pinched the nipples, and Rokki's nostrils flared as he caught the scent of her desire drifting between them.

His mate was close.

Latching onto her hips, he thrust her faster and deeper.

Andrea moaned. The sound filled the night air and his ears.

Rokki's jaw clenched as he gnashed his teeth. The pleasure! Her tight sheesh began to pulse around him, pulling him deeper, readying itself for his seed.

"I'm… I'm about to give you…" His hips bucked in jerky movements as the tightness in his balls grew too intense, and then he came. His seed pumped into her, and Andrea moaned as her sheath pulsed around him, squeezing him and pulling his seed deeper into her body.

Her hands abandoned her nipples and landed on his pecs. She dug her fingernails into his skin as her body took control, pumping and pumping his cock as she sought her blissful release.

Then she collapsed on top of him. Their sweat-soaked skin cooling in the air now that they'd ceased moving.

As they laid there, howls carried through the night air. Other mates had found their release, and later he would shift into his dire wolf and announce to the pack that he too had claimed his mate.

"It's so strange," Andrea murmured, "but I feel so comfortable here like I was meant to be here with you."

Hope soared into his heart. Maybe, just maybe, he could convince her that his clan was the clan for her.

Chapter 19

Andrea stared up at the blue sky above her and watched the fluffy white clouds drift silently above her. They went where ever the wind took them. Placing her hands behind her head, she sighed as she searched the sky for any sign of something black flying her way.

"What are you doing lying on the ground?"

Turning her head to the side, Andrea found Ode standing beside her. "Waiting."

"For?" Ode folded her legs as she plopped down on the grass beside Andrea.

"When I first arrived here, Rokki took me to a seer in a cave."

"Yes, I have heard of her, but I have never seen her before." Ode nodded her head. "I hear she is wise… and scary."

"Her name is Elvira, and she isn't as scary as you might think. She is supposed to send her raven to me when she finishes…" Andrea took a second to find her words since she wasn't sure what all she wanted to tell Ode, "a wooden bracelet."

Ode cocked her head to the side, her brown braided hair tipping past one shoulder. "Why would she make you a bracelet? I'm sure Rokki could carve a bracelet for you."

"I need the seer to create it with her magic."

"A magic bracelet?" Ode's blue eyes danced with excitement as she perked up. "What will you do with a magic bracelet?"

"It's a long story, but I found a wooden

bracelet near my clan, and it brought me here. Then Rokki found me, and when he realized the bracelet might take me home, away from him, he snapped it." Andrea gritted her jaw at the memory. He hadn't been wrong. She would have left him, but still, he broke her way home like an ass.

"He broke your magic bracelet?" Ode asked, sounding horrified that her brother could do such a thing.

"Yes." Andrea heaved a sigh as she focused back on the fluffy clouds above her.

"You want to leave us?" Ode sounded puzzled. "You are a part of our clan now. If the seer finishes your bracelet, would you leave? Would you leave my brother? Your mate?"

Gosh, Andrea wasn't so certain what she would do when the bracelet was finished, which was why she was out here laying in the grass. She needed time to think and process. It'd been at least two weeks since the moonlit jaunt in the woods with Rokki, and she'd fallen in love.

Head over heels.

Rokki had charmed the socks off of her. The man was thoughtful, always catering to her every need, whether it was carnal need or something as simple as hunger in the middle of the night.

"If I don't go home, I won't see my mother or friends again. My clan will be lost to me." She turned her head and looked over at Ode.

Ode nodded her head. "It would sadden me to leave my clan. I fear that someday I will find my mate, and he will want me to leave."

"You don't think you could find a mate

here?" Andrea asked, happy with the distraction from her own troubles.

"If I had a mate here, he would have claimed me by now."

"Are mates instant? Or can something form years after a meeting?"

"My mate isn't in this clan." Ode said matter of fact. "We would have known."

"I'm sorry to hear that your mate isn't here. If I do stay, I'd hate to see you leave." And Andrea meant it. Ode and Zuri felt like sisters. They'd welcomed her with no questions and shown her the ways of the clan with patience and few criticisms.

"Will you leave us?" Ode asked again.

Andrea sighed. "I love Rokki, and I would hate to leave him." She confessed out loud, "But I also can't stay here."

"Why not?"

Andrea widened her eyes as she rolled her head a bit on her hands, which were still behind her head. She had no idea what to say as a response, so she asked a question herself, "Shouldn't I want to return to my family?"

"You should want to, but why would you have to return? Would your mother and clan not want you to be happy with your mate? He is a man who will love you always and see to your safety."

That was true. Rokki always saw to her happiness and safety. And he was the perfect man for her. Tall, strong, handsome, and nice. He was also her mate, which meant she never had to worry about his eye straying, which was kind of nice if she were honest. She wasn't the jealous kind, but it did relieve some fears.

"My mother would want me to find love, but if I don't go back, she might think I'm dead."

"I'm not a mother myself, but I've been taught by many in the clan that mothers have an instinct of when their babes are in trouble," Ode shrugged, "would it not be the same when their babes are happy?"

"Maybe." Andrea couldn't make this decision. It wasn't easy, but no hard decision was simple. Her mother would want her to be happy. There was no doubt in her mind about that. Either way, she would hurt someone, and either way, she would have to live with her decision.

She had thought about going back in forth, but what if the magic ran out and she was stuck in a time she didn't want? And how was she going to explain to people in the future why she kept disappearing? She wasn't even sure if she would arrive back at the same time she left or not. It could get tricky.

Sighing, Andrea looked over at Ode, who leaned back on her hands, her head thrown back so she could also watch the clouds shifting high above them. "Is Rokki still out hunting?"

"He is," Ode confirmed. "He and the hunting party should be back soon."

That would be nice. He had only been gone a few days, but the hut seemed so empty without him beside her in the furs.

When he'd announced that he and some hunters would go out to hunt woolly rhinoceros, Andrea had been eager to join, but Rokki had shot that idea down quickly. Once she was more familiar with hunting, and he was sure she would seek safety if needed, he would let her join. So, with a promise of joining in the future, she'd let him go with a kiss to seal the deal.

The wind shifted, blowing the scent of the woolly rhinoceroses towards the hunting party, which slowly prowled closer to the herd. It was a small herd, consisting of no more than five of the large beasts. Their shaggy coats waved in the cool wind, and the beasts snorted, sensing danger, but unable to detect where the threat came from.

Rokki crouched low to the ground, still in his human form. His dire wolf grumbled in the back of his mind. It wanted to be free, and a part of this hunt, but Darc was here, and in his dire wolf form. They couldn't both be in their dire wolf forms, or their beasts would just fight for dominance and ruin the entire hunt.

Lifting his nose into the air, he scented the rhinoceroses. With a simple sniff, he knew exactly which one to target. One of them was old, and it was time for its end.

When Rokki glanced across the large meadow, he spotted the shifting dots in the tall grass. His brother's side of the hunting party was in position. He glanced around him at the men from his pack who were still in their human forms.

They were ready.

Staying crouched, Rokki waited for Darc to make his move.

The tall grass that hid him from sight waved in front of Rokki as time slowly ticked by.

Then a howl went up, and Rokki spotted his brother and several other dire wolves from the pack running straight towards the rhinoceroses. The herd panicked. It stampeded in the opposite direction, and like Rokki thought, the older woolly rhinoceroses dropped behind.

As the herd galloped past, Rokki and the other men drew back their arms, readying their spears, and then they let loose when the older rhinoceros sprinted past.

Some of the spears bounced off the thick hide harmlessly, but most of them sank deep into the animal's flesh. It went down with a thud, and a sense of accomplishment soared through Rokki.

His clan would eat well tonight!

As Rokki and his men left the tall grass, the woolly rhinoceros struggled back onto his feet. He might be old, but he wasn't ready for death yet.

Grabbing another spear, Rokki pointed the tip at the rhinoceros's face, keeping the beast's back to the dire wolves. Then his brother and a couple of their pack jumped onto the beast's back. They dug their long claws and canines into the beast's skin.

It snorted in pain and charge.

Leaping to the side, Rokki barely dodged the large horns on the front of the beast's face.

Then something seared through his middle. Lurching forward, Rokki dropped to his knees as his mind tried to figure out what was happening. Raising his hands to his abdomen, he felt something wet and sticky, and what felt like the shaft of a spear.

Glancing down, his eyes widened as he realized he'd been speared through. He collapsed onto his side at the same time that the woolly rhinoceros went down, shaking the ground around him.

Then a war cry went up, and right before he blacked out, he caught sight of Neanderthals attacking their hunting party.

"Andrea! Ode!" A female voice called out with urgency, breaking the peaceful silence of nature.

Flipping around and onto her butt, Andrea turned towards the voice and saw Zuri rushing towards them, her arms pumping at her sides as she rushed towards them. Her cheeks were flushed a light pink with her exertion, and her eyes darted around frantically.

"Is something wrong?" Andrea called out as she pushed herself to her feet when Ode stood.

Huffing and puffing, Zuri pulled up in front of them and rested her hands on her hips as she sucked in some desperate gasps of air. "The hunting party is back." She sucked in some more air as her eyes turned to Andrea. "And Rokki has been injured."

"Injured?" Andrea's heart plummeted to the ground at her feet as her knees suddenly felt weak like her bones were constructed of nothing but jelly. "How injured?"

Zuri shook her head as her lips pulled back in a grimace. "The shaman doesn't think he will live. You must come now."

Andrea leaped into action, her arms and legs pumping as she sprinted back to the village. Rokki couldn't die. Fate was not allowed to do this to her. First, it dragged her through time to meet the man of her life, and now it thought it could kill him? Hell to the no.

She left the other women to run after her. If Rokki died, then she wanted to be by his side, holding his hand, letting him know he was loved.

As she crested a small hill, she saw the village laid out in front of her. From the outside looking in, everything was calm and peaceful. The moment she raced down the hill and broke into the village though, she could hear a clamoring of voices. Following the noise, she ran through the huts until she found a crowd standing outside of one hut.

"Move!" Andrea barked as she dashed through them all. The clan parted like a herd of startled animals. She didn't even bother asking for permission to enter the hut and just barged inside.

"Rokki?" Ode's voice was right behind Andrea.

Andrea's eyes searched the semi-dark inside of the hut, and when she saw the shaman leaning over a prone frame, her heart dumped to the ground again, but she straightened her back and marched over. Whatever she saw, she could handle. She had to be here for him.

"What happened? Zuri asked, panic rising in her voice.

Darc melted out of the shadows of the hut. "Half us hunted in our dire wolf forms while Rokki and the others stayed in their human forms and used spears."

Andrea approached Rokki and raised a hand over her mouth so no one would hear her gasp of despair. Blood coated everything. Was he even alive with that much blood loss? Maybe she was too late to say her goodbyes.

Despair welled up in Andrea's chest, and she did her best to hold back a sob. She never realized how much she loved Rokki until now.

"We took down a rhinoceros, but then Neanderthals attacked us. Rokki was speared while we took down the rhinoceros, and no one noticed until we finished with the Neanderthals." Darc sounded pained, and for one second, Andrea realized that despite all his anger and snapping, he loved his brother.

"Andrea?" Rokki croaked as blood trickled out from one corner of his mouth.

"Rokki?!" Andrea cried as she unfroze her feet and flew to his side, where she dropped onto her knees beside the shaman.

Clasping one of his bloody hands, she rose it to her cheek as she tried to smile at him, but the attempt failed as the smile wobbled off her lips. It was hard to smile when Rokki died in front of her. Because die he was. As much as she prayed to the gods above, she knew the shaman couldn't save Rokki. She wasn't even sure a twenty-first century surgeon could save him.

"Darc... will see after... you." Rokki promised as he sputtered blood with every word he uttered.

"I will, brother." Darc pledged from behind her.

"I will not stop healing you until your last breath." The shaman grumped from beside Andrea. "Do not give up your life so easily, Rokki."

Andrea rubbed Rokki's hand against her cheek, finding some comfort in the touch, despite the blood. She glanced over to where the shaman mashed some leaves between a stone and a wooden bowl. "Can you stop the bleeding?" She asked with hope.

"I don't know." The shaman said as he continued at his task. The grizzled man had a long white beard and mustache that almost hid his lips from view. Her eyes skimmed over the tattoos on his face, which moved with his loose skin as he worked the leaves.

Rokki coughed, and Andrea turned her eyes back to him, only to have her throat close up in terror. She couldn't do anything for him. She knew nothing about medicine. Her only hope was that the shaman would succeed in staunching the flow of blood, then she could help with preventing infection. She'd seen plenty of movies and tv shows, so she knew the jist. Prevent infection with clean towels and hot water. She could get those... well, she could get clean furs, which would have to suffice.

Rokki's coughing turned into sputtering as more blood showered out of his mouth.

"Hold on, Rokki. Please stay with us." Andrea begged as she heard horrified gasps from behind her from his sisters. They found this sight just as horrible as Andrea did, which didn't instill a whole lot of hope.

Andrea had never seen a wound like this before, and she'd hoped she never would again. It was one thing to see ghastly wounds on the television, and a whole other thing to see it right in front of her.

The scent of blood, a metallic sweet scent, filled the hut and had Andrea scrunching up her nose. Her mind screamed at her to run from the sight of torn flesh and blood, but she remained where she kneeled. If Rokki died, she would be here with him until he end. He was her mate after all, and he deserved her attention.

Rokki's coughing ceased, and the sudden silence caused her to panic.

"Is he alive?" Andrea leaned in, her eyes searching for the signs of a chest moving under his fur shirt, but she didn't see it rising or falling. "Is he alive?!" She screamed.

The shaman, calm under all the crying and hysteria of three women in the hut, held a hand above Rokki's mouth and right under his nose. Then he pulled his hand away. Turning ever so slightly, he addressed the hut, "Rokki has joined the gods in the Eternal Hunting Grounds."

Ode and Zuri let out wails that would have been howls of pain had they been in their dire wolf forms.

"No!" Andrea screamed at the top of her voice. "You may not leave me!" She slammed her eyes shut and gripped his hand harder. "You may not leave me." She commanded. "Not now. Not ever."

"Come, Andrea. He is with our ancestors and gods." Darc's hands landed on her shoulders as he tried to lift her to her feet.

Andrea shook him off as she focused on Rokki in front of her. She wouldn't leave. She wouldn't leave until he stood up and kissed her again.

She felt something… pull inside her, and then it gave way. With a scream of pain, Andrea collapsed on top of Rokki's body.

Chapter 20

"Andrea?" A light voice asked with concern. "Are you awake?"

Cracking open an eye, Andrea glanced up at Ode. Her head felt like it was split in two, or she'd been binge drinking the night before. "Ode?" Her voice cracked a bit, and her throat felt like sandpaper.

"It is me." Ode patted one of Andrea's hands with her own. "How do you feel? Do you need water?"

Andrea nodded her head slowly, not wanting to exacerbate the ache inside her skull.

Ode shifted on her knees, and when she turned back, she held a wooden bowl up for Andrea. "Can you rise?"

Andrea nodded again as she slowly eased herself onto her bottom. Her head screamed at her in annoyance, and her vision swam before her, but she held herself steady and waited for it to pass.

Once Andrea's vision returned, she took the small wooden bowl from Ode in both of hers and raised it to her lips. Tilting the bowl back, her eyes sank closed in pleasure as the cool water soothed her throat, and there was something else. The water had been flavored with something.

"What's... in here?" Andrea croaked.

"Some leaves and twigs that the shaman thought might ease your throat when you woke."

"Have I been... out long?" Andrea took another swing of the water, her throat already feeling much better.

"A couple of days." Ode smiled. "We thought you may have died in grief, but it seems you just needed time to heal from what you saw and did."

"Is Rokki..." She trailed off. She couldn't finish the sentence.

"Dead?" Ode smiled kindly. "No, he is alive and better than before he was injured."

"He's alive?" Andrea's eyes widened as the wooden bowl slipped from her fingers, spilling the rest of its contents all over her legs.

"He will be here soon. He can barely stay away, but there were some issues with Neanderthals in our territory that drew him away."

Andrea's eyelids closed as she sighed. "He's alive and off trying to get killed again?"

Ode chuckled as she rose. "He is pack leader now, and he must keep us safe. It is what an alpha does." Ode walked over to the fire and stoked it with a stick.

Andrea welcomed the extra punch of heat inside the hut. "I thought he couldn't be pack leader. How is this possible?"

"You will have to ask Rokki. I am sure he will want to be the one to tell you." Ode sent her another smile. "I am glad you are well, Andrea. I must go, though, I will be back later to see how you are."

"Is she awake?" Rokki burst into the hut right as Ode was about to leave, and he caught his sister around the shoulders and spun her around, so they didn't collide.

"See for yourself, brother." Ode said before slipping out of the hut.

Andrea watched Rokki's shoulders rise and

fall as he sucked in breathes, but he hadn't yet turned around. It was like he dreaded what he might see when he turned.

"Rokki?" She asked cautiously. "Are you well?" She had Ode's word that Rokki was fine after the wound he'd been dealt, but she wanted to see for herself.

Slowly, Rokki spun around, and when his eyes landed on her sitting up on her bed of furs, relief washed over his features. His golden eyes soften, and a smile twitched the corner of his lips.

"You are awake."

"I am." Andrea sent him a reassuring smile. "And I have many questions."

"First, let me enjoy this moment." Rokki strode over to her, his long legs eating up the distance between them. He knelt beside her and took her into his arms. "We were worried you might not wake. I fear you might not wake." His voice choked in his throat as emotions overwhelmed him, and her heart went out to him.

"Nothing is keeping us apart." And Andrea meant it. It only took a near death experience for her to realize her life would never have been the same had he died. Reaching up, she placed a palm against his cheek, which had some stubble growing. He usually kept it cut down in the summer with a bone knife, but it appeared he hadn't cared much for himself while she'd been out.

"Thank you for saving me." Rokki placed a tender kiss against her lips before pulling away.

"Save your life? What did I do?" Andrea shook her head as she tried to draw back her memories, but all she could remember was Rokki bleeding in front of her and then darkness.

"You healed my wounds." Rokki slid under the fur that covered her lap and drew her down on the furs so he could wrap his arms around her.

Andrea purred in happiness as his warmth surrounded her. With a couple of fingers, she plucked at the bead work on his leather shirt. "Didn't the shaman heal you?"

Rokki chuckled as he tucked her closer to his body, and she melted against him. "You are a very powerful witch, my mate. You drew me back from the Eternal Hunting Grounds and back into my body."

Andrea rolled her eyes. Not this witch thing again. "Rokki, as much as I would like to say I healed you, I'm afraid you're wrong."

"Darc, Ode, the shaman, and Zuri saw you heal me with magic. There is no other way to explain the bright light that seared through the hut." Then his lips drew into a flat line. "You shouldn't have done it though. You came close to killing yourself."

Andrea rolled her eyes again. "I fainted with fear."

"How do you explain this?" Rokki raised a hand and drew a lock of hair into her frame of vision.

Andrea's mouth gaped as she stared at the lock of hair. "But… but… it's white!" Her hair was pure white! Raising her hands, she grabbed more of her hair, only to find the rest was still auburn. It was just this one lock that was white.

"You used some of your life to save me." Rokki shook his head as his golden eyes took on a hard glint. "Never do it again."

"It could have been fear that caused my lock of hair to go white."

"Explain this then, mate." Rokki pulled back and lifted his shirt to expose a scar… the same place where he'd been speared.

"But…" Andrea placed her hands on his abdomen in wonderment, "I thought I was only out for a couple of days?"

"You were, Andrea." Rokki pulled his shirt down. "You healed me, Andrea."

Andrea pursed her lips. "Then don't injure yourself again." She smacked an open palm against his chest. "I couldn't handle seeing you die."

"I am sorry." Rokki placed his forehead against hers. "I never want to worry you, but our land is dangerous. I never could have known the Neanderthals would attack during one of our hunts."

She realized that the ice age was unpredictable. She'd been targeted a lot since landing here in the past, and she was lucky this white lock of hair was the worst that had happened to her.

"The hunt went like planned until I was speared. I didn't notice the Neanderthals. I didn't scent them." Rokki closed his eyes as he recalled the memory. His face scrunched up as he recalled the pain.

"At least, you're alive." Andrea smiled as she wrapped an arm around him. "I do have another question."

"Yes?" Rokki murmured as he began to kiss her neck and leaned over her, rising up on an arm.

"Ode said you were pack leader, but I…" Andrea giggled, as Rokki's lips tickled the sensitive flesh of her neck. "I don't understand how that is. I thought Darc would end up being leader."

"You must listen to me better, mate." Rokki murmured against her flesh. "Whether you believe it or not, you are a witch, an untrained witch, but you are, and Darc has already been forced out of the village. I am leader of the pack now, and you are my mate."

"Forced out?" Andrea couldn't help but feel a tad sorry for Darc. He wasn't an evil man, just a man who was unwilling to lose the only family he had known, and now he was living on his own. "What will happen to him?"

Rokki shrugged as he slipped under the fur and sucked a nipple into his mouth. He played with the taunt nipple until her mouth popped open on a sigh. Then he pulled away and said from under the fur, "He is an alpha. Darc will be able to take care of himself. There's no need to worry about him. Now… let me give us both pleasure."

Andrea gasped as his hand found her heated center.

"Let me make us feel alive." He murmured from under the fur.

"Oh, yes." She murmured back.

Chapter 21

Caw! Caw! Caw!

Andrea glanced about wildly as she caught the sound of a raven. Turning her eyes to the cloudy sky above her, she spotted a black bird circling above her.

Caw! Caw! Caw!

And then the bird stopped circling and flew back in the direction of the seer's cave. The seer must be done with her bracelet then. Her heart flipped inside her chest at the knowledge, and she wasn't sure whether it was in excitement or dread.

"What are you looking at?" Rokki walked up beside her and draped a muscled arm over her shoulders.

"The seer's raven flew overhead and back to the cave." Andrea turned to face him, searching for what, she wasn't sure.

"Do you want to see the seer?" Rokki asked, his golden eyes giving away nothing.

Andrea still wasn't sure what she wanted. To stay or leave. It was a hard choice, and one she wished she didn't have to make. Maybe the seer would have some answers for her. "It would be rude to not go." She said cautiously.

Rokki nodded his head as he drew his arm back. "We should return to our hut then to gather supplies for the journey. It will take us a couple of days to get there from here."

"Lead the way." Andrea waved a hand in

front of her, and when Rokki started back to the village, she followed hot on his heels.

As they walked back, Andrea stayed a few steps behind him so she could study him unnoticed. She was living in an animal skin hut with a real-life werewolf. It just blew her mind every time she thought about it. She'd gone from being a normal human archeologist to being a witch mated to a werewolf. Life couldn't get any more bizarre.

Surging forward, Andrea reached out a hand and clasped his in her own, entwining their fingers. "I love you, Rokki."

Rokki jerked to a stop, yanking on her arm slightly, pulling her into his embrace as both of his arms snaked around her waist. "What did you say?"

"I love you." Andrea tilted her head up to meet his golden-eyed gaze. "I love you." The words felt good on her tongue.

A slow smile crept across his lips as his head dipped. He placed a gentle kiss on her lips before pulling away and saying, "I love you too, mate. My chest could burst with the emotions I feel for you."

Andrea's heart skipped a beat at his declaration, and a blush decoration her cheeks as she suddenly ducked her head.

"What is it?" Rokki asked as he slipped a hand from her waist and used a couple of fingers to tilt her chin back up.

"I've never felt this way with anyone else." She'd come close a few times, but every time she thought she could grow close with a guy, something would mess it up. Whether it was her, her job, or the guy she'd fallen for, something always interfered with her relationships.

Rokki cupped her face with one of his large hands, and she reveled in the warmth that spread through her face. "Stay with me, and I will make sure you never regret it."

Andrea swallowed. She couldn't say anything to those words. There was no way she could promise anything when she still wasn't sure where she stood on leaving or staying. So, instead, she said, "We should pack and get to the seer before she thinks we forgot about her."

Rokki's dire wolf howled in pain as he watched his mate slip from his grasp and walk towards their hut. Their hut. But he wasn't sure it would be their hut for much longer. Everything had seemed so perfect since she'd saved his life. They'd fallen into a rhythm in the village, and he'd even forgotten about her wanting to go back to her clan.

She was so close, yet she was so far away from him, and he struggled with how to bring her back.

With a heavy sigh of defeat, Rokki walked over to their hut. There were still a few days between them and the seer. He still had plenty of time to convince Andrea that her life was here with him and his pack.

Pushing through the fur entrance of the hut, he found Andrea stuffing a couple of things into a fur pack. She stood and sent him a smile, "I'm done!"

Rokki grunted as he strode over to one side

of the hut and grabbed a pack that he always had at the ready. It had a pack of dried meat and a couple of fur blankets inside. "We should head out before night falls and impedes our journey."

Andrea nodded, "Good idea. I don't like the idea of walking around at night." Then she ducked out of the hut and left Rokki to stand there staring at the waving flap.

Closing his eyes, Rokki sucked in a deep breath as he calmed his dire wolf. The beast wanted to show its face and demand Andrea stay here with them, but Rokki knew his dire wolf would only hinder his attempts at convincing Andrea to stay. Baring his teeth wouldn't get him anywhere.

Opening his eyes, he followed Andrea out of the hut. She was already well ahead of him and about to enter the forest. It pleased him that she felt so comfortable around their village. It had taken her a little time to believe him when he said predators stayed far away from their village. Predators and prey sensed that the village of werewolves was a bad place to stray.

"Where are you going?"

Rokki turned his head to spot his sister, Zuri, standing behind him with her arms crossed over her chest. "The seer has sent us a sign to come to her cave."

"Ode told me about the bracelet." Zuri cocked her head to the side. "Why are you making it easy for your mate to leave you?"

Rokki had been asking himself that very question, and he'd come up with an answer. "The choice to leave is hers. All I can do is hope that I have done enough to change her decision."

Zuri shook her head as she heaved a sigh. "I will look after the pack while you are gone then, and I hope you both return."

"As do I," Rokki said before turning and catching back up to Andrea. "As do I."

Andrea stretched her legs out in front of the fire Rokki had been kind enough to build when they made camp for the night. They'd already spent one night out in the forest, and this would be their last night before arriving at the seer's cave.

"Would you like some?" Rokki held a fur bag up.

"Dried meat?"

He nodded.

"Thank you." Andrea took the bag from him, her fingers brushing his allowing a sear of desire spark through her, and when she glanced up, she saw the same look reflected back at her in his sparkling golden eyes. "I'm actually hungry for something else."

"What is it?" Rokki asked, their hands still touching as neither released their hold on the bag of dried meat. "I will give you what you want, all you need do is ask."

"I want you."

Rokki's hand clenched around her a second before he yanked her into his lap, the bag of dried meat falling to the ground forgotten. "And I will always want you."

Then his lips slanted over hers.

Andrea melted in his lap. Her arms came up to wrap around his neck, pulling him closer.

"Let's take off these clothes." He murmured against her lips.

"Yes." She moaned in excitement.

Standing, Rokki placed her on her feet and backed away. "Shall I go first?" A fire burned in his golden eyes.

"I will go first."

Andrea smiled as she trailed her fingers down the front of her shirt, and cock her head to the side so she could look up at him under her lashes. She wasn't used to being sexy, but she figured anything she did would turn her werewolf on. When she got to the waistband of her tanned leather pants, she slipped her thumbs under the waistband and drew them down her legs. When she reached her toes, she stood back up and flicked the pants away with a jerk of one foot.

Then she trailed her hands up her thighs, across her mound of auburn curls, and then to the hem of her shirt. Ever so slowly, she wiggled her hips as she took the shirt off inch by slow inch.

Once she got it above her head, she twirled it away.

Andrea now stood naked, and she smoothed her hands down her sides until her hands landed on her hips. "It's your turn."

Rokki's golden eyes raked over her body from her toes to her head. He was more eager though, and within a few seconds, he stood naked in front of her. Her eyes fell to his proudly erect cock.

Andrea licked her lips as she watched a bead of cum moisten the tip.

"Excited?"

"Mate, you make me hard with just a whiff of your scent," Rokki growled, and a fire lit in those golden depths as his canines and claws grew.

His body and cock were perfect. Each was strong, and her body quivered at the idea of having him inside her, over her as he claimed her again.

Kneeling on the ground, she presented him her ass while on all fours. Then she reached behind her neck and drew her hair back from her neck. "Claim me."

Her lethal and beautifully built werewolf was on her in a second. His chest covered her back in a blanket of warmth, his hard length pressed up against one of her butt cheeks. She could feel the ridges of his abdomen pressed against her back as she arched below him, enticing him.

Rokki growled in her ear as the tip of his tongue slid against the spot he'd bitten last time. "You are mine."

"I am yours."

She felt him freeze behind her.

"Say it again, mate."

"I am yours."

"What are you to me?"

"I am yours."

Rokki shifted behind her, and then his cock and his teeth sank into her hot flesh. He growled against her as he thrust his hips in and out of her wet center.

Andrea felt like her eyes might have rolled back in her head as her body heated with the delicious feel of his cock stretching and filling her. Could she really give up a love and a lover like this?

Her body took over. She moved with his every thrust, which was slow and deep like he wanted to draw it out... like he was afraid of losing her.

Releasing his hold on her neck, Rokki rose up behind her, placed a hand to the small of her back, and pressed down while reaching out and grabbing a fistful of her hair. Yanking back, he had her back arching, and she shattered.

"Rokki!"

"Yes, mate, come for me." Rokki ground out.

Then she felt him come inside her. Hot and searing. The feeling set her off once again, and she trembled under him until they both collapsed onto the ground. Rokki wrapped his arms around her and drew her back into his chest, his cock still within her pulsing sheath.

How could she ever think about leaving?

The day was pleasant, with a slight breeze that rattled the leaves above their heads. Andrea got the sense that the weather would change soon. The leaves were browning, and she could swear she smelled snow on the air.

"Are you warm enough?"

Glancing over to her side, she smiled over at Rokki, "I'm warm." A little too warm. The moment the winds had come, he had bundled her up in as many furs as he could. Although she wasn't about to protest his concerned attentions. It was cute to watch him fuss over her.

They broke out of the forest, and a rocky area greeted them. When Andrea glanced up a hillside, she saw the black opening of the cave where the seer lived. It seemed like just yesterday when she'd come to this cave with Rokki for the first time.

Nerves rocked through her as her hands trembled a bit. Soon, she would have a choice to make. Her steps slowed as she walked up the rocky trail that led up the hill, allowing Rokki to get ahead of her. Maybe she could spend the rest of the day walking up to the cave and have to make the decision tomorrow.

But that was her just being wishful. There was no time like the present to just get this over with. She had to be an adult and rip the bandage off for the sake of them both.

Trudging up the hill, Andrea's moccasin booted feet kicked random rocks sending the grey rocks clattering around, some falling over the cliff edge and down to the ground below.

When she made it to the top and looked up, a flush to her cheeks after the bit of exercise, she found Rokki standing silently by the entrance, waiting for her. She hated to say his golden eyes looked angry, but there was a steel feel to them as they sliced over her. He definitely wasn't pleased, and she didn't blame him.

Andrea wanted this to be easier on them all, but he wasn't the only one with emotions here. She had a lot rolling through her, and she didn't like him acting like he was the only person affected by her decision.

"Should we go in?" Andrea asked as she peered into the darkness of the cave. "It doesn't look like she is here." She didn't see any flickering of a fire down the rocky corridor.

"She is here," Rokki said, his voice neutral, almost gruff.

Andrea frowned at his gruffness but ignored it. "How do you know?"

Without speaking, Rokki pointed a finger high into the sky, and when her gaze followed the direction, she saw the raven flying high above them. It was circling them, its little black head turning to watch them with its beady eyes.

"It's never far from her?" Andrea guessed.

"The seer and the raven are like one. Unless he is helping her with a task, he is always by her side."

Andrea had always been a bird person, but her lifestyle never allowed her any pets. It didn't feel right to get a pet when she was barely home and always traveling for her job.

When she heard Rokki walking into the cave, she turned her attention away from the raven and back to the entrance. Rushing after him, she darted into the cave, and within a few seconds, she saw an orange light flickering further down the corridor. A few more seconds, and they stepped into the decent sized chamber where the seer lived.

"Hello." The seer said without opening her eyes. She had sparkly gold and black paint smeared over her face and arms. She'd probably made them from minerals in the nearby ground and cave systems. "I finished your bracelet." The seer opened a hand, and sitting on her palm was a wooden ring.

"Thank you." Andrea stepped forward and took the bracelet with a couple of her fingers. "Do I... owe you something?" Andrea asked uncertain what she would give the woman, and not sure how trades went back in the ice age.

"I need nothing from you." The seer said, her eyes still shut.

Andrea fiddled with the bracelet in her hands. The wood was cool, and it weighed heavier than she thought it would. It held the future of her life inside its wooden curves.

"What will you choose, Andrea?" The seer finally opened her eyes and speared Andrea with her all-knowing green eyes. "You don't need the bracelet to be happy."

The seer kept saying that to her. The first time they'd met, the seer had told her that she didn't need the bracelet.

"I don't understand," Andrea admitted as she continued to fiddle with the bracelet.

"You are a witch, Andrea." The seer's gaze dropped to the bracelet. "One day, if you want, you can make your own magical bracelet to take you home."

Or she could keep the one the seer had created for her.

Andrea bit her bottom lip, twisting and turning it with her teeth as she thought about what to do with the bracelet.

"I don't know how to even use my magic." And Andrea still wasn't entirely sure she believed she was a witch. Ever since supposedly saving Rokki's life, which she didn't remember, she'd tried to use magic with no success.

"You will come here to learn from me." The seer sent her a smile, her white teeth a sharp contrast against the gold and black paint all over her face.

"You will teach me what I need to know?" Andrea released her bottom lip, knowing it would be flushed red with all her chewing.

The seer nodded her head. "I will."

"Then," Andrea sucked in an unsteady breath and tossed the wooden bracelet into the fire, "I don't need that."

She trusted the seer. She didn't know the woman, but there was something in those eyes that told her she could trust Elvira. If she learned how to use her magic, then she could always go back home to let her mom know she was good and happy.

"Are you sure about this?"

When she looked over at Rokki, she found him poised, ready to yank her bracelet out of the leaping flames if she said she wasn't. "I'm sure."

And the smile that spread across his face chased all doubts away. She'd made the right choice. Her mom would understand.

Epilogue

"Concentrate."

Andrea closed her eyes and imagined a flame kindling into existence. She'd been training under the seer for a couple of weeks now, and so far, nothing had happened. Although she was impressed with the seer's patience with her. Elvira still had faith in her abilities.

"There you go." The seer whispered in a pleased voice.

"I did it?" Andrea popped her eyes wide as she glanced down at the fire pit. Her eyes grew in size as she watched the small flame grow as it licked hungrily at the twigs. "I did that?"

"Yes, you did." Elvira patted her on the back. "Magic takes time, and since you weren't raised as a child with magic, it might take some time, but never give up."

"Never," Andrea whispered in an awed voice. She could scarcely believe she'd been able to do it. "What next?"

The seer reached behind her back, and Andrea expected her to bring something out that she would practice her magic on, but instead, the seer brought forth an animal skin bag of water and dumped it on Andrea's growing fire.

The fire went out with a hiss and a puff of smoke.

"I just started that!" Andrea complained as her shoulders slumped. Elvira had just undone her great feat.

"And now you will do it again and again until you can do it with a flick of your fingers… or even better, with a single thought." Golden flecks danced in Elvira's green eyes as she smiled encouragingly at Andrea.

Andrea let out a groan. The seer was stern when it came to lessons. Andrea wasn't sure if she spent more time at the pack village or here in this cave.

After a couple more hours of working on her fire magic, she heard steps echo down the corridor of the cave, and she breathed a sigh of relief. Someone was coming, and she hoped it was Rokki come to save her from Elvira.

"Good evening, mate, how are you?"

Andrea spun on her butt and faced Rokki. "Tired." She sighed.

"Come then. It is time for you to come back to the village," he sent her a wink, "so we can warm the furs in our hut once more."

Andrea blushed as she glanced over in the seer's direction, but the woman was already doing something else. "Rokki." She complained as she faced him again. "Not in front of people."

Rokki chuckled. "Your people must be very shy."

"They are private." She agreed. "Now, are you going to just stand there, or will you help me up?" She raised a hand.

Rokki reached out and gripped it, yanking her up to her feet. She dusted off her leather pants and allowed Rokki to lead her out of the cave.

"Thanks for coming to my rescue. I was afraid she would never let me go."

"She is persistent in you learning magic." Rokki agreed. "How did today go for you?"

"Much better." A smile pulled at the corner of her lips. "I started a fire."

"I have no doubts you will make a great witch someday." Rokki threaded his fingers with hers as he held her hand while they walked through the forest on their way back to the village.

And this was the reason she'd decided to stay. She would be hard pressed to find another man like him, and she couldn't wait to spend the rest of her life with him.